MURDER MOST
AUSTEN

ALSO BY TRACY KIELY

Murder Most Persuasive
Murder on the Bride's Side
Murder at Longbourn

MURDER MOST AUSTEN

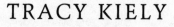

TRACY KIELY

MINOTAUR BOOKS

A THOMAS DUNNE BOOK

NEW YORK

A THOMAS DUNNE BOOK FOR MINOTAUR BOOKS.
An imprint of St. Martin's Publishing Group.

MURDER MOST AUSTEN. Copyright © 2012 by Tracy Kiely. All rights reserved. Printed in the United States of America. For information, address St. Martin's Press, 175 Fifth Avenue, New York, N.Y. 10010.

www.thomasdunnebooks.com
www.minotaurbooks.com

ISBN 978-1-250-00742-1 (hardcover)
ISBN 978-1-250-01735-2 (e-book)

First Edition: September 2012

10 9 8 7 6 5 4 3 2 1

To my grandmother, Winifred Tracy Shanahan,
the original Aunt Winnie

ACKNOWLEDGMENTS

ONCE AGAIN, I find myself in the unbelievably lucky position of being able to publicly thank the many people who helped me bring this book to completion. Their input always makes my work better. Barbara Kiely and Terry Mullin-Sweeney kindly read early versions of the book and offered many valuable suggestions. Toni Plummer's edits always make my books stronger, and Cynthia Merman's copyediting skills are second to none. Barbara Poelle's inspiration and guidance have been enormously helpful. I'd also like to thank Bridget Kiely, Ann Mahoney, Mary Ann Kingsley, Sophie Littlefield, and all the Bunco ladies for their continued moral support. And last, but certainly not least, I'd like to thank my husband, Matt, and our children, Jack, Elizabeth, and Pat, for helping me keep everything in perspective when it all gets a bit crazy.

MURDER MOST
AUSTEN

CHAPTER 1

There is, I believe, in every disposition a tendency to some particular evil, a natural defect, which not even the best education can overcome.

—PRIDE AND PREJUDICE

*I*F I HAD KNOWN that someone was going to kill the man sitting in 4B three days hence, I probably wouldn't have fantasized about doing the deed myself.

Probably.

However, as it stood, I didn't have this knowledge. The only knowledge I *did* have was that he was a pompous ass and had not stopped talking once in the last two hours.

"Of course, only the truly clever reader can discern that it is beneath Austen's superficial stories that the *real* narrative lies. Hidden beneath an attractive veil of Indian muslin, Austen presents a much darker world. It is a sordid world of sex, both heterosexual and homosexual, abortions, and incest. It is in highlighting these darker stories to the less perceptive reader that I have devoted my career," the man was now saying to his seatmate.

I guessed him to be in his late fifties. He was tall and fair, with those WASPy good looks that lend themselves well to exclusive

men's clubs, the kinds that still exclude women and other dangerous minorities. His theories were so patently absurd that at first
I'd found his commentary oddly entertaining. However, as Austen
herself observed, of some delights, a little goes a long way.

This was rapidly becoming one of those delights.

From the manner in which the young woman to his right gazed
at him with undisguised awe, it was clear that she did not share my
desire to duct-tape his mouth shut. Her brown eyes were not roll-
ing back into her head with exasperation; rather, they were practically sparkling with idolization from behind her wire-framed
glasses. While both our faces were flushed from his words, the
cause for the heightened color on her elfin features stemmed from
reverence; the cause of mine was near-boiling irritation.

I closed my eyes and tried to drown out their conversation by
thinking happier thoughts. After all, I was on a plane—and not
just any plane, mind you, but a British Airways flight headed to
London. London! From there I was headed to Bath to attend the
Jane Austen Festival. A week-long celebration of all things Jane,
and attended by Janeites from all over the world. For an Anglophile like me, this was about as close to nirvana as one could get. I
tried to think of scones heaped with clotted cream, red telephone
boxes, gorgeous accents, and the off chance that I might spy Colin
Firth—anything to distract myself from the man in 4B.

And yet, I could not.

"Now I grant you that mine is a special talent," he droned on. "It
is not everyone who can unravel the secret messages—the ciphers, if
you will—that are embedded in each of her works. In fact, it could
be said that I am the Rosetta stone of Austen."

I wondered how much trouble I would get in if I threw my shoe at his head.

Next to me, my aunt Winnie shifted in her seat and cast an idle glance in the man's direction before turning to me. "Is it morning already?" she asked, stretching her arms out in front of her.

"No," I said, checking my watch. "It's still the middle of the night."

Her eyes sought out the man again as if perplexed. "But the cock's crowing."

"Oh, well, in that case," I said agreeably, "it's been morning for a long, long time now."

"Well, I just think it's amazing," the young woman said now. "I studied Austen as an undergrad and no one ever even *hinted* at these other stories. Although some of my professors discussed the moral teachings found in her works, they mainly focused on her social satire. I never saw any of the *intended* stories until your class. I mean, I never realized that in *Persuasion,* Sir Walter Elliot's relationship with his eldest daughter, Elizabeth, was incestuous, or that in *Sense and Sensibility,* Marianne Dashwood's illness was really the result of a botched *abortion* until you pointed it out." She beamed obsequiously at him.

I tried to remember if I'd ever treated any of my professors with such a groveling display of worship. Hmmm. Let me think.

Nope.

Granted, I'd liked and respected a great number of them, but I hadn't had any crushes on any of them. Then again, I'd attended an all-girls Catholic school, largely taught by the Sisters of Notre-Dame, so that last part probably isn't too surprising. I might be somewhat jaded at the ripe old age of twenty-eight, but witnessing this dual display of academic love—for this fool of a man—did not arouse even a minuscule atom of regret at this apparent gap in my academic career.

The man nodded sagely at his seatmate. "I'm not surprised. Unfortunately, most of today's English professors—and I use that term very loosely—are completely ignorant of Austen's true objective."

I gave up trying to ignore them, shifted in my seat, and craned my neck to look for the flight attendant. If I was going to be forced to listen to this drivel, I needed a drink. A Chardonnay drink. Aunt Winnie saw my movement and easily divined my intention. "Order me one, too, sweetheart," she said.

"Already on it," I replied.

The man continued. "They have interpreted her works in a manner appropriate to what they believe a spinster writing during the Regency period intended. While they view her works as containing *some* biting satire, they don't grasp the whole picture! But, as I have diligently maintained, *that* is the true beauty of Austen's work. She was subverting society's precious rules all the while pretending to live by them. She described life as it really was—rough, extremely sexual, and, at times, evil and dark. She dressed it up and let the dull see what they wanted and hoped that the astute reader—a reader like myself—would see it for what it was: a forceful condemnation of the sanctimonious hypocrisy of both society and the church."

Honestly, it was beginning to amount to auditory torture. It almost made me yearn for a teething baby or gassy seatmate. And besides, wasn't this technically a form of assault? Because that's what this boiled down to—assault with an unwanted opinion. And just where the hell was the flight attendant?

"It's all very exciting," the women murmured. "Your discoveries will not only revolutionize how Jane Austen's work is viewed, but how that whole period of literature is viewed."

"Yes, they will," he agreed without modesty. "And I anticipate that after I deliver my latest paper, I will also revolutionize people's views on how her life was *lived*."

"Do you have a copy with you?" she asked, her voice hopeful. "I'd love to read it, if I may."

He dipped his sleek head condescendingly. "I'm sure you would, but unfortunately I don't have it with me. My assistant, Byron, is putting the finishing touches on it. He's already in London tweaking it. We're to finalize the details tomorrow. Perhaps I could show it to you then."

The young woman was silent for a moment. "I see. Of course. Is, um, your wife coming as well?"

He gave a slight nod. "She is. She flew out yesterday."

The woman's eyes fell to her lap in obvious disappointment, but she said nothing. If the man noticed, he didn't let on. "Tell me, Lindsay," he said, "what did you think of my last lecture, where I detailed how Austen's works, when taken in total, are really a kind of early manifesto for the ideals of communism?"

I glanced down at my shoes. No thick boots here, only ballet flats. Even if I threw them really hard, they wouldn't be able to inflict any real damage. I sighed.

"I loved it, of course," the woman answered immediately. "But do you really believe that Austen herself was an atheist?" There was the barest suggestion of doubt now lurking in those adoring brown eyes.

"Believe it? I defy you to prove otherwise! How else do you explain a character like Mr. Collins? He was a pompous, silly egomaniac," was his assured reply.

"There appears to be a lot of that going around," Aunt Winnie said in hearty agreement. She made no attempt to modulate her voice. But to be fair, Aunt Winnie has never been a huge proponent of modulation, whether in voice, appearance, or opinion. One needs only to see her curly red hair and bright green eyes—both of which have intensified in color over the years thanks to Clairol and colored contacts—to deduce that. She is the personification of Tallulah Bankhead's observation, "I'm the foe of moderation, the champion of excess."

Not surprisingly, both the man and the woman turned our way. Aunt Winnie smiled brightly at them. I knew that smile well. It combined all the warmth of Machiavelli with the subtlety of the Cheshire Cat. It also signaled to those who knew her well that it was—as she herself put it—"on like Donkey Kong." I gestured again—a little more impatiently now—for the flight attendant to bring the drinks cart.

The man's full lips drew back into a condescending smile; his teeth were very large and very white. "I take it that you don't concur with my views on Austen," he purred silkily. Next to him, the young woman blinked with owl-like alertness.

"I most certainly do not," Aunt Winnie replied with the cool politeness of a society matron. She then ruined the effect by adding, "In fact, I think they are utter bullshit."

"No, no, I completely understand," he continued with a patronizing air. "Many women—especially women of a 'certain generation'—find my discoveries to be somewhat off-putting."

"Stewardess!" I called out, it having now become paramount that I get her attention if I was going to prevent Aunt Winnie from physically demonstrating just what she did and didn't find off-putting.

Aunt Winnie leaned forward. "Women of a certain generation? Are you suggesting that women of 'my generation,' as you so clumsily put it, are unable to discern reality from perversion?"

Thankfully, the flight attendant arrived, providing a momentary diversion, and no doubt preventing Aunt Winnie from throwing *her* shoes at the man. And as *they* were three-inch platforms, they might have actually done some damage. "May I help you?" the flight attendant politely inquired.

"I certainly hope so," I muttered to myself.

Her round face pulled in confusion. "Sorry?"

"I'd like to order a drink, please—" I began, but the man in 4B cut me off.

"I fear I may have offended you," he said. "Please let me offer the proverbial olive branch and order us all a glass of champagne." Before any of us could answer, he addressed the flight attendant. "Four champagnes, please. Your very best, of course."

"We only have the one kind," she replied.

"Well, nevertheless, put it on my tab," he replied with a lofty wave of his manicured hand. I noticed he was wearing a gold pinkie ring. It suited him.

"It's complimentary, sir," she said and briskly strode to the kitchen area to ready the drinks.

Turning his attention back to us, the man asked, "I gather you are a fan of the dear lady, Miss Jane Austen?"

"We are," Aunt Winnie replied, brushing back her trademark red curls.

"Well then, we are well met!" he replied with a practiced smile. "For I don't think you will meet anyone who reveres Miss Austen or her work more than I." He twisted his long body in his seat, the movement producing nary a crease in his perfectly pressed tan slacks. "May I introduce myself? I am Professor Richard Baines and this is . . . one of my graduate students, Miss Lindsay Weaver."

Lindsay nodded somberly at us. She was a tiny little thing, her pixie features not being limited to her face alone; her thick blue cardigan and wool skirt practically swallowed up her small frame. She wore no makeup, but her complexion was nevertheless clear and smooth, and her jet-black hair was cut short with thick bangs that skimmed the top of her glasses.

"I am Winifred Reynolds," replied Aunt Winnie, "and this is my great-niece, Elizabeth Parker." I produced a weak smile.

"And are you on your way to the Jane Austen Festival in Bath?" Professor Baines asked.

"We are," I answered.

"Excellent! We are, as well. I attend every year, of course. In addition to being a professor of English literature, I'm a frequent lecturer at many of the Jane Austen regional societies."

"I see," Aunt Winnie replied. "And how do they generally react when you tell them that Austen was not only an atheist but a Communist to boot?"

He shrugged, unconcerned. "Some don't like it, of course. They see it as a heresy of sorts. Others, of course, are able to catch a glimmer of the truth. It is to those advanced minds to whom I chiefly address my papers."

"Uh-huh, and do you mind sharing the basis for this rather astonishing revelation that Jane Austen, daughter of a clergyman and by all accounts a God-fearing Christian woman, was actually an atheist, Rich?" Aunt Winnie inquired. I glanced at her in bewilderment. Why was she engaging this man in conversation, especially since it was clear he was a complete dolt? Then I saw the answer. She had finished her Elizabeth Peters paperback and was looking for a new form of entertainment. Inwardly, I groaned. A bored Aunt Winnie was always a daunting prospect.

"It's Richard, actually, and I'd be happy to enlighten you," replied Professor Baines. "Through Miss Austen's character Mr. Collins in *Pride and Prejudice,* we can perceive her true feelings for the church and the clergy. Mr. Collins is, of course, a buffoon and a hypocrite. He is no man of God, which was Miss Austen's way of saying that *none* of the clergy are men of God. They are *all* quacks and charlatans."

Well, if Aunt Winnie was going to play, then I saw no reason not to join, particularly when Jane Austen was the subject. I mentally buzzed in to the game: *Alex, I'll take "The Clergy in Austen" for $800.*

"I agree with you that Mr. Collins is a fool," I said, "but he's just one of the many examples of clergymen that Austen presents us with. We also have Mr. Tilney in *Northanger Abbey,* who is sensible, kind, and wise."

Not posed in the form of a question, perhaps, but still correct.

Professor Baines and Lindsay, however, exchanged glances of

sympathetic derision. "I thought exactly as you did, Elizabeth," Lindsay said kindly but knowingly, "until I realized, thanks to Professor Baines, that Mr. Tilney is an even bigger hypocrite than Mr. Collins. Mr. Collins is a fool, but Mr. Tilney is an educated man, and so his crime is more the worse."

"His crime?" Aunt Winnie asked, her artfully enhanced brows drawn together in confusion. "What crime did poor Mr. Tilney commit?"

"Poor Mr. Tilney, indeed! Why, madam, he helped his father cover up the crime of murdering his mother! He was an accessory after the fact!" Lindsay exclaimed.

I stared at her in horrified amusement. "But his mother wasn't murdered!" I interjected. "That is the whole point of *Northanger Abbey*—to illustrate the dangers of an overactive imagination."

"No, that's what you are *meant* to think," said Professor Baines. "That's the cover story that Austen wrote to hide her true tale— one of murderous deeds and the sins of hiding them. Did you never notice that it's called *NorthANGER Abbey*? Austen is very angry about her topic. It is no coincidence that Mr. Tilney is one of the most heinous of all Austen's villains."

"Mr. Tilney?" I repeated in disbelief. "But that's absurd! He's . . . he's . . . well, he's Mr. Tilney!" Inarticulate perhaps, but true. Aunt Winnie patted my hand in silent commiseration.

"It most definitely is *not* absurd," Professor Baines replied testily. "There is much more than meets the eye in Austen, especially with regard to her antiestablishment views about the church. Take for instance Mary Crawford's comment about the clergy in *Mansfield Park*. Do you recall what she said? 'A clergyman has nothing to do but be slovenly and selfish—read the newspaper, watch the weather, and quarrel with his wife. His curate does all the work, and the business of his own life is to dine.'" He smiled smugly at us. "How do you explain *that* passage, if not as a condemnation of the church?"

"I think that you are forgetting that Mary's not the heroine— Fanny is. Mary's words were meant not as a jab at the church but as evidence of her own selfish character," I said. "Remember, in the end Mary is revealed to be a woman of indifferent morals."

Professor Baines shook his head. "You are incorrect. That's how she's portrayed in the film adaptations, perhaps, but not in the book. You just have to know where and how to look for it. You are like so many of my younger students. You rely only on Hollywood's interpretation of Austen's works to form your opinion."

"I don't, actually," I said, not knowing whether to laugh or scream. "I've read each of her novels many times over—*Mansfield Park* included. And I'm sorry, but I don't see any evidence to support what you are saying."

"Well, it takes a special kind of reader to see the clues," he said.

"'There is, I believe, in every disposition a tendency to some particular evil, a natural defect, which not even the best education can overcome,'" Aunt Winnie quoted rather pointedly.

Professor Baines arched his eyebrow. "Are you suggesting that mine is a propensity to hate everybody?"

"No, of course not," Aunt Winnie answered with a saccharine smile. "Only to willfully misunderstand."

The flight attendant finally arrived with the champagne. After dispensing the glasses, she returned to the kitchen area. Professor

Baines regarded the pale bubbles in his flute suspiciously before lifting it in a kind of salute. "Although we may disagree on Austen's intended message," he said, "we can at least agree that we enjoy her work."

Aunt Winnie lifted her glass in turn and tipped her head in acknowledgment. "Agreed."

Professor Baines's aristocratic nose wrinkled as he brought the glass to his mouth, but then with a what-the-hell smile, he gamely took a large sip. Lindsay was less daring. Her face pulled into an expression of indecision; she reluctantly took a teensy sip before quickly setting the glass back down on her tray table. Professor Baines patted her hand with understanding. "I grant you that it is not a *tête de cuvée,* but we must make do," he said sympathetically.

Catching Aunt Winnie's eye, I indicated my glass. "It is tolerable, but not bubbly enough to tempt *me,*" I whispered.

She grinned. "Good God, man! I would not be so fastidious as you are for a kingdom!" Then, to prove her point, she downed half the glass.

I took another sip without complaint. But then it was rare that I was in such poor humor as to not give consequence to free champagne slighted by pompous pseudointellectuals. Putting my glass down on the tray, I picked up the latest issue of *SkyMall* with feigned interest. I hoped that my apparent fascination with lawn-aerating shoes would deter Professor Baines from continuing the conversation, but he persisted in trying to prove his point. "You have to understand that the general opinion of Austen is incorrect," he said.

Oh, sweet baby Jesus. Really?

"'Where an opinion is general, it is usually correct,'" countered Aunt Winnie.

Professor Baines ignored her and kept talking. "I think that much of the conventional wisdom regarding Austen's work comes from our perception of her chaste, quiet life. Had she been a different kind of woman, her works might be viewed differently. Wouldn't you agree?"

"Not necessarily," I answered, reluctantly putting down the magazine. "Take Hemingway, for instance. He was a bullying, alcoholic misogynist, but knowing that doesn't change his Nick Adams stories and their theme of redemption through dignity in deeds."

Professor Baines shot me an indulgent smile as if I were a petulant child. "That's different, of course, because Hemmingway was a man. Hopefully, you'll figure that out when you're a little older."

Okay, now he had gone too far. *Because he was a man?* He was officially in the boat with Fredo. Aunt Winnie put a restraining hand on my wrist. I paused and put my shoe back on.

Professor Baines continued on, unaware. "That's why I'm so excited to deliver my latest paper. Finally, I will provide the proof that Jane Austen wasn't merely writing clever little romances. After much research and by breaking the codes apparent both in her letters and works, I believe that I have finally discerned something truly shocking, something that the literary establishment doesn't want you to know." His voice dropped ominously. "In fact, what I've discovered is nothing short of a bombshell."

"Oh, I've no doubt it is," Aunt Winnie replied, lowering her voice in turn. "But don't tell me. Let me guess." She leaned forward, her face serious. "You've discovered that Edward Ferris rather 'enjoyed' the company of horses, haven't you?"

While I attempted to mop up the champagne I'd spit all over my chin and sweater, Professor Baines's mouth twisted in annoyance. Despite his obvious irritation, however, he was determined to go on and impress us with his discovery. "I have uncovered proof—although coded proof—that Jane Austen did not die from Addison's disease or tuberculosis." Pausing dramatically, he said, "Jane Austen died as the result of syphilis."

After making this preposterous proclamation, he leaned back in his seat, clearly pleased with himself and his so-called discovery. I'm not sure what effect he expected this "bombshell" to have on us, but I doubted it was the one he got. After a brief moment of stunned silence, I began to giggle. Then Aunt Winnie joined in. Then we couldn't seem to stop. It was like when you're in church and you know you shouldn't laugh but that somehow makes it all the funnier. Soon tears were streaming down my face, and Aunt Winnie was snorting inelegantly and muttering, "Capital! Capital!"

"This is no laughing matter!" Professor Baines exclaimed angrily. Next to him, Lindsay glared indignantly at us on his behalf.

"I'm sorry, but what you are proposing is ludicrous!" Aunt Winnie finally said when she got her breath. "Honestly, I don't know how you think that's even remotely possible. But, Rich"—Professor Baines winced—"I can tell you this, if you plan on presenting that paper during the festival, you are going to find yourself on the wrong side of an angry crowd."

"The uninformed masses do not frighten me," he replied coolly. His earlier spirit of magnanimous condescension had vanished.

His eyes had sharpened while we were giggling until his pupils were tiny black dots anchored in icy blue pools. It would seem that Professor Baines did not like having his "shocking discovery" so openly mocked, especially in front of one of his adoring students. And he *really* didn't like being called "Rich."

"I'm sorry to have wasted your time," he said stiffly. "I can see now that your mind is closed to that which you do not wish to see. I will trouble you no more." With that he turned his back to us and resumed his lecture to Lindsay.

Aunt Winnie shook her head and wiped the moisture from her eyes. "I'll tell you this much," she said to me in a low voice, "if he gives that paper at the festival, he'll be drawn and quartered."

"Which is, I believe, what happened to Mrs. Tilney," I whispered back.

For the next hour Aunt Winnie and I tried to outdo each other with outrageous perversions of Austen's novels. I thought I had her with my "discovery" that Louisa Musgrove didn't jump down the stairs but was pushed by Anne Elliot, until she topped me with her revelation that Jane's cold at Netherfield was actually the clap.

After a while we both fell asleep, neither of us giving any more thought to Professor Baines and his fate once he presented his thesis. Of course, we knew that whatever it was, he wouldn't be drawn and quartered—even though, as Jane herself might opine, his name was Richard. No one was going to do that in this day and age.

CHAPTER 2

*I must endeavor to subdue my mind to my fortune. I must
learn to brook being happier than I deserve.*

—PERSUASION

HE NEXT MORNING my eyes were bleary, my neck was
stiff, and I had a nasty taste in my mouth. But I didn't
care. I was in London! Well, on a plane, on the tarmac, at London's
Heathrow Airport, but that still was—in the lingo of a true Anglophile—a brilliant way to start my day.

As we departed the plane and made our way to the baggage
area, we passed through an area that looked identical to the opening and ending scenes in *Love Actually.* I stupidly found myself
looking for Hugh Grant, Emma Thompson, and, God grant me,
Alan Rickman. Some dreams never die.

After we retrieved our luggage from the carousel, I headed for
the ladies' room to freshen up. Just because I wasn't going to let the
nasty taste in my mouth ruin my morning, that didn't mean I
wasn't going to do anything about it. I had just retrieved my travel
toothbrush from my purse when Lindsay exited one of the stalls,
looking pale and wan. She headed for the sink, where she turned
on the taps and began splashing water on her face. Once done, she

looked up and saw my reflection in the mirror. Meeting my eyes, she dipped her head slightly in acknowledgment, and I gathered she was still upset at the less than serious consideration with which Aunt Winnie and I had received Professor Baines's important "bombshell." However, in spite of her lack of enthusiasm at seeing me, I could see that she wasn't feeling well. I took a tentative step toward her. "Are you okay?" I asked.

Grabbing a paper towel from the dispenser, she patted her face dry. "I'm fine, thanks. I guess I'm not the best flyer," she said quietly.

Suddenly feeling guilty at my giggly reaction, I said, "I'm sorry if we were rude last night. I . . ." There, unfortunately, I stopped. I couldn't think of anything else to say, other than, "But really, the idea that Jane Austen died of syphilis is the most absurd thing I've heard in a long time." And as that hardly seemed apologetic or helpful, I closed my mouth.

Lindsay shook her head. "It's all right. Ric . . . Professor Baines is used to people dismissing him and his ideas. But he is making a name for himself through his discoveries."

Of that, I was quite sure. However, I suspected the name that immediately sprang to my mind—wanker—was far different from the one imagined by Lindsay. I hoped I managed to keep my face neutral, although it wasn't a particularly high hope. Facial neutrality is not a trait that I'm known for, especially first thing in the morning. Fortunately, Lindsay wasn't watching me. She rested her hands on the edge of the sink and closed her eyes.

"Can I get you anything?" I asked.

She took a deep breath, opened her eyes, and shook her head. Staring at her ashy reflection in the mirror, she said, "No, I'll be fine. Too much champagne, I guess. I just need to eat something, that's all." She moved away from the sink toward the exit. At the doorway, however, she turned back to me and said, "But you and your aunt should really reconsider Professor Baines's discoveries. They're all backed up in the books. You just have to know how to look for them."

I had been rude enough already, so I merely nodded and said, "Okay. I hope you feel better."

After I brushed my teeth, I found Aunt Winnie, and we grabbed a much needed cup of coffee and headed for customs. I knew it would be more fitting to get a cup of tea, but I needed the jolt of caffeine that only coffee can promise. Once through customs, we ran into Lindsay and Professor Baines again as they headed for the exit. While she acknowledged my presence with a slight nod, Professor Baines did not. In fact, he practically pushed past me in his haste to move away from us. I was surprised at his rudeness until I saw the unlit cigarette in his hand and the steely determination in his eyes as he closed the gap to the outside smoking area.

By the time Aunt Winnie and I stepped out into the cold morning air in search of a taxi, Professor Baines was greedily sucking on the end of his cigarette, each breath seeming to calm him a little more. Lindsay stood next to him, her pale face etched in misery as she tried without success to avoid the smoky gray tendrils. When the cigarette was halfway gone, his equanimity was restored to such an extent that he was able to bestow a small smile in our direction.

Aunt Winnie and I waved back with equal affability, and then hailed a taxi—one of those iconic black beauties—and headed to

London proper. Although our final destination was Bath, Aunt Winnie had insisted that we spend our first night in London. And she said that if we were to spend a night in London, then we simply had to stay at Claridge's.

Before I knew it, our taxi was in Mayfair and pulling up to the famed hotel on Brook Street. Described by many as "the last word in London's luxury hotels" and "Mayfair's Art Deco Jewel" and by me simply as "awesome," it was by any description stunning. From its relatively humble beginnings in a conventional London terraced house, it has grown both in size and reputation to its current status, that of an extension of Buckingham Palace. I was practically giddy. Pulling out the camera that my boyfriend, Peter, had given me before the trip, I snapped several pictures.

We were helped out of the taxi by a uniformed doorman complete with top hat and led into the Front Hall, a magnificently airy room of yellow walls, intricate white moldings, and gleaming floors of black-and-white marble. I snapped several more pictures.

As we moved to the reception desk, Aunt Winnie said, "I booked us for high tea this afternoon. It's such a treat and I know you'll love it."

"I can think of no better way to end a day after exploring London," I said.

"I didn't think I'd have to twist your arm, but I didn't know how jet-lagged you'd be. But the best thing to do is just keep going and get on local time. I thought we could check in, change our clothes, and then do a little sightseeing and shopping. After all, Bond Street is just a few feet away. Tea is at four, which should allow us plenty of time to explore the city. What do you say?"

"I say that I am certainly the most fortunate creature that ever existed," I replied with a grin.

Although it was my first time to London, it wasn't Aunt Winnie's. In fact, she's been around the world several times. When she was younger, she landed a job as an investor—a vocation for which she apparently has quite a talent. The result was that she made a lot of people, including herself, very wealthy. Several years ago, she retired from all that and bought a house on Cape Cod. She turned it into a B and B—despite having absolutely no experience in hotel management. But just like most things she did, she did it well. The Inn at Longbourn was a huge success, though it did have a rocky start when one of the guests was murdered. But once that was cleared up, with some assistance from yours truly, business picked up. In fact, business was so good that she and her current boyfriend, Randy, recently purchased another property. This one was on Nantucket, and it too was to be converted into a B and B. Like its predecessor, it was to have an Austen theme. Each room is going to be decorated in a manner consistent with one of Austen's novels. Aunt Winnie plans on calling it Aust-Inn-Tatious.

Now that we were finally in London, we immediately made our way to one of the city's most treasured sites: Jane Austen's portrait in the National Portrait Gallery. The unfinished pencil and watercolor sketch was undertaken in 1810 by her sister Cassandra, and it is the only known authenticated likeness of her.

The painting is roughly the size of a playing card, and to set your eyes upon it is simultaneously exciting and disappointing. As a Janeite, to behold an image of her is, of course, wonderful, but sadly, it's not how most fans picture their beloved author. While

Cassandra was considered an accomplished artist, the picture is not a flattering one. Jane, who would have been about thirty-five in the sketch, appears dowdy and has an almost pinched, unanimated expression. It's hard to find the woman whom her nephew, James-Edward, recalled as being "very attractive; a clear brunette with a rich colour; round cheeks, with . . . well-formed bright hazel eyes, and brown hair forming natural curls close round her face." Although her niece, Anna Lefroy, claimed it was an unrealistic depiction, going so far as to call it "hideously unlike" her aunt, most scholars agree that the picture is accurate.

We stared reverently at it for several minutes and then rushed through the rest of the museum catching various highlights. We visited the portrait of King Richard III, the villainous ruler who supposedly imprisoned and killed his nephews in the dreaded Tower of London but whom Aunt Winnie and I think was actually framed by Henry VII. After that we headed over to see Holbein's portrait of Henry VIII, Chandos's portrait of William Shakespeare, and Patrick Brontë's painting of his sisters Charlotte, Emily, and Anne. As for that last one, you didn't need to be a student of the Brontës' work to know they weren't a cheerful bunch. That portrait alone makes it quite clear that a generous dose of antidepressants would have done that family wonders.

After the gallery, we walked through Trafalgar Square, taking pictures of ourselves by Nelson's Column and the four lion statues that guard its base. Then we headed to Buckingham Palace to fight against three thousand other tourists to catch a glimpse of the famous guards. From there, we headed to Big Ben and Parliament, fought the crowds again to catch a glimpse of 10 Downing

Street, and then took a taxi to Tower Bridge. Our last stop was Gracechurch Street, the home to Elizabeth Bennet's Aunt and Uncle Gardiner.

I was close to being overcome with Anglophile fever, not to mention developing some new form of carpal tunnel syndrome from repeatedly snapping pictures.

However, it was getting late and we were both starting to fade, so we headed back to the hotel for tea. We had just crossed the lobby when a voice with a distinctive Midwestern twang called out, "Winnie! Winnie Reynolds! Is that you?"

I turned toward the voice and saw a tall, slim woman who appeared to be in her early sixties. She had frizzy brown hair, cut into an odd triangular bob, and a round smiling face. Aunt Winnie peered at her for a moment and then said, "Cora? Is that really you?"

Cora eagerly nodded and hurried over to us, her sensible shoes making nary a sound on the marble floor. "My goodness, you haven't changed a bit!" Cora gushed to Aunt Winnie, once she was standing next to us.

"Nor have you," Aunt Winnie replied with a smile. Indicating me, she added, "Cora, this is my great-niece, Elizabeth Parker. Elizabeth, this is Cora Beadle. I used to work with her late husband, Harold."

I extended my hand. "I'm pleased to meet you, Mrs. Beadle."

"And you as well, my dear," she said, giving my hand a firm shake. "You know, I believe you're about my daughter's age! Her name is Elizabeth, as well, although everyone calls her Izzy." Indicating a young woman now striding our way, her black kitten heels making rhythmic taps as she strode across the marble floor, Cora smiled brightly. "Why, here she is now!"

I turned and saw a woman who did appear to be in her late twenties. However, she was a good two inches taller than my five foot seven and a good ten pounds thinner than my weight of 125. Her hair was flaxen and cut in one of those super-short cuts that look good on only one percent of the population. She was a member of that one percent. The one time I cut my hair that short, people assumed I'd fallen ill. I now wear it shoulder length. Half the time it looks like I've just been caught in an unexpected windstorm, but it's better than having your coworkers take up a collection for you.

"She's a lovely girl, if I do say so myself," Cora gushed to me in one of those artificial whispers that can be heard clear across a room. "Of course, she doesn't look a thing like me, so it's not like I'm bragging. I'm sure you two will get along wonderfully!"

Several male heads turned in admiration as the fair Izzy not so much walked but glided to where we stood. I had a twinge of doubt about the accuracy of that statement. Women like Izzy always made me feel like Mary Bennet must have felt as the only plain sister among so many pretty ones.

"Hello, Mama," said Izzy when she finally got to us. "Are you ready for tea?"

"Yes, dear," replied Cora, "but first I'd like to introduce you to an old friend of mine, Winifred Reynolds, and her great-niece, Elizabeth Parker."

Izzy turned and smiled at us both. Even her teeth were perfect.

"It's very nice to meet you both. Are you joining us for tea?" she asked politely.

Cora turned to us, her expression hopeful. "Oh, yes!" she exclaimed. "That's a wonderful idea. Can you join us?"

Aunt Winnie paused only a split second before saying, "Absolutely. We actually have reservations ourselves. We'll just push together."

We headed to the area just off the foyer, which was set up for afternoon tea. The staff immediately accommodated our request to be seated together. While I glanced in happy contentment at the elegant green-and-white–striped plates, each topped with such goodies as scones with clotted cream and cucumber sandwiches, Cora said, "Well, what brings you to London, Winifred? Holiday or business?"

"Holiday. We're going to the Jane Austen Festival in Bath."

Cora's round face lit up with joy upon hearing this. "Really? Why, what a coincidence! That's where we are heading!"

"Really?" replied Aunt Winnie. "I didn't know you were a Jane Austen fan."

Cora scoffed. "Fan! My dear Winifred, I am the president of our local chapter! And Izzy here is the secretary!" she added proudly.

Izzy turned to me, equally eager. "Are you a Janeite, as well?" she asked.

"I am—" I had just got out, when Izzy clutched my hand in excitement.

"Oh, I just knew when I saw you that you and I would be the best of friends," she gushed. "Tell me, which of the novels is your favorite?"

"I guess I'd have to say *Pride and Prejudice*," I said, "but—"

Izzy's loud squeal of happiness stopped me. It also caused several heads to turn our way. This time minus the male admiration.

"But that's *my* favorite, too!" she announced with a small gasp, as if finding someone who professed that *Pride and Prejudice* was her favorite Jane Austen book was somehow an anomaly. "Oh, I just love Mr. Darcy. I broke up with so many men over the years because they just couldn't compete with Mr. Darcy."

I smiled. "He did raise the bar rather high," I admitted.

"But now you finally have your own Mr. Darcy," Cora said to Izzy. Turning to me with obvious satisfaction, she said, "Izzy recently got engaged to the most wonderful man. Allen Tucker. He is a real-life Darcy. He's on his way to becoming a top realtor in New York. They make the perfect pair; they both go after what they want."

Refusing to dwell on the rather incongruous image of Darcy as a hustling New York realtor, I offered my congratulations as Izzy stuck out her left hand for us to admire her ring.

"So tell me more about you," Izzy said to me after we finished oohing and ahhing over the large diamond. "What do you do for a living?"

"Well, you might say I'm unaffiliated right now." I explained that until recently I was an editor for a small newspaper, but when my boss decided to blame the failure of his pet project on the untimely death of my relative and hold me accountable, I'd quit. "I guess you could say that I realized that I could no longer be intimidated into anything so wholly unreasonable," I added with a laugh.

Izzy regarded me wide-eyed. "So you just quit? Wow. What are you going to do now?"

Before I could answer, Aunt Winnie chimed in. "I'm trying to convince her to open up a detective agency, as she seems to have a knack for catching criminals."

Aunt Winnie was teasing, of course, but the truth was that I'd had some odd experiences over the last few years, and they included being involved in three murder investigations. Although I did not purport to be some kind of Nancy Drew—not out loud, anyway—I had been able to provide real assistance to the police in all three investigations. And while the experiences were a tad more scintillating than ensuring proper subject-verb agreement, I wasn't really seriously thinking of a career change.

"A detective!" exclaimed Izzy, her eyes bright with interest. "How exciting! But how do you expect to meet your Mr. Darcy if you're off chasing criminals?"

I laughed. "First of all, you should know that I'm not a detective. My aunt is prone to hyperbole. And second, I think I've already met my Mr. Darcy. His name is Peter. We've been together for about two years now."

"And is he The One?" asked Izzy.

I paused. It was a question I'd been asking myself a lot lately. Just before Aunt Winnie and I left for this trip, Peter had asked me to move in with him. I'd said no, but it wasn't a decision I'd come to lightly. I love Peter, but in addition to just having quit my job, I'd been forced to move in with my pregnant sister, Kit, and her family thanks to a rampant mold problem in my apartment. I didn't want to move in with Peter because I was desperate. And trust me, jobless and living with Kit—pregnant or not pregnant—was enough to make anyone desperate. When Peter and I took our relationship to the next step—whatever step that was—I wanted it to be because it was the right decision for us, rather than the most convenient decision for my personal situation.

Or, to paraphrase Jane Austen, I didn't want to be accused of pursuing a man merely for the sake of a situation.

Peter was disappointed but said he understood. I hoped that was true, but I had a horrible feeling that I'd blown something. That's about when Aunt Winnie called and told me we were going to Bath. Since then I'd let myself be distracted with travel details.

"I think so," I said to Izzy now.

"Well, then, you should take a page of advice from dear Jane Austen and show more affection than you feel if you are to secure him," Izzy advised teasingly.

I laughed. "Somehow, I don't think Austen meant for us to take that remark seriously," I replied, taking a sip of tea.

"Oh, but I think she did," exclaimed Cora. "Remember, Charlotte Lucas gave that advice for Jane Bennet. And if Jane *had* initially shown more affection to Bingley, then his sisters and Darcy wouldn't have been able to convince him that her heart was untouched!"

"Well, yes," I conceded, "but then Charlotte took her own advice regarding Mr. Collins and ended up married to one of the stupidest men in all of England."

Cora shook her head. "But she was finally *settled,* and that's all she ever cared about. It didn't matter to Charlotte what her husband was like. She just wanted to be comfortably established and married. And that's what she got. As Austen demonstrates in all her books, there were only a few options for women with regard to marriage. Really, one could say that that was the intent and guiding theme in all of her books."

I remembered Professor Baines and his perverted suppositions. "Speaking of Austen's intent," I said, "we met someone on the flight over who had the most bizarre theories on that. He said there were two stories in her books: one obvious and one hidden. But his ideas about these hidden stories were absurd!" I started laughing as I remembered the details. "He claimed that Marianne Dashwood had an abortion, and that Sir Walter Elliot and Elizabeth had an incestuous relationship."

To my surprise, Cora did not seem amused. Her face froze in an expression of disgust and she said with icy disdain, "Let me guess. Professor Richard Baines."

"Why, yes," I said in surprise. "I take it you know him?"

"Unfortunately, I do." Cora's nose wrinkled as if she'd suddenly caught a whiff of raw sewage. "He is a revolting man with revolting ideas and he is perverting Austen's legacy. I cannot stand him. Unfortunately, I have to see him every year at the festival. He considers himself an expert on Austen and is determined to convert people to his way of thinking. It's disgraceful."

Izzy winked at me and said, "Mama would prefer it if he would not go out into society. She thinks he only makes people uncomfortable."

"Do not tease me, Izzy," Cora replied. "You know that what I'm saying is perfectly true. If it wasn't for his money, which came from his father and not from his own efforts, most people wouldn't tolerate him. But because he is rich, he gets away with more. He stirs things up and upsets people."

"He upsets *you*," corrected Izzy. "You've made it your life's objective to ban the man from any Austen gathering—both here and at home. You pick a fight with him every year at the festival and then proceed to get into a huge public screaming match. I'm surprised that it isn't advertised in the brochure as one of the main events."

"You exaggerate," Cora said dismissively, while Izzy mouthed, "No, I don't," to me. "Even his first wife, Gail, left him because of his crazy ideas," Cora continued.

"That's not the only reason Gail left him," said Izzy. "If I remember correctly, his current wife, Alex, had something to do with *that* decision." Turning to Aunt Winnie and me, Izzy said, "It was quite the scandal at the time. Richard had run around on Gail for years, and it's rumored that their son, Ian, is not an only child, if you catch my drift."

Cora flushed and looked away in apparent disgust.

"Anyway," Izzy continued, "Gail and Richard Baines ran one of the best Austen magazines in the States, *Forever Austen*. Then Richard started in with all his secondary story theories and making the most outrageous claims. Some people ignored him, some—like my dear mama," Izzy added with an indulgent smile at Cora, "frothed and foamed at him, while a few others actually entertained his ideas."

"Did Professor Baines's wife—Gail—agree with him?" Aunt Winnie asked.

"God, no. She thought they were complete crap, of course," said Izzy. "But she loved him, I guess, so she put up with it. But then Richard claimed that Darcy and Bingley had been lovers and that was the real reason behind Darcy's dislike of Jane. As you can imagine, all hell broke loose. Gail took his name off the magazine and filed for divorce. At first everyone thought that it was because of his crackpot theories, but within a month or two he'd married his current wife, Alex—who, I might add," she added archly, "is a good ten years younger than Gail."

"The man's a pig on all levels," muttered Cora. "And what made it all the worse for Gail was that as part of the divorce agreement, Richard was still given a monthly column in *Forever Austen*. He's no longer an owner, but he is a contributor. I find that particularly distasteful, because I write a monthly column for the magazine as well. To be published in the same periodical as him is humiliating."

"But surely people don't take him seriously," said Aunt Winnie. "I mean, the stuff he claims to have unearthed is pretty outrageous."

Cora shook her head. "But that's just the problem—he's starting to collect quite a following. Most are stupid little sycophants from his classes hoping to curry favor and a decent grade, but there are others in his camp who ought to know better."

"Such as?" asked Aunt Winnie.

"Well, Byron Chambers, for one," replied Cora. "He serves as a kind of secretary or assistant to Richard. Byron's a smart guy. I've known him for a few years, mainly through the festivals. I don't know why he ever took a position with Richard in the first place. I thought he was better than that."

"Mama, I've told you a thousand times—ignore the man," said Izzy with more than a little frustration. "You sabotage your own cause by constantly engaging him and reacting to him."

"I know, I know, but he makes it so hard. He's always proclaiming some new scandalous find, and I just lose my head," Cora said with a rueful shake of said head.

"Well, maybe this will be the year he won't unleash any new discoveries," Izzy offered.

I have often been told that I have an easy face to read. This is usually articulated to me with the advice, "For God's sake, I hope you don't play poker." Over the years, I've tried to control my expressions, but without much success. Too late, I now felt my face pull into an expression of grave misgiving. Of course, Cora saw it.

"What? Did he say something?" she said to me. "Please tell me that he doesn't have some new cockamamie theory he's going to foist on us during the festival."

"Well, um, he may have mentioned something—" I began, but Aunt Winnie cut me off.

"He sure as hell did," she replied with a laugh. "He claims that he's discovered the real reason that Jane Austen died."

Cora stiffened in anticipation, her teacup frozen halfway to her mouth. "And?" she inquired ominously.

Eyes sparkling with laughter, Aunt Winnie leaned over. "He claims she died of syphilis!"

While Izzy gave a snort of laughter, Cora's reaction was much less lighthearted. Her eyes narrowed and she angrily slammed her teacup down onto her platter. "I'll kill the son of a bitch," she said.

CHAPTER 3

It would be an excellent match, for he was rich,
and she was handsome.
—SENSE AND SENSIBILITY

Izzy ROLLED HER EYES. "Oh, Mama. Please, don't be so dramatic. You know he only says these things to shock people and get attention. You're just playing into him."

It seemed pretty sound advice, but Cora was having none of it. "The man is the devil incarnate," she said. "He's bent on ripping down Austen's reputation just so he can build up his own. It isn't right!"

Izzy appeared as if she were about to respond when her eyes focused on something just beyond Cora's indignant left shoulder. "Well, don't look now, but he's here."

Of course Cora did just the opposite and twisted around in her seat. "Who's here? Richard?" she asked.

Izzy didn't need to answer because it was immediately clear that the "he" in question was indeed Professor Baines, aka "Richard." He was also heading our way. He hadn't seen us yet as he was too engrossed in a conversation with another man. Professor Baines's companion was tall with an average build. He had sandy blond hair and a square jaw. His face wasn't classically handsome, but the deep laugh lines that ran from the corners of his brown eyes to the tops of his cheeks made it an appealing one. "Who's that with Professor Baines?" I asked Izzy as the men, still in deep conversation, took a seat at a table not far from us.

"That's Byron Chambers," Izzy replied in a low voice. "He's Richard's assistant, the one we were telling you about before. Mama is right about him, at least. He is a really nice guy. I've no idea why he's working with Richard."

I turned to study Byron again, wondering if he'd been named for Lord Byron. He certainly didn't look "mad, bad, and dangerous to know." But then again, it's generally hard to look any of those things while wearing a blue blazer and gray wool pants. Actually, if anyone resembled Lord Byron it would be Professor Baines. He had the strong profile, the shiny hair, and even the curling lip. All that was missing was an extravagant ensemble of velvet and lace.

No sooner had Professor Baines taken his seat than he noticed Cora glaring at him from our table. A slow smile formed on his lips, and his eyes narrowed with an expression of pleased anticipation. I'd seen that look several times before on Aunt Winnie's cat, Lady Catherine, usually right before she pounced on some unsuspecting victim. It's also a look commonly found on that particularly nasty set of girls in junior high who enjoy ruthlessly tormenting their counterparts on the social ladder. Different species, perhaps, but the same look.

"Why, Mrs. Beadle," Professor Baines purred at Cora. "What a pleasant surprise. It's always lovely to see you. Are you in town for the festival?"

"You know that I am," Cora snapped back. "Tell me, Baines, is it true?" she asked without preamble.

"Is what true?" Professor Baines raised his groomed eyebrows in apparent cheerful confusion at her question. His companion, Byron, however, made no such pretensions. His shoulders hunched slightly as if he were readying himself for an attack.

"Is it true that you are seriously proposing to spread this filthy theory about Jane Austen's death?" Cora demanded.

Professor Baines's blue eyes twinkled in amusement. Whether it was from his enjoyment at Cora's vexation or it stemmed from an egotistic appreciation at his own purported cleverness wasn't clear. What was clear, however, was that the man was relishing every second of the confrontation. Cora by now was too furious to notice.

"My filthy theory?" he repeated, glancing at Byron in seeming bewilderment. Byron pretended not to notice and studied the papers on the table in front of him. "Theories are either true or false. I don't see how they can be 'filthy,'" continued Professor Baines. Cora huffed noisily. "But perhaps," he said with a meaningful glance at Aunt Winnie and me, "you are referring to what I told your companions on the plane last night? My *discovery*—which, my dear Mrs. Beadle, I must point out, is very different from a *theory*."

Next to me, Cora clenched her fists until her knuckles showed white. Izzy rolled her eyes in annoyance, seemingly more at her mother's reaction than from Professor Baines's condescending behavior. "You know damn well what I'm referring to, you arrogant . . . ," Cora began, then stopped herself. Taking a deep breath, she attempted to calm herself before continuing. "Are you seriously claiming that Jane Austen died of . . ." Her voice petered out, unable to form the word.

"Syphilis?" Professor Baines supplied politely.

Cora closed her eyes and visibly shuddered at the sound of the word. "How can you possibly claim such an outrageous perversion?" she asked, but Professor Baines cut her off by forcefully tapping his long forefinger on the thick pile of papers that lay in front of Byron.

"I do not 'claim,'" he said, "I prove. I establish. I demonstrate. With my findings, I will once and for all validate my long-standing claim that Jane Austen was not a blushing virginal spinster but rather an experienced woman of the world who wrote about the hypocrisy of Regency England. For her to not only die from syphilis, but for it to be covered up by the establishment with bogus tales of Addison's disease, only serves to prove my broader point that her novels were also willfully perverted and misconstrued to fit the prudish norms of her day."

Cora's round face was flushed from anger, and her eyes blazed. "This time you've gone too far, Richard. We've tolerated your ridiculous theories about Austen's real stories, and God knows we've tried to be polite—"

Professor Baines cut her off with a snort. "Polite? Last year, you threw a glass of wine in my face. A pink Zinfandel, of all things, if I remember correctly," he added with a shudder.

"I said we've *tried* to be polite," Cora retorted. "I didn't say we've always succeeded. Sometimes you simply make it too impossible. But my point is that if you present this filth, you will have pushed us too far. We will be forced to take the appropriate steps."

Professor Baines leaned back into his upholstered chair and non-chalantly took a sip of tea. "We? And who, may I inquire, is this il-lustrious 'we'?"

"The true Austen fans," Cora replied confidently. "The fans with brains in our heads. We will not sit idly by and let you besmirch her name and reputation. You will be laughed out of every society."

Professor Baines only smiled. "But not laughed at by the press, I think."

Cora leaned forward, her body tense. "What's that supposed to mean?"

Professor Baines shrugged. "I thought it was clear, but then you and I have very different opinions on what is clear and what isn't. However, I am always happy to provide edification for you—*again*. I have taken the liberty of inviting various members of the press to attend my little announcement. I think that most will be quite happy to come out and record the reaction of the . . . as you called them, 'true Austen fans.' I believe that in itself will make quite a news splash."

Cora blanched. "You would, wouldn't you? You'd make some trashy public spectacle just to get your name out there, just to get your precious publicity," she spat out with revulsion. "You're hop-ing for some horrible public display so you can get your lousy fif-teen minutes of fame."

Professor Baines's smile grew wider. His teeth really were al-most abnormally white and large, I thought. "On the contrary," he said, "I assure you. I just want to share my findings with everyone who is interested in Jane Austen, not just those who are fortunate enough to be in Bath."

What little was left of Cora's self-control now broke. "Why, you repulsive, dirty-minded . . . ," she began but was interrupted by the arrival of a woman.

"Oh, dear. Has the fun started already, Richard?" she asked in a tone of bemused surprise. "I thought you were saving *that* for the festival." Turning to our table, she said, "Hello, Cora. Hello, Izzy. It's nice to see you again."

While Cora struggled to get her emotions under control, Izzy shot a wry smile at the woman. "Hello, Alex. Nice to see you, too."

Alex returned the smile. She was very pretty. She was wearing a creamy white cashmere sheath dress and brown suede boots. Her dark brown hair was pulled back into one of those loose, casual-looking ponytails that are anything but. She was maybe about five foot nine and could have been anywhere from thirty-nine to forty-nine years old. It was hard to tell; she had that dewy, fresh skin that is hardly ever seen without the aid of expensive treatments—not after the age of six, anyway. Poor Lindsay, I thought; she hadn't a snowball's chance in hell against a woman like Alex.

Alex turned her attention back to Professor Baines. She leaned in close to his face to place a kiss on his cheek, but then crinkling her nose in disgust, she abruptly pulled back. "Ugh. Darling, you smell like an ashtray. You promised me that you were going to try to quit."

Professor Baines rolled his eyes. "And I will, but not right after a transatlantic flight. A man's got to know his limitations."

Alex produced a small pout. "I thought we were going to have tea, darling," she said with a pointed look at Byron. "Or are we once again to be graced with Byron's presence? Honestly, you two spend so much time together of late I wonder if I should be jealous."

Byron took the hint and immediately stood up. I noticed that his face was slightly flushed, but whether from embarrassment or anger, I couldn't tell. "I was just leaving, Mrs. Baines," he said with cool formality. "Please excuse me." Turning back to Professor Baines, he added, "Richard, I'll make the changes we discussed and get you the final draft tomorrow." With a polite nod in our direction, he left the restaurant.

Next to me, Izzy whispered, "As you can see, Mrs. Baines and Byron are not the best of friends."

As Alex settled into the chair just vacated by Byron, I whispered back, "Why don't they like each other?"

Izzy shrugged. "I'm not sure, really, but I get the impression that Byron doesn't think Alex is terribly bright. I once heard him say that she gives flibbertigibbets a bad name. I think Alex senses that and it chafes because in lots of ways she's been living in Gail's shadow ever since the divorce. Gail is really well liked and respected among the Janeites."

"Gotcha," I said.

Alex turned to Cora now. "I see that you've heard about Richard's findings regarding Jane Austen's death," she said, her tone almost playful.

"You mean his *fabrications,*" Cora shot back. "I've never heard of anything so ridiculous! I will not let him spread this vile story, not while I have breath in my body."

Alex's delicate brows pulled down in a frown. "Oh, for goodness' sake, Cora. Can't you for once just leave him alone? If you don't agree with him, fine. But he is entitled to his opinion just as you are entitled to yours." Unfolding a crisp linen napkin and lay-ing it gently on her lap, she continued, "Honestly, I don't see what the big fuss is about, anyway. Who really cares how the poor woman died? She wrote a few very nice books—some nicer than others, of course." Picking up a cucumber sandwich from the plate on the table, she took a delicate bite before continuing. "I, for one, was never a fan of *Mansfield Park*. Fanny was *such* a dreary little mouse. But in any case, the fact remains that Jane Austen has been dead for about one hundred years. Let it go, already!"

Alex's little speech did have the intended effect of defusing the tension. However, that effect was twofold: while Cora and Richard seemed to have momentarily forgotten their war with each other, both now seemed equally annoyed with Alex.

Jane Austen ironically penned in *Northanger Abbey* that "a woman especially, if she have the misfortune of knowing anything, should conceal it as well as she can." Somehow, I doubted that this was what Alex was doing. Instead, I rather suspected that Byron was right: she was merely a fledgling flibbertigibbet and, as such, apt to annoy her more serious sisters.

CHAPTER 4

I have always maintained the importance
of Aunts as much as possible.
—LETTERS OF JANE AUSTEN

HEN OUR TEA WAS FINISHED, Cora and Izzy seemed loath to part from us. Izzy, in particular, seemed almost distressed that we wouldn't see each other again until the next day. "Promise that we will meet at eight thirty for breakfast. Then we can all go to the train station together," she implored of me. I agreed, of course, because it would be rude not to, but I was still surprised when she hugged me and said, "Oh, this will be such a fun week, especially since *you'll* be with me!"

I wasn't positive, as Izzy seemed a reserved sort of girl, but I think I'd just made a new best friend for life.

We were just leaving the restaurant when Cora gave a sudden yelp of alarm. "My purse is gone!" she cried.

"Really, Mama," Izzy huffed with a practiced roll of her blue eyes. "You lose *everything*!"

Cora ignored Izzy and began to frantically search the area. Happily, her purse was found within a few minutes, shoved under a nearby chair. "But how on earth did it get there?" Cora asked us with a bewildered face.

"You must have somehow pushed it with your foot," offered Izzy.

"But I didn't!" came Cora's indignant reply.

"Well, then elves must have done it," Izzy retorted. "Or perhaps Richard Baines did it. Lord knows you fight with him about everything else; perhaps you should add malicious mischief to his list of crimes."

Cora muttered something under her breath while Izzy continued to tease her. Aunt Winnie and I took advantage of their distraction to quickly pantomime our good-byes and dashed upstairs to our room.

I have to say, I have never been in a room like our room at Claridge's. It opened into a small, elegant foyer where we were greeted by a side table upon which there was an arrangement of purple and white orchids and a complimentary platter of grapes, dried apricots, and figs. The room itself had a high double tray ceiling and walls the color of thick cream. The patterned rug continued this neutral color theme with shades of toffee and champagne, offering a contrast to the gauzy purple of the bedspread and furniture upholstery. And the bathroom! The bathroom was an art deco masterpiece of marble and glass. I could live in that bathroom for a week and be quite content with my situation. I added several more photos to my growing collection.

Flopping on the soft bed, I let out a sigh of happiness. "You have a sweet room here, Ms. Reynolds. I do not know a place in the country that is equal to Claridge's," I said.

Aunt Winnie laughed. "And I would not think of quitting it in a hurry," she said, "were it not for the exorbitant cost." Examining the fruit platter, she chose a plump fig and popped it into her mouth.

I propped myself up on my elbows. "Yes, about that. Would you please let me chip in for this? I have money and, as much as I appreciate the gesture, I don't need or want you to pay for everything."

Aunt Winnie waved away my words while she finished chewing. "I never said you did," she said once she'd swallowed. "But this is my treat. Besides, you just quit your job. Now is not the time to be spending money foolishly."

While it was true that I had just quit my job as an editor for a D.C.-based newspaper, a publication that was nothing more than a vanity project for the odious owner, I wasn't without funds. Not totally, anyway. One of the unexpected perks of having a rampant mold problem in your apartment is not being saddled with a pesky rent bill while the landlord fixes the "unfortunate trouble." Of course, not having a place to sleep was a definite drawback. And while my sister, Kit, had kindly taken me in, that came with its own set of difficulties. Kit is the personification of the "smug marrieds" that Helen Fielding wrote about, especially since she became pregnant with her second child or, as I privately refer to it, "the Second Coming." In her spare time, she likes to tell me what's wrong with my life.

Kit has a *lot* of spare time.

The main thing that bugs Kit about me is my involvement—my *helpful* involvement—in a few murder investigations. Not out of any fear for my safety, mind you. No, what really bugs Kit is that on her private scorecard, she wins in the categories of house, husband, and family, but she can't compete with me on murder investigations. It's that—no pun intended—which kills her.

"Spending money to attend the Jane Austen Festival in Bath could never be considered foolish," I retorted. "It isn't right for you to pay my whole way, Aunt Winnie. I'm a grown woman. I simply can't let you do it."

Aunt Winnie snorted. "There is a stubbornness about me that never can bear to be frightened at the will of others. My courage always rises with every attempt to intimidate me."

I was not to be outdone. "I have had the pleasure of your acquaintance long enough to know, that you find great enjoyment in occasionally professing opinions which in fact are not your own," I quoted back.

"True," Aunt Winnie replied with a dip of her red head. "But, I'm resolved on the matter, so keep your breath to cool your porridge. Or, in other words, shut your pie hole," she added with a grin. "Besides, you need to get dressed for dinner. We have reservations downstairs at Gordon Ramsey's restaurant."

"How did you manage that?" I asked, momentarily distracted from the topic. "We only found out last week that we were coming— don't you need to make reservations there several months in advance?"

"You do," Aunt Winnie replied smugly as she plucked a silky dress from the closet. "However, a friend of a friend pulled some strings and got us in. Which is why you need to stop yakking and start getting dressed."

"Okay, okay, but our conversation is not over." I hopped off the bed and headed for the shower. "I'll be ready in a flash."

Forty-five minutes later (okay, okay, so I'm not the Scarlet Speedster), I was showered and ready. I was wearing a new dress, one that I had bought especially for the trip. It was a black square-necked sheath with horizontal pleats and short sleeves and an illusion back. I thought I looked rather elegant until I saw Aunt Winnie. As usual, her ensemble far outshone my own simple one. So much so that I suddenly felt like the main character in *Cousin Bette*. Her dress was bright sapphire. It was also skimpy and clingy and, judging by its incandescent glow, spun from silkworms suffering from radiation poisoning. It also offered an almost indecent amount of cleavage. Silver and rhinestone platform pumps with four-and-a-half-inch heels completed the look. In short, she looked like she'd been poured into her dress by an overzealous bartender on ladies' night. Which, when I stopped to think about it, was a typical outfit for Aunt Winnie.

"How do you like it?" she asked, happily twirling in front of me.

"Would you be offended if I told you that you look at once expensively and nakedly dressed?"

"Of course not, silly. That was my aim."

"Oh, well, in that case—well done. Full marks."

My subsequent suggestion of a shawl was rejected as prudish, so we made our way downstairs and crossed the lobby to the famed restaurant. Decorated with a nod to 1930s opulence, the room is furbished in warm shades of caramel, burgundy, and honey. I closed my eyes for a moment to soak in the atmosphere, from the faint tinkling of expensive crystal to the hushed accented murmurings where nary an *r* was rolled and several *t*'s were elegantly dropped. It was as if I'd stepped into an episode of Agatha Christie's *Poirot*, one in which Poirot and Hastings were seconds away from the civilized confrontation of the wealthy killer, all while enjoying a delectable amuse-bouche. I may have sighed with happiness.

Oh, who am I kidding? I *did* sigh with happiness. I was finally in London, damn it! I was floating in a giddy tea-infused, strawberries and scones, Burberry tweed dream come true.

Okay, so maybe I was a bit jet-lagged. And I guess there might be some truth to the oft-repeated observation by some that I watch entirely too much PBS and *Masterpiece Theatre.*

Whatever. As if there is such a thing as too much *Masterpiece Theatre.*

Once we were seated at our table, we were attended by a seemingly never-ending parade of exceedingly polite waiters. After our orders had been placed and the wine had been served, I leaned back in my chair and said, "So, seeing as how I have the strong feeling that Izzy is to be my constant companion over the next week, tell me again how you know them?"

Aunt Winnie laughed. "Well, I don't really know Izzy. When I last saw her, she was a little bit of a thing. She's grown into quite a nice-looking girl, though."

"I gather she takes after her father in looks," I said, remembering Cora's earlier comments.

Aunt Winnie paused to consider the question. "No, actually. She doesn't look a thing like Harold, which, God forgive me, is actually a blessing. Harold was short, bald, and terribly nearsighted. Or was it farsighted?" Aunt Winnie mused. "I can never remember which is which. Oh, well, it doesn't matter. I just remember he wore these enormous glasses, a bit like the ones Charles Nelson Reilly used to wear. But Cora is relatively harmless," Aunt Winnie said with a smile. "She's just very excitable. She was never one to take a deep breath and think before speaking or acting—as you saw for yourself today."

"Yes, I sort of caught on to that whole theme of her being eager in everything and her sorrows and joys could have no moderation."

Aunt Winnie nodded. "Cora means well, but Lord, how she used to fray poor Harold's nerves. He was the complete opposite of her, of course. Always cool, calm, and rational. Bit of a bore, actually, now that I stop to remember him."

"Well, it should be an interesting week, then," I said, after taking a sip of wine. "I get to attend my very first Jane Austen Festival with my new best friend, Izzy, her excitable mother, Cora, and then watch the fun unfold when Professor Baines announces to the world his discovery that Jane Austen was apparently something of a Commie tart."

"Yes," agreed Aunt Winnie. "You will have to keep a journal, for how are your absent cousins to understand the tenor of your life in Bath without one?"

I laughed at that and then immediately dismissed it from my head as the first of our courses arrived. It's hard to stay focused on anything but your stomach when a bowl of Thai-spiced lobster ravioli, lemon grass, lime, and coconut broth is placed before you.

But by the week's end, I would find myself wishing I *had* kept a journal. It might have helped in making sense of the coming calamity.

CHAPTER 5

Oh! Who can ever be tired of Bath?

—NORTHANGER ABBEY

HERE YOU ARE!" cried Izzy the next morning as I crossed the lobby to her. "I've been waiting forever! Where have you been?"

Surprised, I found myself apologizing. "I'm sorry. Have you been waiting long?"

"Ages."

Confused, I glanced at my watch. "But didn't we say eight thirty? It's just eight thirty now."

"It doesn't matter. I'm just glad that you're finally here, and I can join Mama at the table and get away from those horrible men over there." She tipped her blond head to the far end of the lobby. "They have been practically *gawking* at me this whole time. I grant you, they *are* very good-looking, but still, I am surprised. Englishmen aren't usually so forward."

I turned in the direction indicated and saw two conservatively dressed businessmen intently reading the *London Times*. I inwardly agreed with Izzy that they were very good-looking; however, they appeared to be anything but gawking. After a moment, one looked up and glanced rather vacantly in our direction. Seeing us staring at him, he nodded politely and returned to his paper. "See what I mean?" Izzy hissed. "It's disgraceful!"

Either I was still jet-lagged or Izzy was delusional. "Where's your mother?" I asked, hoping to change the subject.

"Mama went to get us a table," she said. "Where's your aunt?"

"Checking out. Oh, here she is," I replied, as Aunt Winnie made her way to us.

"Good morning, Izzy," said Aunt Winnie. "How are you today?"

"Fine," Izzy said, shooting a coy glance in the direction of the men who were again absorbed in their papers. "Mama's gotten us a table."

Aunt Winnie followed Izzy's gaze and then glanced back to me. I shrugged. "Well, let's join her," Aunt Winnie said. With one last lingering look at the men, Izzy turned and made her way to the breakfast area. Cora saw us and waved us to the table.

"I hope you don't mind, but I already ordered us tea," she said. "I don't want to risk being late to the train station."

"Tea sounds fine—" began Aunt Winnie.

Cora cut her off. "I was up all night, trying to figure out our problem. I imagine you were, too, and I think if we put our heads together, we can find a solution by the time we get to Bath."

Aunt Winnie responded with a blank look. "What problem?" she asked.

Cora's eyes opened in surprise. "Why, Richard, of course! What are we going to do to stop him from spreading his filthy lies about Jane?"

Aunt Winnie sighed. "Cora, anyone who believes his drivel is no Austen fan with any sense, and all true Austen fans have sense, so don't worry. Besides, I don't think there's anything we can do. If the man wants to make his claims, we can't stop him. It's a free country, after all."

Cora shook her head in disagreement. "No, it's not. That's America."

I stifled a laugh. "I don't think free speech is exactly frowned upon here," I said.

Cora shot me a level look. "Well, his particular brand of speech is frowned upon by *me,* I can tell you that."

"Yes, Mama," said Izzy, pulling her still hopeful gaze away from the lobby. "Despite your rather cagey behavior, I think we all managed to decipher your true feelings about Richard Baines."

"Well, what do *you* propose we do about him?" Cora countered.

"Nothing. Tease him. Laugh at him. Please, for once, don't rise to his bait. You make it worse. Every blessed time you make it worse." From the way Izzy uttered these words calmly and without emotion, I gathered it was an oft-repeated speech. From the way Cora kept proposing ideas, I also gathered it was an oft-ignored speech.

And so it continued for the rest of the morning. Cora could be steered to no other topic but how to thwart Richard Baines. As we headed outside to hail a taxi for Paddington Station, I saw with delight that it was a perfect, crisp autumn day—made all the more lovely by virtue of it being a perfect, crisp autumn day in *London.* Cora, however, seemed oblivious of our surroundings and prattled on. Could we steal his paper? Could we somehow get to Byron? Could we preempt him by calling the press ourselves?

It went on and on. After offering a few polite responses, I gave up and largely ignored her. So did Aunt Winnie and Izzy. I don't think Cora noticed, so consumed was she by her topic. She only briefly stopped her rant when she thought she'd lost the train tickets, but upon discovering them in her coat pocket, she quickly resumed her tirade.

Soon the taxi deposited us at the station. While Cora continued to fret about "our" problem, we quickly made our way to our assigned track and soon we were on board the ten-thirty high-speed train to Bath.

Bath!

I got a happy little chill at the very thought of it. Home of the famous Roman baths, the glorious Circus, and, of course, the Jane Austen Centre. An hour and a half later, our train was pulling into Victoria Station in the city's center. As we emerged from the station, I glanced all around me, afraid to miss one single sight. While Anne Elliot is perhaps second only to Elizabeth Bennet as my favorite Austen heroine, I have to admit I did not share her dismal view of the city. I neither entertained a very determined disinclination for Bath, nor did I hold a disinclination to see more of the extensive buildings. Rather, I was like Catherine Morland—all eager delight. My eyes were here, there, everywhere, as I approached the city's fine and striking environs. I was come to be happy, and I felt happy already.

All around us was evidence of the upcoming festival. Banners and posters were everywhere. The streets were crowded with tourists, many of whom were clutching well-worn copies of Austen's novels as if they were the Holy Grail of travel guides. As we were staying at a different hotel from Cora and Izzy, we said our temporary good-byes, which were mingled with fervent entreaties from Izzy to swear that we would meet later.

I admit it was with some relief that I saw their forms disappear up the street and out of sight.

"Dear God," said Aunt Winnie with a weary sigh. "I'd forgotten what an excellent talker Cora is and how she can get so completely rattled over nothing."

"I wouldn't let her catch you saying that defending Jane Austen's reputation is a mere nothing."

"Good point. I'm beginning to remember why Harold was so quiet. I attributed it to dullness, but I think I've done the poor man a disservice. He probably just gave up trying to get a word in edgewise."

"Do you think she's really going to try and stop Baines from presenting his paper?" I asked, as we threaded our way through the crowd toward our hotel.

"I sincerely hope not," Aunt Winnie replied. "I have a suspicion that that is exactly what he hopes she *will* do. As much as I think the man is full of it, he is right on one count: the press would love a story of some crazed Austen fan attacking an English professor over his scintillating views on Austen."

"Do you think he's intentionally goading her?"

Aunt Winnie paused in front of a poster. In large print, it proclaimed THE TRUTH BEHIND AUSTEN'S DEATH: A COVER-UP EXPOSED. Below it, in smaller letters, it read, JOIN RENOWNED ENGLISH LITERATURE PROFESSOR, RICHARD BAINES, 7 P.M. SUNDAY AT 3 UPPER CAMDEN PLACE, CAMDEN ROAD, TO HEAR HIS GROUNDBREAKING REVELATIONS. In the background, there was a faded watercolor sketch of a busty woman provocatively sprawled on a bed, the neckline of her tissue-thin chemise millimeters away from indecency.

Aunt Winnie tilted her head. "I think I'd better keep an eye on Cora," was all she said.

OUR HOTEL WAS on Henrietta Street, an elegant avenue lined with stately Georgian homes. I was convinced it served as the setting for Camden Place in the 1995 film adaptation of *Persuasion,* but Aunt Winnie disagreed. We argued the point for several minutes until the proprietor, a middle-aged woman with a kind heart-shaped face who appeared used to hearing such meaningless topics so hotly debated, politely interrupted to inform us that while her hotel was *not* the location in question, she would be happy to show us where it was. She pulled out a walking map of Bath and circled the location, Number One, Royal Crescent, and provided us directions on how to get there. Having been proved correct, Aunt Winnie smirked. I, as is also my habit in these situations, ignored her.

Our room key and map in hand, Aunt Winnie and I were about to head upstairs when a man who had evidently overheard our conversation came toward us. "I take it you ladies are in town for the festival?" he asked in a booming voice.

He appeared to be in his early thirties. He wasn't particularly handsome; his forehead jutted out from a receding hairline over eyes that were set too close together. He was only a few inches taller than I am, and from the looks of his wiry build only a few pounds heavier as well. His tweed blazer was close to being threadbare, and his jeans were ripped. However, his Rolex was obscenely large, and his shoes hinted of Italian beginnings at the gentle hands of a gloved master. Taken all together, it gave the impression that he was intentionally trying to lessen the potential of his appearance. Why, I couldn't begin to imagine.

"We are here for the festival," Aunt Winnie answered. "Are you?"

"Yes indeed. I never miss it. I've been coming for the last fifteen years at least."

I paused. "But I thought the first festival was held in 2000?"

"Good God, no! It must be older than that! I'm sure of it. I should know, after all, I've been coming to them all this time, haven't I? No, no, you must be mistaken. But it's a frightfully good time. You must let me show you some of the better sights. I'm quite an expert, you know. How could I not be, after coming to them for so long? I'm John Ragget, by the way."

We shook hands all around, and Aunt Winnie and I introduced ourselves. "Well, you must let me show you Bath," John continued. "You won't find anyone more knowledgeable. And I have a car, of course. It's a Jaguar convertible, actually." Addressing me, he asked, "Do you like Jaguars?"

I really didn't care one way or the other. I wanted only to get away from this blowhard and go to our room, but my mother raised me to be polite. "They're very nice," I offered. Apparently, my offering missed the mark entirely.

"Nice?" John cried in a loud tone of outrage. "They're a damn bit more than just nice, I can tell you. They're bloody brilliant! I just got mine last week. Paid through the bloody nose for it, but, damn it, I didn't care! I simply had to have it. When I see something I want, I'm not one to dither about. No, indeed. I act!"

"You're perfect," Aunt Winnie said, her eyes bright. I surreptitiously nudged her, hoping she'd rein in the sarcasm, but I needn't have bothered. John missed her meaning entirely.

"Well, as you Americans are fond of saying, that's how I roll," he informed us with a straight face. Aunt Winnie was right. He *was* perfect. Unintentionally so, and for all the wrong reasons, but nevertheless, he was indeed perfect.

"So, is it a date?" he asked, jolting me out of my thoughts.

"Date?" I repeated, confused. Surely I had misheard.

"Yes. To show you around Bath. In my car," John answered.

I turned to Aunt Winnie for assistance, but she was of no help. Instead, she considered me, her eyes merry and her mouth spread in a wide grin. I could have killed her. "Oh, well, that's very nice of you," I finally managed, "but I'm afraid we already have plans today. We're meeting friends."

John was not deterred. "Oh, who are you meeting? I probably know them. I know practically everybody here."

"Cora and Izzy Beadle," I replied hesitantly, hoping that he did not know them. Seeing his blue eyes light up, I knew that hope was in vain.

"Izzy! Why, Izzy is one of my closest friends here! This is perfect! We can all go together."

My brain, still tired and suffering from the draining effects of jet lag, drew a complete and utter blank. I gaped at John in frustrated confusion. Thankfully, Aunt Winnie finally came to my rescue.

"That's a lovely invitation, John," she said now, as she took my arm to steer me toward the stairs, "but I am afraid that we will have to decline it. However, I'm sure we will run into you later during the festival. Now, if you will excuse us."

John called out something about getting in touch with Izzy, but Aunt Winnie kept us both moving steadily up the stairs until we were out of his sight.

"Dear God," I muttered when we were out of earshot.

"What are you complaining about?" Aunt Winnie teased as we continued down the hall to our room. "I thought you loved the English. If I'd told you a week ago that an Englishman, complete with a tweedy blazer and posh accent, would be practically begging to take you for a drive in his convertible, you would have been thrilled."

"First of all, I am quite happy with Peter, thank you very much. And second, that man gives all Englishmen a bad name. They should take away his passport." I paused. "I have to admit, that while Catherine Morland isn't my favorite of the Austen heroines, she does have one trait that I envy."

"Really, what?"

"When *she* first came to Bath, she didn't have a single acquaintance. I, on the other hand, have not only acquired a new best friend but have secured the attention of a blowhard with a Jaguar."

Aunt Winnie laughed. "Remember, if adventures will not befall a young lady in her own village, she must seek them abroad."

"That very well may be true, but I am neither seeking an adventure nor am I Catherine Morland," I pointed out.

Both were true, of course. Only I forgot that sometimes you don't need to seek out an adventure to find one.

CHAPTER 6

*Insufferable woman! . . . A little upstart, vulgar being . . .
and all her airs of pert pretension and underbred finery.*

—EMMA

*O*UR ROOM WAS another high-ceilinged wonder, only this
time the décor was faded floral prints rather than crisp neu-
trals. Tall windows afforded us a view of the back courtyard. After
unpacking our things, we headed back out to the center of town.
Happily, John was nowhere to be found.

Our first stop was to the Jane Austen Centre. Located on Gay
Street, where Austen herself once lived, it's set between two of
Bath's highlights, Queen Square and the Circus. Outside the door
to the centre is a mannequin of Jane Austen, so Aunt Winnie and
I were delayed several minutes from entering because we had to
take numerous pictures of each other standing next to "Jane."

Inside, we toured the costume museum, had tea upstairs in
the Regency Tea Shop, collected our information for the festival,
and then hit the gift shop. Aunt Winnie bought—among other
things—a reproduction of the large oil painting of Mr. Darcy/Colin
Firth while I bought several books and more I ♥ DARCY parapher-
nalia than was perhaps strictly necessary. Our final bill was shock-

ing, and that was before we calculated the exchange rate. However, we left the store secure in the knowledge that our feelings of guilt would pass, and no doubt more quickly than they should.

We spent the remainder of the afternoon happily wandering through the streets of Bath and returned to our hotel in the late afternoon only to shower and get ready for our dinner with Cora and Izzy. However, I had forgotten that Aunt Winnie is a shower singer. A loud shower singer. Her choice of song depends on her mood. For instance, if she's stressed, she sings country. If she's feeling silly, she belts out bad '70s love songs. (Her favorite being "A Little Bit More" by Dr. Hook. Try hearing *that* without gagging.) But when she was happy, as she apparently was now, she became a "Fanilow." Which was why I was being assailed with every verse, every lyric of Barry Manilow's opening act at Caesars in Vegas.

By the time she got to "Mandy," I could take no more. As I was already ready, I headed to the hotel's reading lounge where I could escape the jukebox from hell and call Peter.

"Hey! How are you?" he said when I got through. "How's Bath?"

"Wonderful," I said. "Aunt Winnie and I went to the Jane Austen Centre and had tea, and we took our pictures next to the Austen mannequin."

"Of course you did. When does the festival start?"

"Tomorrow. There's a costume promenade in the morning and then a fancy dress ball tomorrow night. Tonight we're going to dinner with an old friend of Aunt Winnie's and her daughter. I think they might even be bigger Austen fans than Aunt Winnie and I—and that's saying something." I told him about our encounter with Richard and his crazy theories and Cora's subsequent fury.

"Well, I'm glad that you're having fun," he said, "but be careful. Knowing your luck, someone will kill this Richard guy, and you'll get all caught up in another murder investigation."

I laughed. "Highly unlikely. These are Janeites we're talking about. We're too civilized for such base behavior."

"Well, be careful anyway. I miss you."

"I miss you, too," I said, wondering for the hundredth time if I made a stupid decision in not moving in with Peter. As I cradled the phone close to my head, I found myself regretting that decision. "Peter?" I said.

"Yeah?"

I paused. Now was not the time to bring it up or change my mind. "Nothing. I love you."

"I love you, too."

I hung up and stared blankly at my phone. What was the matter with me? I was a reasonably intelligent adult. Why couldn't I figure out what I wanted with Peter? He was perfect—at least he was perfect to me. Although I had disliked him when we were little, mainly because I had misinterpreted his adolescent teasing as evidence of a cruel nature, that was all long ago and long forgotten. Okay, mostly forgotten. Peter was intelligent, kind, and funny. At six feet, with brown hair and brown eyes, he was also very handsome, which, as we Janeites know, a young man ought likewise to be, if he possibly can.

So just what the hell was my problem?

I decided not to try to analyze that right now and instead pulled out the itinerary for the week. After tomorrow's promenade and ball, the festival offered various sessions for attendees. There were walking tours, dance workshops, fencing lessons (for fans of Colin Firth's portrayal of a frustrated Darcy), plays, and numerous lectures. Several of the more popular sessions such as "Dueling Mr. Darcy," "Dressing Mr. Darcy," and "A Regency Wedding" were offered daily. I was reading the write-ups on these when another couple entered the lounge.

I gauged them to be about my age. The woman wore a long-sleeved, high-necked dress that appeared to be constructed entirely of black doilies. She was petite and very pale, with almost colorless blond hair that hung in tight ringlets about her long, narrow face. Honestly, if I didn't know such things didn't exist, I would have pegged her as one of the living dead. Her companion, too, had blond hair and pale skin, but his look was more waspish than deadish. His outfit, a blue blazer and crisp jeans, was also less funereal than hers. His expression, however, was similarly disconsolate. After hearing a few minutes of their conversation, I understood why.

"Ian," said the woman, her nasal twang turning the one-syllable word into three, "it's not that difficult. Just do as I say and ask him. It's very simple. We need the money. He has the money. It's your right to have some of it. He's family, for goodness' sake!" She paused to study the silver tray laden with complimentary goodies for afternoon tea. There was an assortment of small cookies, some powdered, some jam filled, and some sugar encrusted, in addition to a variety of grapes, figs, and nuts. Next to the tray was another, this one holding a squat blue teapot and an intricately cut crystal decanter.

"What is this?" the woman asked, lifting the stopper of the decanter and lowering her hooked nose close for a suspicious sniff.

"Sherry? Yuck. And I suppose *this* is tea," she grumbled, indicating the porcelain teapot. Lifting the lid, she peered inside, her pale blue eye doubtful. "Just as I suspected," she pronounced with a kind of proud resignation. "Tea. Why can't they ever have coffee at these places?"

"Well, it *is* called tea—" began Ian, but Ms. Living Dead cut him off.

"I know that, Ian. I'm not stupid. But it's not 1772, is it? Haven't they heard of Starbucks? No wonder they aren't a superpower anymore. They are hopelessly stuck in the past."

"Well, some might say—" began Ian, but again he was not allowed to finish.

"Where was I? Oh, yes. I want you to promise me that you will talk to him," she said, settling on the damask-covered love seat in the far corner of the room and arranging her skirt. "If you don't, then he is going to spend it all on *her,* and that can't happen. She has no need for the money, whereas you do! You can put it to good use. What is she going to do with it? She's only one person, her expenses are nothing, where you have a *family.* What about little Zee? Have you considered his future? Honestly, it's no contest."

"You have a point," the hapless Ian agreed.

"Of course I have a point! And I'm sure that he will see *your* point once you explain it to him. He can't mean for you to be left out." The woman paused to thumb through the pile of magazines spread out on the low coffee table before her. "I haven't heard of any of these. They're all foreign. Don't they even have *People?*"

"I imagine that they just carry the local magazines."

"Well, that's shortsighted, then. Most of the people who stay at these places aren't from here, are they? No, they aren't," she continued, answering her own question. "Nine times out of ten, they are Americans, and the people who run these types of establishments should remember that."

"If you say so," said Ian, staring miserably at the floor.

Another person entered the room now. Unfortunately, it wasn't Aunt Winnie. It was John. I immediately ducked my head and intently studied the festival guide. Happily, I was not John's focus. "Ian! Valerie!" he called out. "It's splendid to see you again! How are you? How's *Forever Austen* going?"

I peeked up. Ian? *Forever Austen*? This was Richard Baines's son? Well, well. Better and better.

"Hello, John," said Valerie. "We're fine. The magazine's going splendidly, of course. Why do you ask?"

"Oh, no reason," John replied. "One hears things, is all. Economy's in the tanker, you know."

"Well, not for *Forever Austen*," Valerie replied testily. "*It's* doing just fine."

"Excellent, that's excellent." John's eyes now landed on me. "Well, hello again!" he boomed. "I was hoping to find you." Both Ian and Valerie now seemed to notice my presence in the room. Ian smiled politely at me. Valerie did not.

"Hello," I offered with a quiet smile.

Turning to Ian and Valerie, John said, "Ian and Valerie Baines, I'd like to introduce you to Ms. Elizabeth Parker. She is also here for the festival. Elizabeth, the Baineses run the magazine *Forever Austen*."

"It's very nice to meet you," I said before glancing back down at my festival guide. My hope that this move would deter further attention from John was, as it turned out, a rather silly one.

"Is that the guide for the festival?" asked John. "Why, you've no need for that! Not with me around. I'm the best guide there is! You are going to the ball tomorrow, aren't you?"

When I reluctantly nodded, John clapped his hands. "Excellent! Then I will claim a dance! I know them all, of course. Many of my partners consider me to be one of the best Regency dancers."

I paused. Unlike Catherine Morland, I experienced no reflection of felicity in being already engaged for the evening, for I knew that to go previously engaged to a ball does not necessarily increase either the dignity or the enjoyment of a young lady. Besides, I think I'd rather stick needles in my eyes than stand up for an hour with John; it would be insupportable.

Oh, I missed Peter.

Realizing that John was waiting for an answer and that Ian and Valerie were watching me as well, I produced a strangled cough and muttered, "Well, I'm not sure what our plans are right now . . ."

Aunt Winnie entered the room. I don't think I've ever been so happy to see her. "There you are!" she said upon seeing me. "Are you ready?"

"Yes," I said, quickly getting to my feet, but John wasn't ready to end our encounter.

"Ah, Ms. Reynolds," he said, "I was just introducing your lovely niece to my friends, Ian and Valerie Baines. As you probably know, they run the magazine *Forever Austen*."

Aunt Winnie said her hellos and then turned back to me. "Well, we'd better be off, if we don't want to be late meeting Cora and Izzy."

"Late?" repeated John. "Oh, but I was hoping to show you around Bath this evening!"

"You were?" I asked with some astonishment.

"That is very gallant of you, John," said Aunt Winnie, "but I'm afraid that we'll have to take a rain check on your kind offer." Grabbing my arm, and moving quickly to the doorway, she said, "Ian and Valerie, it was nice to meet you. John, I'm sure we'll see you around."

"You can count on it," he called out after us.

WE WERE MEETING Cora and Izzy at the Dower House situated in the renowned Royal Crescent Hotel. The hotel occupies two buildings of the iconic crescent that is featured in just about every movie filmed in Bath, but the restaurant was just as impressive. Located in a renovated coach house behind the hotel, the restaurant boasts large windows swathed in mink-colored silk and trimmed in light olive, which afford a view of the famed secluded one-acre garden. You could almost envision Captain Wentworth and Anne Elliot strolling along the grounds.

Cora and Izzy were already at the table when we arrived. "I have so many things to tell you," Izzy gushed to me when I sat down. "I saw the most gorgeous dress today while out shopping. I want to get your opinion on it, but really, it's like a bright shiny diamond in my head. I really think I must have it."

I laughed. "Well, if it's a bright shiny diamond, then I think you will *have* to get it."

"Which reminds me," Izzy continued, "what are you wearing tomorrow?"

There were two costume events scheduled for the first day of the festival. In the morning there was the Regency Costume Promenade through the streets of Bath, followed in the evening with the Regency Masked Ball.

I was just about to ask her if she meant the promenade or the ball, when she went on, "Because I was thinking, wouldn't it be fun if we wore the same outfit? We could say we were sisters!"

I stared at her, incredulous. First, there was simply no way anyone would ever mistake us for sisters and, second, what grown woman wants to invite comparisons by dressing as a twin? "Um, I'm wearing a simple white frock for the promenade and a blue one for the ball," I said.

"Oh, that *is* too bad. Mama and I got these gorgeous silk gowns last year in London. Mine is this amazingly deep shade of pink with a kind of feathery headdress. If Gucci were alive during the Regency, he would have made this dress."

"It sounds lovely," I said. "I guess the modern-day equivalent for my dress would be the Gap."

"Oh, I'm sure it's wonderful. Besides, with *your* looks you can pull anything off. It's women like me who need the Gucci to elevate us a bit."

I laughed out loud at that. "You're nuts. I thank you for the compliment, of course, but you're still nuts."

Izzy affected an expression of disbelief. "It's true! Fine, then, to prove my point, I will tell you this. The other day when we were having tea at Claridge's, I saw Byron staring at you. And from the look on his face, it wasn't because he found fault. So what do you say to that? Or do you only have eyes for Peter?"

"I say that your eyes deceive you, and that, yes, mine are indeed only for Peter."

Across the table, Cora let out a little exclamation, and I turned her way. "Well, well, look who's here," she said, indicating a table not far from us with a nod of her head. "It's Gail Baines."

We all looked where directed and saw a trim, blond, middle-aged woman. Her face was attractive, with high cheekbones and full lips. With her were Ian and Valerie. "I wonder if she's heard about Richard's latest stunt," Cora continued.

"Mama," Izzy said, a warning note in her voice.

Cora turned, her expression innocent. "What?"

"You know perfectly well what. Stay out of it. Do not stir up trouble."

Cora sniffed. "Me? Me stir up trouble? The very idea. I beg to differ. It is Richard Baines who is stirring up trouble."

"Fine. Then let's leave the subject alone for now. Shall we order?" Izzy said, indicating our menus.

We all studied our options in momentary silence. "Oh, the Irish stew looks good," said Aunt Winnie.

"So does the steak and chips," agreed Izzy.

Although Cora kept her eyes on the menu, I could sense that her mind was on neither the stew nor the steak. With a swift motion, she put down the menu and stood up. "Excuse me," she said. "I'll just be a moment."

"Mama!" Izzy hissed, her annoyance quickly turning to anger. "Sit down. Don't you dare stick your nose into this! You will only make it worse!"

"Make it worse!" Cora retorted. "How on earth could I make it worse? There is strength in numbers, and the more people we have ready to fight Richard, the better we will be."

She strode away from the table and toward Gail.

Izzy put her head in her hands. "I want it noted for the record that I tried to stop her. When this all goes to hell, which I've every assurance of it doing, just please mention to whoever is the proper authority that I did try to stop it."

"Of course," I said. "What are friends for?"

Aunt Winnie winked and added, "And after all, a friend in need is a friend indeed."

Izzy raised her head and looked at us, a faint smile on her lips. "That may be so, but as the song goes, 'A friend in need is a friend indeed, but a friend with weed is better.' And if Mama keeps this up, I just might need that kind of friend."

CHAPTER 7

Most children of that age, with an imperfect articulation,
an earnest desire of having their own way, many cunning
tricks, and a great deal of noise, are sure to please.

—SENSE AND SENSIBILITY

E WATCHED IN SILENCE as Cora set upon Gail. I could
hear only snippets of the conversation: "terrible news,"
"outrageous," and of course, "syphilis." At first, Gail regarded Cora
with a blank expression. However, within minutes, her eyes narrowed into annoyed slits, and her lips pressed together into a hard
thin line. Whether the change in her mood was due to the message
or the messenger, however, was unclear.

Izzy saw the transformation and let out a low groan. "Well, that's
Mama for you."

Aunt Winnie considered Izzy with sympathy. "Never mind,
dear. You must allow your mother to follow the dictates of her conscience on this occasion, which leads her to perform what she looks
on as a point of duty."

I giggled while Izzy stared vacantly at Aunt Winnie. "Huh?"
she replied.

"Think of her as Mr. Collins introducing himself to Darcy," I clarified.

Izzy's mouth pulled into a grimace. "Oh, right, because that went *so* well. Perfect. Thanks. I feel loads better."

I laughed while Cora finished her conversation and returned to our table. "Just as I suspected," she said as she seated herself with the pleased air of one who has fulfilled her duty. "Gail was most upset to learn about Richard. She fully agrees with me that something must be done."

"Which would be what exactly?" inquired Izzy.

"We didn't go into the particulars," Cora replied with a vague wave of her hand, "but it was clear that we were on the same page."

"Right," Izzy replied with a doubtful glance in Gail's direction. "Dear God, but Valerie looks even more anemic than usual. You know, with her dead white skin and those horrible yellow ringlets, I bet she could pass for Matilda from *The Monk*. She definitely has the personality for the role."

"Wasn't Matilda the devil in disguise?" I asked.

Izzy nodded. "Yep. And that's Valerie—a modern-day she-devil."

Cora cast an uneasy glance in Valerie's direction before hushing her daughter. "Izzy! Keep your voice down. That is not only untrue, but unkind."

"It is not," Izzy persisted. "You've seen the way she treats Ian. It's contemptible. She's nothing but a nasty little mercenary social climber."

"I think they're staying at our hotel," said Aunt Winnie. "We met them just before we came here."

"Then you must know what I mean," said Izzy, turning to Aunt Winnie for confirmation.

Aunt Winnie shook her head. "We only met her briefly."

Izzy turned to me. "You must back me up on this, Elizabeth. With your insightful ways you must have detected the kind of woman she is." I paused, uncomfortable. Valerie *had* seemed a bit of a shrew, but I didn't feel right saying so. After all, I'd only seen her for a few minutes. Izzy caught my hesitation. "I knew it! I knew it!" she crowed. "You saw the same as I! I knew we thought alike! See?" she said, turning to Cora. "Elizabeth thinks she's a she-devil, too!"

I held up a hand in protest. "Whoa! Wait a second. I didn't say that. I didn't say *anything,* actually. I only caught a quick impression of her."

"But it wasn't a good one, was it?"

"Well, no, but . . ."

Izzy laughed. "No 'but's. Admit it, I'm right. You think of her as I do. If she's not channeling Matilda, then she's trying out for a role in *Pride and Prejudice and Zombies.* God, I don't see what Ian ever saw in her. She's a nasty little freckled thing but without the freckles. If I were him, I'd spend every day praying for the sweet release of death."

"Izzy!" Cora said, scandalized. "That's enough!"

Izzy arched an eyebrow at Cora. "You can trash Richard all you want, twenty-four/seven, but I can't say anything against Valerie? Why is *she* so special?"

Cora glanced downward and shifted awkwardly in her seat. "I didn't say she was special, I just don't think you're being nice. It's . . . it's not becoming behavior for a Janeite."

Izzy let out a yelp of laughter. "Oh, please! Becoming behavior, my ass. Jane Austen was the queen of the cutting remark. That's one of the many reasons I love her."

Cora shot Izzy an expression of pained frustration. "Izzy, *please*. Do as I say and let it go."

Izzy's mouth pulled down in a mutinous line, and it was clear that she had no intention of letting anything go. However, before she could continue, Aunt Winnie said, "Ladies, I think the discussion of the essential character of Valerie Baines will have to wait. Professor Baines himself has just made an appearance."

I glanced up, and sure enough there was Richard strolling through the restaurant with the air of a man who knows himself to be a celebrity but feigns embarrassment at the inevitable attention. Alex trailed along a half step behind him. Seeing Gail and his son and daughter-in-law, Richard altered his path and headed their way. I watched the reactions of the table as he did so. Gail's expression remained pleasant, almost indifferent to the sudden appearance of her ex-husband and his new wife. Either she truly did not care about Richard or, like Jane Bennet, she united with great strength of feeling, a composure of temper and a uniform cheerfulness of manner. Of course, a monthly injection of Botox could also be the reason for her lack of expression. Valerie was easier to read. Stretching her mouth into a wide smile, she directed an urgent whisper to Ian before waving to her father-in-law. Ian gave a nervous start and turned his body around in his chair. He noted the approach of his father with almost palpable dread.

Once at the table, Richard murmured something to Gail before turning his attention to Ian and Valerie. Valerie dove into her purse and quickly pulled out a handful of pictures, which she waved at Richard. From my vantage point, I could see they were of a boy about two or three years old. It wasn't a Sherlockian leap to deduce that he must be "little Zee" who was so deserving of his grandfather's money.

"She is *so* obvious," said Izzy with a snort of derision. "She trots out either the boy or his pictures any chance she gets. I swear to God she uses that son of hers as a meal ticket."

"Izzy, would you please lower your voice?" Cora begged.

Ian stood up and fumblingly shook his father's hand before Valerie shoved the pictures at him. While Alex stood awkwardly at his side with a painted smile on her face, Richard thumbed through the pictures. Whatever you thought about Valerie's motives and tactics, they seemed to be successful, for a fond smile now played on Richard's lips.

Snippets of Valerie's comments floated our way. "So much like you—so clever!" "Can't wait to see you again." "Talks about you so much!" Beside me Izzy made gagging motions. I tended to agree.

Once the pictures had been properly studied and fawned over, Richard handed them back to Valerie, who then prodded Ian. Ian coughed and muttered something about "getting together later to discuss a few things."

Richard gave him a jocular slap on the back. I heard "busy week" and "see what I can do." Even from where I sat, I could tell that Ian had just been blown off. Valerie's face pinched in anger. Richard and Alex then said their good-byes and headed for their own table, seemingly oblivious of the emotions they'd created.

The instant they left, Valerie turned in her seat to berate Ian for his lack of success. Ian tried to defend himself, but after a few interrupted attempts he fell quiet, his head bowed low.

Throughout it all Gail sat quietly, her face serene and calm. I was just thinking that I would never be able to remain so cool and collected around Richard and Valerie—and they weren't even my family—when I noticed Gail covertly reach into her purse. I saw a flash of a pill bottle, and a second later, Gail popped something into her mouth and took a quick sip of water. She briefly closed her eyes and exhaled slowly.

I revised my earlier opinion of Gail. She was no Jane Bennet. She was a self-medicator.

CHAPTER 8

My black cap was openly admired by Mrs. Lefroy, and
secretly I imagine by everybody else in the room.
—LETTERS OF JANE AUSTEN

*Y*OU LOOK VERY PRETTY, LIZZY," Aunt Winnie said to me
the next morning, as I put the finishing touches on my appearance.

I grinned at her from underneath my straw bonnet and coquettishly flicked the skirt of my white muslin dress. "Thank you," I replied. I was about to compliment her on her frock—a feathery print of pale blue and ivory—when she added, "But pull your shoulders back, dear! A man could go a long way without seeing a figure like yours, if you could only make the most of it!"

"Like you, I suppose," I said with a laugh, as I stared pointedly at her chest. Like me, she was wearing a dress of thin muslin that was cinched up high, just under the breasts. Underneath, she wore a linen chemise. However, unlike me, Aunt Winnie had chosen to dampen hers down. It was a popular trend among the Regency's more daring women who were aping the natural look made popular in France during the revolution. It was, I suppose, an early form of the wet T-shirt.

73

Aunt Winnie's lips curved into an innocent smile. "You know me, dear. I'm a stickler for accuracy."

"Uh-huh," I replied, my gaze straying from her dress to the large assortment of cosmetics on her dressing table.

"Women in the Regency used makeup!" she protested defensively.

"True," I agreed, "but did they wear colored contacts?"

She shrugged her shoulders apologetically, the small movement emphasizing the "naturalness" of her costume. "It was a struggle between propriety and vanity, but vanity got the better," she admitted.

"As it usually does," I said in agreement, as I added a touch more eyeliner to my own face.

WE LEFT THE HOTEL and headed to the Pump Room, the meeting point for the start of the promenade. From there, we would stroll through the streets of Bath until finally ending in the Queen's Square. The day promised to be a good one; the sun was shining and there was a crispness in the air. Arriving at the Pump Room and seeing so many Janeites all done up in their Regency finery gave me a quirky little thrill. It was akin to being at a giant amusement park for Austen fans.

In spite of the large crowd, we located Izzy and Cora with little difficulty. Like Aunt Winnie, Izzy had opted for the authentic look and had wet down her chemise within a millimeter of decency. And, just so it's clear, that millimeter was on the south side of the line of decency.

"Oh, you look marvelous!" cried Izzy upon seeing me. "You

were simply made for these fashions!" Linking her arm through mine, she said, "I fear I shall make a shabby shadow to you today."

I was about to contradict the sentiment, when Cora called out behind me, "Mr. Baines! Ian! There you are! I was hoping to find you this morning!"

Turning, I saw both Ian and Valerie. Valerie wore an ivory promenade gown with matching Spencer coat. Unfortunately, the color did nothing for her pale complexion and only served to suggest that she suffered from a severe case of iron deficiency. Ian, however, looked very dashing in a reproduction of the red regimentals that Wickham and Denny wore; the cut flattered his build and somehow made him appear taller. Beside me, Izzy extended a gloved hand to him and with a mischievous smile said, "My goodness! How handsome you look today, Ian. I hope you don't think me forward, but I must admit I am quite partial to a man in regimentals!"

Ian's cheeks turned crimson, clearly flattered by her words. He accepted her hand and bowed low over it. Valerie watched the interaction between them, her eyes narrowed in suspicion. "I hear that you are to be congratulated on your recent engagement, Izzy," she said pointedly.

Izzy aimed a dazzling smile her way. "Why, thank you, Valerie. You heard correctly. I am engaged." Shooting Ian a teasing gaze of longing, she added with a dramatic sigh, "With all the really lovely men already taken, I had to either lower my expectations or end up a lonely spinster."

Ian's response at hearing this was a comical mixture of stuttering and blushes. Valerie's glower deepened. "Really?" she said. "I thought to be a spinster, one also had to be a—"

Happily, Valerie's catty response was drowned out by the arrival of Richard and Alex. He was wearing a long gray linen coat with a blue vest and black top hat. She was wearing a white striped gown with a pumpkin-colored Spencer coat and matching bonnet. I thought they made a striking couple until it dawned on me that they were wearing exact replicas of the outfits that Jennifer Ehle and Colin Firth wore on the walk during Mr. Darcy's second proposal. I did not like it. Not one little bit. It wasn't so much that it seemed to show an abominable sort of conceited independence, or even a most country-town indifference to decorum. To be honest, it just smacked of sacrilege. And besides, Mr. Darcy would never smoke. To see Richard happily puffing away while wearing the Darcy garb vexed me greatly.

Byron was with them, but I hadn't noticed him at first. Now that I did, I saw that he wore a fitted blue coat with a white cravat and snug cream britches. And I mean *snug*. I quickly looked away before I could be accused of staring. Between the cut of those pants and the habit of dampening one's chemise, Regency fashion wasn't nearly as chaste as I'd once imagined.

Richard greeted us all in the manner of a gracious lord who has come upon sightseers on his land. "Why, we meet again!" he called out to Aunt Winnie and me, his previous annoyance at us seemingly forgotten or forgiven. Cora glared at him, her straw bonnet practically vibrating with anger. If Richard noticed, and I suspect he did, he didn't let on.

"I don't think you've met my wife, Alex," Richard said, with a courtly gesture in her direction. "Or my associate, Byron Chambers."

Introductions were made, and Byron said to me, "I believe I saw you in London. At Claridge's?"

"Yes, that's right. At tea."

"I never forget a face," he said with a friendly smile. "I'm horrible with names, but not faces. But seeing how your name is Elizabeth, I think I can manage to remember *that,* given our surroundings." Izzy shot me a knowing expression and mouthed, "I told you." I ignored her.

"Well, shall we begin?" asked Richard, as the town crier indicated the start of the promenade with a hearty bellow. I had just taken a few steps when I heard my name being shouted from several feet away. I did not immediately turn around because my first thought was that it was something to do with the festivities. However, I soon realized that I was indeed the intended "Elizabeth" being hailed.

With a sinking feeling, I turned and saw none other than John Ragget bearing down on me. Like the other men, he was wearing snug britches. It wasn't a pretty sight. It wasn't just that his legs were scrawny; rather, like Aunt Winnie and Izzy, John had opted to replicate another dressing habit of Regency times. In a manner not unlike *Spinal Tap*'s Derek Smalls and his infamous zucchini, John had knotted the long ends of his shirttails and stuffed them down the front of his pants.

"Elizabeth!" he called out again. "There you are! I thought we were going to meet this morning at the hotel and head out together."

"You did?" I asked, stunned. "But I never . . ."

"No need to apologize," he said with a magnanimous wave. "I

am here now. No harm done." Taking my arm, he said, "Now, you must be dying to know the history behind our little promenade . . ."

Byron caught my eye and gave me a sympathetic smile just before I briefly closed my eyes and sighed. I couldn't very well yank my arm away without appearing rude. I would have to politely submit to John's lecture with good humor. I would have to channel Elizabeth Bennet herself when stuck with a loquacious Mr. Collins. I would also have to have a large drink when this was done.

As we strolled along the glorious streets of Bath, I tried to focus on anything other than my blowhard guide. John didn't really expect a response from me, as he was apparently content with the numbing buzz of his own voice, so it wasn't too hard. I was pretending that I was Anne Elliot newly arrived in Bath and had just spied Captain Wentworth when I heard Ian, who was directly behind me with Valerie, say, "Yes, I know that the magazine needs money. But that's not what's worrying me . . ."

Next to me, John's voice interrupted. "The first promenade set out from the Jane Austen Centre . . ."

". . . surely, you've noticed a difference?" Ian said, his voice low and worried.

"Not really," came Valerie's indifferent reply. "She's a bit quieter, I suppose, but that's not a crime. What *is* a crime is not fighting for your family's welfare. Ian, you *promised* you'd talk to him!"

"I was, of course, an integral part of it," continued John.

"I said I would, and I will," hissed Ian. "But right now, I'm worried about Mother and those damn pills!"

"I really don't see the problem . . . ," Valerie said.

"In 2009, the promenade . . . ," said John.

"... if she seems happy," finished Valerie.

"Happy?" cried Ian. "How can you say that? She's practically catatonic!"

"... specifically asked me to lead the arrangement of . . ."

"Oh, Ian. Do be sensible. She's a grown woman. She is not our concern. Our concern is—and should *only* be—with little Zee and *his* future."

"... drummers, dancers, military and naval men!" John said with a flourish. "Shall I continue?"

"I'm all ears," I said, quite honestly.

We continued along until we got to Queen's Square. There we all gathered to have our picture taken, and I could finally let go of John's arm without rudeness. However, it wasn't without a price. I had to first promise him a dance later at the ball. I fear I did so with little grace. I only hoped that the dances weren't historically accurate, otherwise I'd be forced to hear more of his incessant chatter for a full half hour.

After finding Aunt Winnie, we headed for the luncheon in the Guildhall's Banqueting Room. I paused at the entrance to take in the impressive interior. Before me was an enormous room with spectacular plasterwork and gilding, Corinthian columns, magnificent chandeliers, and original royal portraits. I pulled out my camera and took several pictures. However, as my eyes were focused on the viewfinder, rather than where I was supposed to be walking, I crashed right into Byron.

"Oh! I am sorry!" I said. "I'm looking up instead of where I am going. I just can't get over this room! It's beautiful!"

"Don't apologize," he said. "It is an amazing room. I would tell you a bit of its history, but I imagine you've had your fill this morning of Bath trivia."

I smiled. "That is true."

Byron paused. A faint smile played on his lips, causing the laugh lines around his eyes to crinkle. "Mr. Ragget's conversation is very . . . wholesome."

"And there is so much of it to be had." I laughed in agreement.

He paused. "Are you going to the ball tonight?"

"We are."

"Perhaps then I could be so bold to ask for a dance? Maybe by then you might be up to hearing more about Bath," he added with a smile.

"Sure, that would be nice. See you there," I said, then headed over to Aunt Winnie and our table. As I settled into my chair, I said to her, "Dear God, but John Ragget can talk."

"I thought you made a pretty pair," said Aunt Winnie with a saccharine smile.

"Just because you're wearing a bonnet doesn't mean I'm not above slapping you around a bit," I said. A waitress wearing cap and serving outfit came by and placed small plates of salad in front of us.

"Oh, come on now. It wasn't so bad now, was it?"

"Only if you think Austen was serious when she said that 'stupid men are the only ones worth knowing.'"

As Aunt Winnie bit into her salad, I saw Lindsay rush by and head for Richard, who was seated at the table next to us. Alex had just vacated it, and Lindsay apparently was determined to lose no time in chatting up her professor in private. She slid into Alex's vacated seat, her face flushed. "I need to talk to you," she said in a low voice.

"I'm rather busy right now," replied Richard with cool indifference. "Perhaps we can talk later, after my lecture. I've set aside a substantial amount of time for questions and answers."

Lindsay's response to this went unheard by me, but whatever it was, it did not seem to please Richard. "I think you are being rather melodramatic," he said. "I really don't have time to indulge these schoolgirl antics."

Lindsay gave a little gasp. "Schoolgirl antics!" she repeated indignantly. "This is serious. You have to listen to me . . ." But whatever knowledge she was about to impart was interrupted by the return of Alex and Byron to the table.

"I sent off that fax for you," said Byron as he took his seat. "Hello, Lindsay," he added politely.

"Hello, Byron," she muttered, and ignoring Alex completely, she excused herself and left.

Alex resumed her seat. After watching Lindsay's hurried retreating form, she turned to Richard with a knowing smile. "Dear, don't tell me that you've conquered the heart of *another* one of your students? Really, you should cut the poor thing loose before she falls violently in love with you, and you are forced to break her heart."

Richard gave a short laugh and shook his head. "You exaggerate, I'm sure. Lindsay is passionate about one thing only and that is Jane Austen."

"Don't be so modest, darling," teased Alex. "It's clear the girl has a crush on you—just like *all* your students. Just like *me,* not so many years ago." She pressed her hand on his arm and leaned in close. "But seriously, Richard, let the poor girl out of her misery, or I'll have to do it for you." Batting her eyes at him, she added, "Besides, you know how jealous I can get."

Placing his hand over hers, he said, "Trust me, darling. You have nothing to worry about."

I happened to glance at Byron as he said this. Byron observed Alex with an expression I couldn't quite read, but if I was pressed, I'd have to say it was pity.

CHAPTER 9

My hair was at least tidy, which was all my ambition.
—LETTERS OF JANE AUSTEN

"Now, LIZZY," Aunt Winnie said to me some hours later as we readied ourselves for the ball, "I hope you'll not keep Byron to yourself all night. I want to dance with him as well, you know."

"I promise I shall not. Even if I wished to, I *could* not. I have to dance at least one with Mr. Ragget," I replied.

"Oh, Lord, yes. He's threatened to dance with us all."

I sighed and put down my tube of mascara. "You know, this would be funnier if it weren't for the fact that I'm the one dancing with the Official Tour Guide of Bath—which wouldn't be so terrible in itself if it weren't for the fact that nearly everything he says is incorrect." I looked in the mirror and studied my handiwork. "Do you know that he actually told me that the Catholic church imports the waters of Bath for their Holy Communion water?"

Aunt Winnie giggled and patted my shoulder sympathetically. "I am sorry, Elizabeth. Try and bear it as best as you can. If it makes you feel any better, you look very nice."

I glanced back at the mirror. I did love the Regency fashions, I thought as I admired my pale blue gown. It had a low square neck, short sleeves, a high waist, and a short train. Unlike authentic gowns (or Izzy's), mine was not made of silk but of a heavy cotton. I didn't care. It was fabulous. I had parted my hair down the middle and curled the bangs. I twisted the back into a kind of loose bun. For a final touch, I ran a ribbon embroidered with seed pearls around the crown of my head.

Aunt Winnie's ensemble was—of course—more elegant. Although her dress was a similar cut to mine, rather than a pale shade, it was a turkey-red paisley print, and instead of a ribbon in her hair, she wore a plume. An enormous purple plume.

Think Cher at the Oscars, but Regency style, and you have Aunt Winnie's outfit.

We grabbed our reticules and headed back to the Guildhall for the masked ball. The variety of costumes we encountered was amazing. Many wore dresses similar to mine—relatively simple cotton frocks; however, others had gone all out for the occasion. Luxurious silks in brilliant colors swirled around us, with many attendees wearing gowns identical to those worn by the actors from the 1995 version of *Pride and Prejudice.* In fact, many had not only copied the outfits but had taken it a step further. Rather than the simple eye masks that Aunt Winnie and I wore, some were wearing actual face masks of the actors: Darcy/Colin Firth, Elizabeth/Jennifer Ehle, and even a few of Wickham/Adrian Lukis were wandering around.

While Aunt Winnie and I were getting ourselves glasses of wine, we ran into Izzy and Cora. Izzy hadn't been exaggerating when she'd described her dress as something Gucci would have made had he been around during the Regency period. It was a deep golden silk with intricate jeweled braiding across the chest and down the front. On her head, she wore a turban of the same gold material with a jeweled cockade in the front.

Cora was one of the guests wearing a reproduction of a gown from *Pride and Prejudice*. It was the silk gown of creamy white that Elizabeth wears for the ball at Netherfield. Cora had even donned a brunette wig and face mask to complete the illusion that she was Elizabeth Bennet. By my modest count, this brought the total number of Elizabeths I had spotted so far to twenty-three. It was strange enough to be in the room with one Elizabeth Bennet, let alone twenty-three.

No sooner had I said hello than Cora burst out, her voice shaking with anger, "Have you seen them? It's horrible!"

"Seen who?" I asked.

"Richard and Alex! They're dressed as Darcy and Elizabeth! Look at them." She swung her arm out to point to a far corner of the room. Turning, I saw them. The man was wearing a Darcy costume and mask, and the woman was wearing the same dress and mask as Cora. At first I couldn't see how Cora could discern the couple's identity, but then I noticed Richard's pinkie ring.

I was about to mention that Richard and Alex had also copied the costumes from the movie at the promenade when I thought better of it and shut my mouth. Izzy rolled her eyes and handed Cora a glass of wine. "Mama, calm down. Here's your wine. I suggest you drink it. You're practically frothing."

Cora took the proffered glass, pushed her mask up, and took a large sip. If Izzy had hoped that the drink would calm Cora down, she was disappointed; in fact, it had quite the opposite effect. She glowered in Richard's direction. "Look at him. Preening about like he's actually Darcy. And the whole time he's getting ready to sully Jane Austen's name with his ridiculous theory. Well, I, for one, won't stand for it!"

"Cora, you've got to let this go," Aunt Winnie said. "It's not your battle. People who hear him will have enough sense to know that he's wrong."

"But what if they don't?" she retorted. "What if the press gets hold of this? You know they'll have a field day. This could ruin our upcoming membership drive."

"Oh, not necessarily," replied Aunt Winnie with a smile. "Who knows? It might actually increase membership."

Cora did not return the smile. "Oh, no," she said with a determined shake of her head. "It will ruin it. You don't know how conservative the ladies in my town are. Any hint of a scandal and they attack." She glared in Richard's direction again. "I really hate that man!"

Izzy ignored her mother and moved to stand next to me. From somewhere in the large hall, a voice boomed over the microphone that the dancing was about to begin. Linking her arm through mine, she said teasingly, "I am resolved to stay with you tonight, dear Lizzy. You have such a calming effect on me and will stop me from smacking my dear mama upside her thick head. Besides, we are both women whose sweethearts are not here. We will keep each other company."

We turned our attention to the couples as they paired off for the dance, commenting on the various outfits. "None are as pretty as yours," Izzy said loyally. "You make me feel like a gilded lily in all this finery. I should have remembered, simple is always better."

I paused, wondering if that really was a compliment. For some reason, I doubted it. A second later, Ian was next to us, smiling shyly at Izzy. "Well, hello again, Ian," Izzy said brightly. "Don't you look handsome tonight! Where is Valerie?"

"Oh, she's with my mom. Valerie wanted to ask her a few questions about Zee."

"So you are not dancing, then?" Izzy asked. "Well, then, you must stand with Elizabeth and me. We are determined *not* to let the fact that we are overlooked wallflowers dampen our spirits. Besides," she added with a mocking smile, "the rewards of observation and reflection are much greater."

I laughed. "Indeed, they are. We will have to be philosophers."

Ian's lips pressed together as if he were fearful of saying the wrong thing. Finally, he overcame his indecision and said, "Well, I'd be honored to dance with you, Izzy."

Yep, I thought wryly. I was living proof that there was just no beating that "simple" look on a woman.

"Oh!" said Izzy with a little gasp of surprise. "Ian! How sweet! Well, I would be delighted. Thank you!"

Then, taking his arm, she said to me, "I won't be gone long, Elizabeth!" A second later, they were out of sight, caught up in a brightly clad swirl of dancers.

I looked around and noticed Valerie peeking furtively around the side of an open doorway. Her cheeks were flushed, giving her a most unusual appearance of life. After a quick glance around, she reentered the ballroom, putting her phone back into her reticule as she did so, and then headed toward the bar.

Next, I looked over to where Aunt Winnie stood talking to Cora. They were just out of earshot. However, from the annoyed set of Aunt Winnie's mouth, I gathered she was still trying to calm Cora down. From the way Cora kept angrily gesticulating, I also gathered it was a losing battle. Although I had a twinge of guilt at leaving Aunt Winnie to deal with Cora alone, I remained where I was. I simply was not up for another rehashing of the evil that was Richard Baines. I quite preferred the solitary role of philosopher.

"Um, this is probably bad timing," said an apologetic voice behind me. "I just came over to say hello."

Then again, I got a C in philosophy, I thought, as I turned with a welcoming smile. It was Byron, looking very handsome in his blue coat and cream britches. "Hello, Byron. Why would it be bad timing?"

He shot an uneasy glance in Cora's direction. "I'm probably considered part of the enemy's camp, aren't I?"

Before I could answer, Cora saw him and rounded on him. Stepping away from Aunt Winnie, she said, "Byron, how could you let him do this? You always seemed such a nice, sensible young man. How did you ever get mixed up with the likes of Richard Baines?"

Byron gave a half shrug. "You'd be surprised the jobs one considers when faced with mounting grad-school debts." Then, with a guilty glance over his shoulder, he quickly amended his traitorous words. "But Professor Baines really does have some interesting theories, and they are not without merit. He takes his subject very seriously."

"He takes himself very seriously, you mean," Cora shot back. "All of these so-called theories of his are nothing more than thinly disguised vehicles to call attention to himself."

"I'm sorry you're so upset," Byron said. He seemed earnest, but then again he was working for the man, so who knew what he really thought.

"I take it he really is going to announce his belief that Jane Austen died of syphilis, then?" asked Aunt Winnie.

Byron nodded, his expression sympathetic. "I'm afraid so. I must admit, that's one of his theories that I'm not convinced of, but he is quite determined to publish it."

The small orchestra took up their instruments and began a piece by Mozart. Music swelled through the room, drowning out Cora's next words. From the expression on her face, I suspected it was just as well that we couldn't hear them. Downing the rest of her wine, she stomped off to refill her glass, the curls of her wig bouncing in irritation with each step. I had just turned back to Byron when I heard another voice behind me. This one was less welcome.

"Well, Elizabeth! There you are!" said John. "Are you ready for our dance?"

A feeling of dread overcame me, and I had more sympathy than ever for Elizabeth Bennet when she had to dance with the odious Mr. Collins. As I was still facing Byron, he must have seen my expression of dismay. I was just turning around to politely accept my fate, when Byron stepped forward. "Oh, I am sorry, John. I just made Elizabeth promise to dance this one with me."

John muttered something about it being a shabby trick as Byron grabbed my hand and led me out onto the crowded dance floor. "I hope you don't mind," he said as he took his place in the long line across from me. "But your face looked so miserable, I couldn't in good conscience hand you over to him. My mother would never have forgiven me if she learned I'd left a lady in distress."

I laughed. "Your mother would be proud. But I'm going to have to dance with him at some point. He practically made me promise earlier."

"Have you danced a country-dance before?" he asked as we queued up.

I nodded. "My aunt Winnie and I took a lesson before we left." I moved forward when it was my turn, performing the simple steps before returning to my proper place in line. "I'm curious. Do you really like working for Professor Baines? He seems a rather polarizing character."

"You don't expect me to admit otherwise, do you?" he asked with a laugh.

"So he is a man without fault?" I asked teasingly.

Byron finished his steps before replying. "No, of course not. I suppose one might say that there is, perhaps, a slight disposition to vanity and pride."

I affected an expression of amazement. "Are you suggesting that Richard Baines is vain and proud? I'm all astonishment."

Byron assumed an intentionally blank face. "You may very well think that. I couldn't possibly comment."

"Oh, a fan of Francis Urquhart, are we?"

Byron let out a laugh and shook his head. "I shouldn't have said anything. Now I must give one smirk, and then we may be rational again." He produced the promised smirk and then added, "Honestly. I do need this job. It's not perfect, but it pays well."

"Don't apologize. I just quit one of those jobs myself. The resulting giddy feeling of emancipation is wonderful until you look at your checkbook." I was just completing another step-and-turn routine when I was thrown off balance as someone ran past me. Thankfully, Byron caught my arm and righted me before I fell down. Turning, I saw that it was Lindsay who had pushed past me. I almost didn't recognize her. Gone was the meek creature I'd met on the plane. Underneath her cable-knit sweaters and wool skirts, Lindsay was hiding a very sexy figure. The clingy gown she was wearing tonight made that perfectly clear. However, her figure wasn't what caught my attention; it was her face as she threaded her way through the crowd and out of the room. It was splotchy with high emotion. I glanced up at Byron. His eyes stayed focused on her before seeking out another figure in the crowd. I followed his glance. It was to Richard he looked. Richard was adjusting his Darcy mask, which seemed to have been pushed (or slapped?) askew. Looking back to Byron, I saw that his face was dark with anger.

"What was that all about?" I asked.

Byron didn't answer immediately. "I don't know," he finally said.

"Lindsay seems upset. Should someone go after her?"

Byron seemed to debate this as we continued our steps in time to the music. "I wouldn't know what to say. I think she's developed something of a crush on Richard."

I scoffed. "Yeah, you think?"

Byron raised his eyebrows in surprise.

"It's kind of obvious," I amended.

He sighed. "She's a nice kid, but she doesn't seem to get the fact that Richard is married. And he'd never divorce Alex."

"Really?" I asked. "I guess I have a hard time picturing Richard as an until-death-do-us-part kind of guy, especially as it sounds like he left his first wife for her."

Byron's mouth opened in surprise. "Jesus! The gossip mill *has* been churning, I see!"

"What do you expect? After all, we are at a festival of voluntary spies."

"True," Byron agreed. "Well, let's just say that Richard no longer believes in divorce. He'd rather not give any more of his money to divorce lawyers."

"Does that mean there is trouble in the Baines marriage?" I asked.

He shook his head. "Far from it. Alex is devoted to him, and he seems quite happy with her . . ." He trailed off, leaving me with the impression that he couldn't quite fathom why that latter part was true.

"She's very pretty," I offered.

His eyes sought out mine. At the moment, the laugh lines around them were especially deep. "Yes, well, as to that—what was it that Austen said? Oh yes, 'Woman is fine for her own satisfaction alone.' I think that sums Alex up rather nicely."

"What sums me up, if I might be so bold to inquire?" inquired a hard voice.

Byron and I whirled around. Before us stood Alex in all her

Elizabeth Bennet finery. She really did look lovely. Although she had a face mask, she wasn't wearing it at the moment. Unlike many of the other women wearing the Elizabeth costume, Alex didn't need a wig. She had curled and styled her own hair into a sophisticated coif. I felt my own "simple" appearance more acutely than ever.

Byron quickly covered his gaffe. "Elizabeth here was just saying that you seemed a very genteel, pretty kind of girl, and I quite agreed."

Alex smiled archly, in a manner more in keeping with Lady Catherine than Elizabeth Bennet. "But of course, you were," she said with a condescending tone. "Now, I hate to break up such a charming couple, but Richard asked me to find you—which took some time in this crowd, I can tell you—and ask that you finalize his notes from earlier and send out the e-mails to the societies."

Byron's face registered annoyance. "Where is Richard?"

"He ducked out for a cigarette," Alex said with a faint trace of irritation.

Byron sighed and glanced regretfully in my direction. Alex noticed and added sweetly, "Of course, if you prefer, I can always tell Richard that you are too busy to do your job just now."

"Of course not. I'll get right on it," Byron muttered.

"Excellent. I'll let him know," she said with a satisfied smile. Her task completed, Alex turned back to push through the crowds and return to Richard. As Byron apologetically made his excuses to me and left, I was dismayed to see none other than John Ragget bearing down on me, his intention to claim his dance clear. Putting on a brave smile, I tried to think of a topic to mentally distract myself from John's otherwise mind-numbing conversation.

It didn't take me long, for I quickly found myself wondering if the reason Richard sent Alex to find Byron wasn't so he could have a cigarette but so he could have his little conversation with Lindsay without her knowledge.

CHAPTER 10

I was as civil to them as their bad breath would allow me.

—LETTERS OF JANE AUSTEN

Y THE TIME my dance with John was over, I was seriously rethinking my partiality for English accents. And as I'd once joked that an Englishman could read me the phone book and I would still lose all capacity for rational thought, that was really saying something.

On the other hand, even a dry recital of the phone book would be more interesting than John's incessant cataloging of his finer points. Among the fascinating tidbits I learned was that John's horses and dogs were the "bloody best" in England and that the beer he brewed got you "completely arseholed."

Oh, be still my beating heart.

After claiming that a slight headache unfortunately prevented me from another dance, I let John escort me back to Aunt Winnie. Cora joined her just as we did, with another glass of wine in her hand. She stumbled toward us, and it was with some surprise that I realized that she was quite tipsy. Aunt Winnie stared at the glass with obvious annoyance.

"Cora, please. You need to eat something. One shouldn't drink her dinner. Not after the age of eighteen months, anyway."

Cora waved away Aunt Winnie's suggestion as if it were nothing more than an irksome fly. "I'm fine, Winifred. Please stop fussing over me." Her words would have been more believable if her wig wasn't askew. "Anyway, I'll eat *after* I talk to him."

Aunt Winnie's green eyes opened very wide at this. "You can't be serious! Cora, have you heard nothing I've said? For God's sake, leave it and Professor Piano Teeth alone!"

John looked from Cora to Aunt Winnie to me. "What's going on?" he asked. "Perhaps I can be of assistance?"

"No, it's fine . . . ," I began, hoping that he would just leave, but Cora, of course, had other ideas.

"I'm going to demand that Richard not present his paper tomorrow," she said. "I'm going to tell him that if he does, I will do everything in my power to discredit him."

I rolled my eyes at Aunt Winnie. Dear God, Cora was almost as bad as John in terms of dull, repetitive conversation. John stared at Cora in confusion. "His paper on Austen's death? Why on earth *shouldn't* he present it?"

"Because it's obscene!"

John shrugged. "I guess. But it's just an opinion."

"But what if people believe it?" she asked, aghast.

John narrowed his eyes in concentrated thought as he mulled over this puzzle. "Then they believe it," he replied some moments later. "You know, I actually had suggested some of the very things myself a few years back at one of our meetings."

I stifled a groan. Of course John would claim that he'd thought of Richard's theories first. John was so full of himself that it wouldn't surprise me if he claimed to have somehow influenced Austen herself. "I happened to fully agree with him that there are more to Austen's stories than meets the eye," he went on. "Of course, no one listened to *me* as they seem to do *him*." Cora opened her mouth to interrupt. "My point is," John quickly continued, "that you can't control what people think or when they decide to think it. Just as you can't control what people will do with ideas gleaned from others."

I regarded him with something akin to amazement. It was the most sensible thing I'd heard him say since I'd met him. And trust me, he'd said a lot.

With a low bow, John politely excused himself, no doubt in search of other women more appreciative of his dubious charms.

Cora stamped her foot in irritation, the movement sending her wig farther askew. "Well, we'll just see about that." Without another word, she turned and headed toward where Richard stood talking to Alex. Neither Aunt Winnie nor I tried to stop her. Frankly, we were both sick to death of hearing about her outrage.

We watched in silence as she made her way to them, her body swaying to an unheard beat as she crossed the room. From where we stood, we couldn't hear what she said, but she must have called out to Richard as she approached because Alex turned around in apparent surprise. The whole scene was strange enough, but seeing one Elizabeth Bennet confront her twin only increased the oddness. Just as Cora drew near, she lost her footing and lurched forward into Alex, spilling Alex's glass of wine in the process. Cora appeared to apologize and then handed Alex her fresh glass before turning her attention on Richard.

Watching her angry gesticulations and finger pointing while Richard calmly observed her from behind his Darcy mask was strangely comical. It was like watching an outtake from *Pride and Prejudice.* Soon Richard began to laugh, if his shaking shoulders were any indication, and Cora yelled something in obvious irritation. It appeared that Alex attempted to calm Cora down, but rather than listen to her, Cora turned and, thankfully, headed out of the hall and away from all of us. As uncharitable as it may sound, I honestly don't think I could have listened to any more of her complaints with a polite face. Aunt Winnie must have had the same thought, because she said with a sigh, "I suppose I should go after her. But then again, I suppose I should also bake my own bread and grow my own vegetables, and that sure as hell isn't happening either."

"Let her go," I replied. "She doesn't listen to anything we say anyway. Let Izzy deal with her for a while."

"Speaking of Izzy," said Aunt Winnie, as she peered around the room, "where is she? I haven't seen her in a while."

I shrugged. "I don't know. After promising me that she wouldn't leave my side this evening, she promptly left my side."

Aunt Winnie smiled. "Perhaps she was in no humor to give consequence to young ladies who are slighted by other men."

I wrinkled my nose at her. "Somehow I doubt that was the motivation."

The orchestra began another piece and the dancers took their positions, among them Richard and Alex. With their masks and costumes, they really did resemble Darcy and Elizabeth. What made it even more "realistic"—if you could even use that word—was that despite what people might say about them—namely, that he was an arrogant ass and she was a flibbertigibbet—it was clear from their interactions as they danced that there was real affection between them. You didn't need to see their faces—their body language said it all.

I wasn't the only one watching them. A little distance from where I stood was Gail Baines. Wearing a dark green dress with a coordinating turban, she leaned against the wall, her face pale. With glassy eyes, she followed the movements of Alex and Richard as they performed their dance. Next to her, Ian tried without success to divert her attention.

"Mother?" he said, his face anxious. "Why don't I take you back to your room? I think you should rest. You don't look well."

"I tried to talk to him," Gail muttered in response, her voice thick. "Bastard wouldn't even answer me. Who the hell does he think he is? He can't hide that money forever. He can't!"

Ian gently took his mother's arm. "Mom? Come on. Let's go. I'll take you up to your room. I think you should lie down."

Gail shook him off. "I'm fine. I don't need to lie down." Still glowering at Richard, she took a sip of her drink. "Who the hell does he think he is? He's a fraud! He's nothing but a lousy fraud! Did you try to talk to him?"

Ian gave a reluctant nod of his head. "I tried but he, um, he, um . . ."

"He blew you off, didn't he?"

Ian's long face was a portrait of misery. "Mom, really, it's okay. It doesn't matter. We'll figure it out later. But now, I really think that you . . ."

"He is such a bastard!" Gail said, with a sudden burst of energy. She pushed herself off the wall and seemed intent on heading toward Richard. Ian reached out and grabbed her arm.

"Where are you going?" he asked in alarm.

"To tell him exactly what I think of him," she said, trying to break free of his grasp.

Ian's eyes grew wide, and he kept a firm grip on Gail's arm. "I don't think that's a good idea," he said, his voice tense. "Not here. Not now."

However, Gail was in no mood to listen to any advice. She twisted away, the movement catching Ian by surprise. He hurriedly grabbed out for her but ended up pushing Gail off balance. As she tried to right herself, her glass dropped to the ground, breaking into several pieces as it hit the floor. Gail stared at the mess, her expression confused. Ian took advantage of her bafflement and quickly steered her toward the doorway behind us. As he passed by me, he said, "Elizabeth! Can you tell Valerie that my mom wasn't feeling well, and I've taken her back to her room."

"Sure," I answered as Ian continued to steer Gail out of the room.

"So, are you enjoying your first Regency ball?" Aunt Winnie asked in a bemused voice once they were gone.

"Honestly, I feel like I stumbled into a scene penned by Julian Fellowes." I shook my head. "It's not only pretty to look at, but it's chock-full of drama. I half expect Alan Cummings to pop out any moment and provide me with a brief synopsis."

Aunt Winnie laughed and said, "And don't forget. This is only the first day of the festival. We have a whole week ahead of us."

No sooner had she said this than Alex suddenly bent over awkwardly, clutching her stomach in apparent pain. Richard quickly escorted her away from the other dancers. Tipping her mask back on her head, she closed her eyes and took a deep breath. After a brief conversation with Richard, Alex turned and left the ballroom. Richard walked back to his empty table and sat down.

Within a matter of minutes, however, Alex reappeared, her mask firmly back in place. From the way she strode briskly across the floor to where Richard sat, it was clear that whatever had been ailing her had passed. It dawned on me that she seemed angry. Her movements were erratic and her posture combative. As she drew near, Richard stood up in apparent surprise. Alex grabbed him roughly by the wrist and dragged him through the back exit and out of the room.

"Oh, dear. Do you suppose that there is trouble in paradise?" murmured Aunt Winnie.

"It would appear so. I wonder what caused the sudden change," I said.

"Maybe she realized that she's married to one of the stupidest men in England."

"I'll drink to that," I agreed. "And speaking of which, my glass is empty. Would you care for a refill?"

Aunt Winnie and I were just returning from the refreshment table when a voice behind me called out, "Elizabeth!" I turned. To my surprise, I saw Byron and Alex. Byron had changed out of his costume and was now wearing jeans and a T-shirt. He had an arm around Alex, who was leaning heavily against him. She was still in her Elizabeth costume, but her hair had come undone and now hung in limp curls around her damp face.

Seeing me, Byron said, "Elizabeth! Have you seen Richard? I can't find him, and Alex is really sick. I think he needs to look after her."

"He just left through that door." I pointed to the exit in question.

Alex moaned. "I wish to God he'd stop smoking. He's been popping in and out of this room all night."

I shook my head in confusion. "I don't think he went outside to smoke. In fact, I thought he was with you."

Alex looked at me in confusion. "With me? That's impossible. I've been in the bathroom. Getting sick."

"Where did you see him go?" Byron said to me.

I again pointed to the doors. "Over there. He left with someone."

Byron glanced at Alex before mouthing to me, "Lindsay?"

I shook my head.

"Come on, Alex. Let's go see where he is," Byron said. Alex nodded weakly.

"Here, I'll show you where he went," I offered and moved in the direction of the doors. Aunt Winnie followed behind me.

I'll admit that when I reached the doors, I had a brief premonition of something ugly lurking behind them. Unfortunately, my thoughts veered toward interrupting a lovers' embrace or a lovers' spat.

Of course, it was neither.

No, it was far worse than that.

We pushed open the heavy doors, entered a narrow service hallway, and stared at the grim scene before us. There, among extra table linens and serving carts, lay a body. And not just any body, but a Mr. Darcy body. For a dedicated Janeite such as myself, it was bad enough to see Mr. Darcy sprawled on the floor; it was even worse when you saw the dark crimson stain that spread across his chest.

CHAPTER 11

*Where there is a disposition to dislike, a motive will never
be wanting.*

—LADY SUSAN

ALTHOUGH THE MASK was still in place, it wasn't hard
to guess who lay behind it; not many Darcys sported a
diamond pinkie ring.

Alex let out a piercing scream when she saw the body. "Is
that? Is that . . . ?" she gasped, breaking away from Byron and
running to the unmoving figure on the ground. Crumpling into
a heap beside it, she gently pulled back the mask. Richard Baines
returned our horrified stares with his own vacant one. "Oh, my
God!" sobbed Alex. "No! *No!* This can't be happening!" Grabbing his hand, she cried, "Richard? Can you hear me? Richard,
answer me!" She then cradled his face in her hands as she continued to call out his name.

Byron broke out of the stunned daze that still held Aunt Winnie and me immobile. Moving quickly to Richard's side, he felt for
a pulse. Finding none, he turned frightened eyes first to Alex, then
to me. "Call the police," he said.

"Police?" cried Alex, looking at him aghast. "No! Call a doctor!

We have to help him!" Turning her tear-stained face up to me, she said, "Please, we have to help him. Somebody get a doctor. Now!"

Byron reached out and gently took her hands away from Richard's face. "Alex?" he said, his voice low, "he's gone. We need to call the police."

Alex stared back at Byron, but her eyes didn't register his words. "Richard," she repeated.

Aunt Winnie went to Alex. Taking her hand, she said, "Come here, dear. You shouldn't look anymore. Let's get you away from this."

Alex stubbornly shook her head. "No. I'm not going to leave him. He's not . . . he's going to be fine. I'm not leaving him."

Aunt Winnie patted Alex's shoulders sympathetically while she firmly eased her away from the body. "Call the police, Elizabeth," she said as she helped Alex to her feet.

Finally, the spell of finding Richard's body lifted. I turned and ran back into the ballroom, shouting for someone to call the police.

TWENTY MINUTES LATER, the police arrived. Various men and women of the force moved about with brisk authority, dusting for fingerprints, taping off areas, snapping pictures, and taking names of those present. Although someone had placed a white tablecloth over Richard's body, it didn't hide the fact that there was a dead body not twenty feet from where we stood. The situation was made all the more surreal by the almost comical contrast between our Regency garb and the police's modern-day uniforms. It was a little like that scene in *Monty Python and the Holy Grail* when the police descend on King Arthur and his men and haul them off to jail.

Now, I have always been very up front about my Anglophile

tendencies—despite the rather vocal protests from some of the more conservative members of my Irish Catholic family. It is my dream to live in England, surrounded by tweed, crumpets, and tea. To say that I have idealized life across the pond would be an understatement. A case in point would be my preferred pastime of watching episodes of *Miss Marple* and *Hercule Poirot*. Sure, the characters stumble across dead bodies with an alarming regularity, but they are dead bodies in *England*. It's somehow more civilized—and less frightening—when tea and cucumber sandwiches are served while the kindly inspector conducts his investigation.

I wonder when I will ever learn that fiction and reality are really two very, very different things.

I had no tea. I had no cucumber sandwich. What I did have was a very grumpy-looking woman by the name of Inspector Middlefield asking me all sorts of questions, with nary a kind word *or* expression. Of course, it probably didn't help that the poor woman had to lead her inquiry surrounded by a roomful of people dressed like extras from a fluffy BBC period piece.

I guessed her to be about fifty-five. She was tall and reed thin, with long, thick salt-and-pepper hair that was pulled into a tight bun. Her face was all sharp angles, except for her eyes. These were a brilliant cornflower blue, their saucerlike shape made even more so by the prescription glasses that now perched precariously on the tip of her nose.

"I understand that you were one of the people to discover the body," Inspector Middlefield now said to me, pushing her black-framed glasses back up the bridge of her long nose and regarding me intently.

"Yes. I saw Professor Baines leave through those doors," I answered, indicating the ones behind me. "A few minutes later, Alex asked me where he was. I showed her." I glanced over at Alex, who was slumped in a chair, staring blankly at the floor. Byron stood next to her, his hand placed awkwardly on her shoulder in an apparent effort to comfort her. Inspector Middlefield saw my glance and lowered her voice slightly.

"Yes," she said. "I understand that you stated that Professor Baines exited the ballroom with his wife? And that it appeared that they were in the middle of an argument?"

I nodded—somewhat reluctantly, as Alex was not three feet from me. "I *thought* it was Alex. It certainly looked like her. I mean, whoever it was, was a similar height and build."

"But it was definitely a woman?" asked Inspector Middlefield.

I nodded. "I think so. I mean, I guess so. I thought it *was* Alex until she came in a few minutes later and asked where Richard was, so maybe I was wrong."

Alex's head snapped my way upon hearing that. "You *are* wrong! It wasn't me! You have to believe that," she cried, her eyes wide and still wet with tears. "I was in the bathroom getting sick. Richard and I were dancing when my stomach suddenly cramped up. I left to go to the ladies' room. I ran into Byron on my way, and he saw that I was really sick, and so he waited outside the bathroom for me."

She tilted her head up at Byron, a beseeching expression on her face. Byron nodded at the inspector. "That's true. She was pretty sick," he added with a rueful glance at his right shoe. I followed his glance. There was a beige blob of . . . something on the toe. Feeling bile rise in my throat, I quickly looked away.

Alex continued. "I got really sick in the bathroom. I can't remember ever being so sick in my life. When I came out, I asked Byron to help me find Richard. I wanted to go back to the hotel, and I didn't think I could make it alone."

Inspector Middlefield turned to me to corroborate that statement.

"That's what she said when she asked me where Richard was," I said.

"So why did you think it was Mrs. Baines who was fighting with the deceased?" asked Inspector Middlefield.

"The costume, I guess. The woman was wearing the same Elizabeth Bennet costume and mask as Alex. And she was about the same height as Alex."

Inspector Middlefield's eyes strayed to Alex again. They were filled with doubt.

Alex buried her head in her hands. "Oh, this is unbelievable!" she cried in frustration. "I didn't kill my husband! I loved him. Why would I want to hurt him? I don't know who took him out those doors, but I swear to you, it wasn't me!"

Inspector Middlefield took a deep breath and exhaled it slowly through her nose. "You say that you left the ballroom and went directly to the bathroom?" she asked.

Alex nodded fervently. "Yes. That's when I ran into Byron. He waited for me, and then we both went back inside the ballroom to look for Richard."

"And what were you doing, Mr."—Inspector Middlefield glanced down at her notebook and then back at Byron—"Chambers? I understand you left the ball early. Why was that?" Although her voice was bland, it still didn't hide the fact that Inspector Middlefield viewed Byron as a suspect.

Byron's face slacked with shock as the same impression seemed to strike him. "Richard asked me to see to a few tasks he wanted completed by tomorrow," he said, his voice a shade higher than it had been a minute ago. "I was just coming back to ask him a question about one of his notations when I bumped into Alex."

Inspector Middlefield's brows knitted together in concentration as she noted this down. "Were you in costume earlier this evening?" she asked.

"Yes," replied Byron. "But I knew that I wouldn't be able to finish what Richard needed before the end of the ball, so I changed into my street clothes."

"I see." Inspector Middlefield said nothing else, letting silence fill the room, as she calmly regarded him. Byron began to fidget under her gaze.

A constable gave a sudden shout of excitement from down the hallway, breaking the tension. "Inspector," he called, "I think I've found something!"

Inspector Middlefield turned in his direction, her expression studiously controlled and calm. This couldn't be said for the rest of us.

Hurrying over to the inspector, the constable held out a black wig in his gloved hands. I recognized it immediately. I'd seen several identical ones earlier. It was the wig that went with the Elizabeth costume. However, this one had an added feature. Tucked inside was a bloody knife.

CHAPTER 12

We do not look in great cities for our best morality.
—MANSFIELD PARK

LEX LET OUT A LITTLE MOAN and covered her mouth. "Is that . . . is that what he was stabbed with?" she asked, her eyes wide with horror.

Inspector Middlefield studied the knife with a practiced eye. "It certainly appears to be," she said slowly. Taking her pen, she poked it at the wig. "I'd say this seems to go with a costume." Turning to Alex, she said, "You don't appear to be wearing a wig, Mrs. Baines."

Alex shook her head. "No. I didn't need one. I did my own hair." Inspector Middlefield looked dubiously at the lank strands that fell haphazardly around her face. Sensing her suspicion, Alex said, "It didn't look like this earlier, obviously. It came undone while I was in the bathroom."

"That's true," I said.

Inspector Middlefield shifted her gaze to me. "Were you in the bathroom as well?" she asked.

"Oh, no," I said. "I meant it's true that Alex didn't wear a wig tonight. There were several women dressed in costumes similar to hers, but they all wore wigs. I remember noticing that she didn't."

"So there were several women dressed like Mrs. Baines?" Inspector Middlefield asked.

"Yes. It was a pretty popular costume. A lot of women also wore the mask with it. Now that I think about it, the woman I saw wore a wig." I paused and then stated the obvious, "I guess I must have seen one of those women approach Richard. He must have had the fight with another guest in an Elizabeth costume."

"Yes, it would seem so," Inspector Middlefield said with the mild sarcasm at which the British excel. I felt my face flush. Turning back to Alex, Inspector Middlefield said, "Did your husband have any enemies that you know of?"

Alex shook her head. "No. I mean, I don't think so. He upset a lot of people with his theories on Jane Austen, but no one ever got really mad. Well, no one other than that woman Cora."

"I'm sorry. What woman? Who is Cora?" asked Inspector Middlefield.

I snuck a glance at Aunt Winnie. Her face wore the same expression of dread that I suspected mine did.

"Cora Beadle," replied Alex. "She was very vocal about her disgust at Richard's theories. She and he have never seen eye to eye, but this year it was worse. My husband was going to deliver a paper that argued that Jane Austen didn't die of Addison's disease but rather syphilis, and Cora was livid."

Inspector Middlefield made a noise not dissimilar to a strangled cough. Behind her glasses, her blue eyes were shuttered with professional detachment, but I thought I still detected a faint look of amusement in their depths. "I see. Well, that is quite a discovery. What did Cora say about that?" she asked.

"She yelled a lot and said she was going to try and stop him from giving the paper . . . ," Alex began and then broke off as the implication of her words sank in. "Oh, dear God! Could *she* have done this?" She turned to Byron, her eyes wide. "I mean, I knew she was angry, but do you think she could have killed him?"

Byron shook his head. "I don't know. I don't think so. But I really don't know."

Inspector Middlefield tapped her notebook with her pen. "Where is this woman now?"

"I don't know," replied Alex. "I haven't seen her since she yelled at Richard during the ball. She seemed a little drunk, to be honest. She bumped into me and spilled my wine. She then insisted I take her glass. After that she lit into Richard."

"Do you remember what she said?"

Alex gave an apologetic shrug. "Not really. Cora yelled at my husband a lot. After a while, I just tuned it out. So did he, for that matter. As best I can remember, she was angry about the effect his paper would have on Austen's reputation. She was also going on about some group back home and what they would do."

"And what was your husband's reaction?" asked Inspector Middlefield.

"He just laughed at her. I tried to calm her down, but she was furious. She called him a bastard and then left."

"Did you see her after that?" Inspector Middlefield asked.

"No. Richard and I joined a dance, and then soon after that my stomach started to cramp." Alex looked down at her lap. Twisting her hands, she said, "If only I hadn't gotten so sick. I might have been able to stop whoever did this."

"Oh, I don't know," said Inspector Middlefield mildly. "I rather wonder if your getting sick wasn't part of the plan."

Alex looked up, her expression confused. "What do you mean?"

Inspector Middlefield did not answer her. Instead, she asked, "Do you happen to remember what Ms. Beadle was wearing to-night?"

"Yes," said Alex. "She was wearing an Elizabeth costume."

"Like yours?"

"Yes. Why? You don't think that—" Alex began, but Inspector Middlefield cut her short.

"I think I need to talk to Mrs. Beadle," was all she said.

FINDING CORA PROVED something of a challenge. No one at the ball had seen her, and Izzy was nowhere to be found either. After several minutes of searching various rooms, we finally found her slumped in a chair under the grand staircase. Her chin was resting on her chest and she was softly snoring. In her hands, precariously balanced, was an empty wineglass. As my mother would say, she was in the arms of Morpheus. But seeing how Morpheus was the god of dreams, I think it was more accurate to say that Cora was in the arms of Bacchus. And seeing how long it took us to rouse her (which happened only after Aunt Winnie gave her a less-than-gentle slap across the face), he was certainly hanging on tightly to Cora.

When she opened her bleary eyes, it was clear that her little nap had not erased the effects of the wine, and her confusion at finding herself in a circle of people that included representatives from the local police was evident from the manner in which she gaped at us.

"Cora, you need to wake up," Aunt Winnie ordered in a firm voice. "The police are here. They need to talk to you."

Cora rubbed her eyes and stared back at Aunt Winnie without comprehension.

"Can we get her a cup of coffee or something?" Aunt Winnie asked Inspector Middlefield. The inspector nodded and jerked her head at one of the constables, who promptly trotted off in search of an appropriately caffeinated beverage.

"Cora, do you understand me?" Aunt Winnie asked, bending down low so her face was only inches from Cora's.

Cora's brows pulled together. "Why are the police here? What's happened? Where's Izzy?" she asked thickly.

"There's been an incident. The police need to talk to you," replied Aunt Winnie, her eyes never leaving Cora's.

There was a flicker of emotion in Cora's bloodshot eyes at hearing this. Fear? Panic? I couldn't tell.

"Where's Izzy? Is she okay?" she asked again, just as the constable returned with a large cup of coffee. He handed it to Cora, who took a grateful sip.

"We haven't been able to find her, but I'm sure she's fine," said Aunt Winnie. "Do you know where she might be?"

Cora shook her head.

Inspector Middlefield now stepped forward. "Hello, Mrs. Beadle. My name is Inspector Middlefield and I'd like to ask you a few questions, if you don't mind."

"I don't mind," Cora said slowly.

"I understand that you had a disagreement with Professor Baines earlier this evening. Could you tell me what it was about?" The inspector's voice was almost conversational.

Cora shot a wary glance at Alex. Alex stared suspiciously at Cora with her arms wrapped protectively across her chest.

"Why do you care about that?" Cora asked.

"Because he's been murdered," came the harsh reply.

Cora's link with Bacchus now snapped. She sat up in her chair and stared back at the inspector, her eyes finally alert. They briefly landed on Alex with an expression of horror, before refocusing on the inspector. "Wait a minute. What? Richard's been killed? But how? Why?"

"That's exactly what I'd like to know, Mrs. Beadle. Now, perhaps you could help me by explaining what your fight with him was about."

Cora blinked. Several times. She glanced at Aunt Winnie, as if hoping she somehow had the answers. Aunt Winnie gave her a reassuring smile but said nothing.

"Wait. You think I had something to do with his death?" Cora finally got out.

Inspector Middlefield shook her head. "I didn't say that. I merely wondered if you could tell me what your argument was about."

Cora blanched and stared at her cup of coffee. After a moment, she looked back up at Inspector Middlefield. "Well, first of all, I wouldn't call it an argument—"

"It most certainly was!" interjected Alex, her eyes flashing with anger.

Inspector Middlefield held up a cautionary hand. Alex fell silent. "We have several witnesses who called it just that," Inspector Middlefield said.

Cora took a deep breath. "Oh. Oh, I see. Well, yes. I did talk to Richard tonight. I admit that I was upset with him. He was planning on giving a paper tomorrow that claimed some really horrible things about Jane Austen. I told him that he was a disgrace to the Austen Society." Cora stopped. Turning pleading eyes to Inspector Middlefield, she said, "Look, I admit that I didn't like the man, but I didn't kill him! That's insane!"

Inspector Middlefield produced a thin smile. "Well, someone did. In the meantime, could you please tell me your movements this evening? When did you have this argument with Professor Baines?"

Cora hesitated. I wasn't sure if it was because she was hiding something or just having trouble remembering. Either way, it didn't look good. I glanced at Aunt Winnie. She stared back at me with worried eyes.

"I saw him at his table. The dancing had just started," said Cora slowly. "I went over to him, and I told him what I thought of his theories. I admit I was angry, but that's all. I didn't want him to present his paper, but I certainly wouldn't kill him to stop him!"

"What did Professor Baines say to you?" asked the inspector.

"Nothing, really. Nothing at all. He just laughed at me. That made me even angrier, so I left. I got another glass of wine, and I came out here to get hold of my emotions. I . . . I must have fallen asleep. I must still be a little jet-lagged or something."

"Or something," the inspector agreed. Cora flushed. Inspector

Middlefield continued. "I understand that when you first approached Professor Baines, you accidentally bumped into Mrs. Baines, spilling her drink in the process, and that you gave her yours instead. Is that correct?"

Cora nodded. I suddenly saw where this was going, and my own stomach began to cramp in anticipation of the inspector's next question.

"Could you tell me what was in your drink?"

Cora had no reason to understand the significance of the question, as she—in theory, anyway—didn't know that Alex had gotten sick soon after drinking from Cora's glass.

Cora's brows drew together in confusion, but she readily answered, "White wine, why?"

"Mrs. Baines was suddenly taken rather ill after drinking it," came the reply.

"Well, I certainly don't know anything about that!" Cora cried defensively.

"One more question. You wore an Elizabeth Bennet costume this evening, correct?"

Cora looked down at her costume, perplexed. "Yes, why?"

"I understand that this costume came with a wig. Did you wear one this evening?"

"Well, of course I did," Cora said, reaching for her head. "It's right here."

But it wasn't there, as Cora's groping hand quickly discovered. She gasped as she discovered what we already knew: Cora's head was bare.

"The reason I ask, you see," said Inspector Middlefield, "is that a wig similar to the kind belonging to your costume was found near the body. With the murder weapon neatly tucked inside."

Cora frantically looked around for her wig, but it was nowhere to be found.

"I'd like to continue this conversation somewhere a bit more private," continued the inspector. "I think now might be a good time to come to my office."

CHAPTER 13

My mother means well; but she does not know, no one can
know, how much I suffer from what she says.

—PRIDE AND PREJUDICE

ORA LEFT WITH A CONSTABLE, still protesting her innocence. "Find Izzy!" she repeatedly called to us as she was led
away. Inspector Middlefield stayed behind to obtain a few more
statements before she joined Cora at the station for additional questioning. She quickly completed her task and then left for the station, leaving one of her associates, a short, stocky man by the
name of Sergeant McDunna, in charge.

I glanced over at Alex. She still stood with her arms wrapped
around her, her gaze vacant and unblinking. Byron caught my eye
and took a few steps toward me. His voice barely above a whisper, he
said, "I can't believe this is happening. I mean, I knew that Richard
could be annoying at times, especially to those who disagreed with
his theories, but to kill him? It's madness!"

"So you have no idea who might have done it?" I asked.

He shook his head, his eyes wide. "None. My mind feels like it
shut down. I think I must be in shock or something."

I peered over his shoulder to where Alex still stood staring off into space. "I think Alex actually is in shock," I said.

Byron turned and looked as well. "I think you may be right. You know, she's never been my favorite person, but she did love Richard. I can't imagine what she's going through."

"Is there anyone we can call? A relative or friend?"

Byron's forehead crinkled as he thought. "She has a sister, I think. But of course, she lives in the States. I'll see if I can get hold of her. In the meantime, I wonder if I could get her a sedative or something. She should probably lie down."

I nodded my agreement. "If you can't find a sedative, try a stiff drink. She looks as though she could use it."

"Good idea. I'll do that." Walking back over to Alex, Byron gently touched her arm. "Alex?" he said. "Why don't I walk you back to your room? You should probably lie down."

Alex remained rooted to the ground. She neither moved nor indicated she'd heard him. Byron tried again, his voice a tad louder. "Alex? Alex, let me take you back to the hotel. You can talk to the police some more later."

This time his voice penetrated the fog that seemed to cloud her brain. With an almost robotic movement, she gradually turned her head until she was facing him. "Okay," she said in a flat, dull tone.

Byron reached out his hand and awkwardly pulled her next to him. Wrapping his arm around her shoulders, he steered her toward the doorway. "If the police need either me or Mrs. Baines," he said to Sergeant McDunna, as he continued to guide the zombielike Alex from the room, "you can find us at our hotel."

"I'd prefer it if you would stay here, sir. At least until I hear from Inspector Middlefield," said Sergeant McDunna.

"And I would prefer to get Mrs. Baines back to her room before she collapses to the ground from shock. We aren't going anywhere, just to the hotel. Now, if you will excuse me," Byron said firmly.

Sergeant McDunna's brown eyes registered uncertainty at this arrangement, but Byron's tone broached no argument. "I'll have someone escort you there," the sergeant finally conceded. "I'm afraid that I will also need you both to surrender your passports until we've cleared up this matter."

Byron's step did not waver as he led Alex away. "Do whatever you think you need to do," he said. "It's not like either one of us is going to want to leave before this matter is cleared up."

Sergeant McDunna said nothing else, but from the frustrated glare he aimed at the doorway just vacated by Byron and Alex, I suspected that he wasn't impressed with Byron or his chivalrous instincts. When I heard him mutter, "Arrogant American," under his breath, I was sure of it.

I found myself starting to defend Byron but then I stopped. While he seemed a nice enough man, I really didn't know him. Could he have killed Richard? And if so, why? Since Richard seemed to stir up all sorts of animosity, I decided to skip the latter question and focus on the former. However, try as I might, I couldn't see how Byron—or anyone over five foot eight—could have committed the crime. Whoever had burst into the ballroom wearing the Elizabeth costume had been of slight build and average height.

Byron was at least six feet tall and broad shouldered. There was simply no way that it could have been him in the costume.

But I still didn't say anything to Sergeant McDunna. I suspected that he would have thought I was an "arrogant American" as well and would look at me with undue suspicion.

Turning to Aunt Winnie and me, Sergeant McDunna asked each of us a few more questions before finally indicating that we, too, were free to return to our hotel. Like Byron and Alex, we were instructed to turn over our passports.

Just as we were gathering our things to return to the hotel, Izzy appeared, out of breath. Her face was flushed and her turban was askew. "Izzy!" I cried when I saw her. "Where on earth have you been?"

"Why?" Izzy stammered, her voice a shade high. "What's wrong?"

"Someone killed Richard Baines!" I answered.

Izzy's eyes grew wide and her mouth fell open. "Killed him? But who? How?"

"He was found stabbed in the alcove behind the ballroom," I answered. "Actually, I was the one who found him."

"Dear God," Izzy said, gripping my hand. "How ghastly! Who did it?"

Aunt Winnie and I cast uneasy glances at each other. "Um, well, they don't know for sure—" I began, but Aunt Winnie cut me off.

Never one to mince words, she blurted out, "The police think your mother is involved. It's ridiculous, of course, but they've taken her to the station for further questioning."

The flush in Izzy's face drained away. Her hand flew to her

mouth. "Holy shit! You're kidding, right? No, I can see from your faces that you're not. But that's absurd! It's impossible! She would never do such a thing."

"I know that, of course," agreed Aunt Winnie, "but unfortunately the police seem to have other ideas."

Izzy shook her head as if she could will the situation away. "But why Mama? It doesn't make sense . . ." She stopped and considered. After a pause, she said, "No, actually it makes a lot of sense. She's gone on about precious little other than how much she despises Richard and his work since we got here. Of course, they suspect her. If I didn't know her myself, *I* would probably suspect her." She let out a sigh, her graceful shoulders slumping. "Stupid, stupid woman. She just couldn't let it go," she muttered as she rubbed her face tiredly. Raising questioning eyes to ours, she then asked, "But why did they home in on her so fast? It couldn't be just because she disliked him. There must be more to it than that."

Aunt Winnie succinctly explained about Cora's drunken outburst, subsequent disappearance, and the loss of her wig.

Izzy's mouth pressed into a thin line. Righting her posture, Izzy looked at us with steely determination. "I see," she said. "Well, I suppose I'd better get down to the station and see about getting her a lawyer or barrister or whatever they're called here." With an amused glance down at her costume, she added, "But perhaps I should slip back to the hotel and change before I do so. I have a feeling they'll take me more seriously if I'm not dressed like a BBC groupie."

"We'll walk with you," I offered.

She shot me a grateful smile. "Thanks. I appreciate that."

We'd just left the ballroom and were heading for the doors

when Valerie ran up to us, her usually deathly white pallor now a blotchy red. Whether the change was from excitement or horror, I couldn't tell. Next to me, I sensed Izzy tense up, no doubt dreading Valerie's reaction to the news that Cora was a suspect. "Dear God!" Valerie said. "I've just heard the news about Richard. Is it true?"

Aunt Winnie nodded. "I'm afraid so. We found him, actually."

Valerie stared at us in disbelief. "But why? Why would anyone want to kill him? And where are Ian and Gail? Do they know? I've been looking for them everywhere."

Oops. "Oh, Valerie," I said apologetically, "in all the commotion, I completely forgot to tell you. Gail . . . wasn't feeling too well, so Ian took her back to her room. I'm so sorry. He did ask me to tell you."

Valerie's small mouth twisted in annoyance. "I see," she said with a sniff. After shooting me an icy stare, she turned her attention to Izzy. "I heard they took someone into custody. Do you know who it is?"

Izzy cleared her throat uncomfortably and produced a wan smile. "Um, well, that's a bit of an awkward point. They've taken my mother in for questioning."

"Cora!" Valerie exclaimed. "Oh, dear God!"

"If you are heading for the hotel, we are going back as well," Aunt Winnie said kindly. "Why don't you walk with us? You've had a terrible shock, I think it's best that you have people around you."

Valerie didn't answer immediately. She seemed lost in thought. "Huh?" she finally answered, when Aunt Winnie repeated her offer. "Oh, sure. Whatever," Valerie said, her manner distracted.

The four of us walked back through the dark streets of Bath in relative silence as both Valerie and Izzy seemed too preoccupied to respond to Aunt Winnie's few attempts at conversation. When we were a few streets from our hotel, Izzy stopped. "I'll see you all later," she said. "I'm going to my hotel to change and then see what I can do about Mama. I'll call you once I know something."

"Okay," I said. "Please remember to call me, no matter the time. And let us know if we can do anything to help."

Izzy nodded. "Thanks. I'll do that." She turned and quickly walked down the street and soon was swallowed up by the darkness.

Valerie, Aunt Winnie, and I resumed our journey in silence. Valerie seemed especially preoccupied, and I forced myself to push away the uncharitable thought that she was mentally spending Ian's inheritance.

At the hotel, we stepped into the brightly lit lobby, an act that caused us all to suddenly blink like startled owls. When my eyes adjusted, the first thing I saw was Ian. From the distressed expression on his face, I assumed that he'd already learned about Richard's death, but his greeting to Valerie made me think otherwise. "What are you doing here?" he asked.

Valerie exhaled impatiently. "I might ask the same of you."

Ian flushed but didn't answer her question. Instead, he said, "I don't understand. The ball isn't over already, is it?"

"No, the ball isn't over," Valerie replied. "You don't know why I'm here?"

Ian shook his head, his expression anxious. "No. Why?" His eyes widened. "Earlier, I saw some police cars with their sirens on race by—what's happened?"

Valerie stepped forward, her face softening as her anger at him evaporated. "I'm afraid that I've some terrible news for you. It's about your father."

Ian's brows drew together. "What about him?"

Valerie took a deep breath. "He's . . . well, he's dead. Killed."

Ian's mouth dropped open in disbelief. "What? But no, that's impossible!" His eyes sought out mine and Aunt Winnie's for verification. I gave a weak nod. Ian turned back to Valerie. "How?" he asked.

Valerie grabbed his hand. "He was stabbed."

Ian closed his eyes as if to ward off Valerie's words. "Who did it?" he finally asked, his voice thick with emotion.

"The police think that terrible woman, Cora, did it," came Valerie's reply.

"Cora!" Ian exclaimed, opening his eyes in surprise. Some of the tension left his face. "Cora? But why would she kill him?"

"Who knows?" Valerie responded indifferently, waving her hand as if to brush away the question. "It doesn't really matter. Anyone can see that she's unhinged, always going on about Richard's theories being perverted. She probably killed him to prevent him from presenting his paper."

Ian glanced at us, as if asking for our opinion. Aunt Winnie dipped her head in silent acknowledgment. "Unfortunately, the police do seem to have their suspicions about Cora's involvement," she said. "She did drink too much tonight, and she got into a fight with your father. The fact that she ran around telling everyone who would listen how much she disagreed with his theories doesn't help her, either. But for what it's worth, I've known Cora for a very long time. She can be a bit excitable at times, but she's not a killer."

Ian nodded but said nothing.

"Where's Gail?" asked Valerie.

"She's in her room, sleeping. She got . . ." Ian broke off and glanced at me and Aunt Winnie. I knew that he was about to say "loaded," and I tried to keep my face neutral. However, Ian still shot me a funny look before pressing on with his modification of events. "She felt unwell, so I brought her back to the inn so she could lie down," he said quickly.

Valerie gave him a knowing look that was tinged with more than a little exasperation. "Is she sleeping?" she asked.

"Um, yeah. She's sleeping," Ian answered.

"Well, we'd better wake her and tell her the news," said Valerie. "I imagine that the police are going to want to talk to her as well. It might not be a bad idea to get some coffee in her, too. That is, if this place even *has* any coffee."

"I'll go see what I can find," Ian volunteered and disappeared down a corridor.

Valerie let out a huff of irritation. "Which leaves me, I guess, with waking Gail. Perfect," she groused as she headed for the staircase. "I swear to God, I have to do everything around here."

Aunt Winnie called after her, "Valerie, please let us know if there's anything we can do to help."

Valerie turned back to us, her expression baleful, and started to say something, but she was interrupted by the ringing of her cell phone. Looking down at the display, she grimaced and answered it. "Look, I can't talk now," she hissed into the receiver. "We'll have to do this later." Turning away from us, and resuming her ascent up the stairs, she continued to speak in a low, annoyed tone before abruptly hanging up on the caller.

Aunt Winnie watched her go, a faint smile on her face. "Our Valerie is all politeness, is she not?" she asked me as we headed for our own room.

I gave an inelegant snort. "I'd as soon call John Ragget a wit."

CHAPTER 14

Which of all my important nothings shall I tell you first?
—LETTERS OF JANE AUSTEN

ACK IN OUR ROOM, Aunt Winnie and I changed out of our Regency costumes and into our modern-day clothes. While I missed the flattering cut of my high-waisted gown, I was nevertheless happy to no longer have to compete with Aunt Winnie's dampened-down cleavage. It was bad enough to be small chested; it was frankly demoralizing to be put to shame by a woman in her seventies.

While Aunt Winnie finished changing, I ducked out into the hall to call Peter. I dreaded his reaction when I told him that—just as he predicted—Richard had been killed and that I was once again in the midst of a murder investigation.

"Hey there," I said with a forced tone of casualness when he answered.

There was the briefest of pauses, and then he said, "What's wrong?"

"Wrong? Nothing. I mean, there's nothing wrong with me, that is. But, um . . . there was an incident earlier."

"Incident?"

"Yes. An incident. That guy I was telling you about—the professor with the crazy ideas? Well, he died."

"He died?"

"Well, he was stabbed."

Peter swore. "Elizabeth! First of all that's not an 'incident.' That's a murder! Goddamn it! I can't believe this! Come home now! Promise me that you will get on the next plane out of there and come home!"

"Peter, calm down. I'm fine. Really. There's no need for me to come home."

"Do it anyway."

"I can't."

"Why?"

I took a deep breath. "Well, I'm sort of the one who found the body."

There was a very long pause, and I heard Peter mutter something. I didn't ask him to clarify as I think I got the general gist of it. "Peter, I promise you I'm fine. But the police took Aunt Winnie's and my passports. They want us to stay around while they sort this all out."

"I'm coming over, then."

"Really? Can you?" My mood lightened considerably at that prospect.

He sighed. "No. Not really. But it doesn't matter. I'll move a few things around and get over as soon as I can."

"I do love you," I said, smiling.

"And I love you, too, which is why I want you to stay as far away from this investigation as you can. Stay safe."

I giggled. "You sound like Daniel Day-Lewis in *The Last of the Mohicans*. 'Stay alive. I will find you!'"

Silence met my imitation.

"Elizabeth, I'm serious," he said finally. "A man has been killed!"

"I know, Peter. I'm sorry. I guess it's easier to joke than think about what happened. It was pretty awful." I closed my eyes and saw Richard's lifeless body on the floor. I pushed away the gruesome image and focused instead on the happier one of Peter joining me in Bath. "I really hope you can get over here," I said.

"Don't worry. I will."

We hung up after a few more minutes of talking, and when the little click that signaled our connection was broken sounded, I was suddenly filled with unease. Peter was right. A man had been killed. And I very much doubted that Cora had anything to do with it. Which meant that whoever had killed Richard was still out and about, enjoying the sites of Bath.

ONCE AUNT WINNIE had finished changing, we decided to get a drink at the lobby bar, a cozy room with wood paneling and thick green carpet. When we arrived, I saw that John, Valerie, and Ian were already in attendance. The three of them huddled somberly together at a low wooden table in the corner. Ian stared blankly at the flickering votive candle on the tabletop, seemingly ignoring both John's incessant chattering and Valerie's sour expression. I didn't blame him. They were the last people I'd want to spend time with, too. If hell has a bar, people like John and Valerie will always be there.

I furtively tugged on Aunt Winnie's blouse and nodded in their

direction. She caught my meaning, and we began to quietly back
out of the bar. Unfortunately, Ian happened to glance up just as we
neared the door. His face practically lit up. I didn't for one minute
flatter myself that Ian found our company so entertaining. Rather,
he was merely glad for companions in his little corner of hell.

"Elizabeth! Winifred!" he called out. "Please come join us." Valerie looked our way as well, but unlike Ian she did not issue a similar invitation. In fact, for once I sensed that she and I were in perfect
agreement in that she and I both wanted me to leave.

John stood up and flamboyantly waved his arms to catch our
attention. As they were the only people in the small bar, it was an
unnecessary move at best.

"We just came down to get a quick drink, Ian," I said when we
were at their table. "We wouldn't dream of imposing on you right
now. I'm so sorry for your loss."

Ian stood up and said, "Thank you, but there's no reason you
shouldn't join us. After all, you know what they say, 'Misery loves
company.'"

He pulled out a chair for Aunt Winnie, while John did the
same for me. I noticed that even though Ian appeared in control of
his emotions, his eyes were still faintly red from recent crying. In
contrast, Valerie's eyes were quite dry, making the little napkin she
used to randomly dab invisible tears wholly superfluous.

Aunt Winnie and I reluctantly sank into the worn leather chairs.
"Have you talked to the police yet?" I asked after John took our
drink orders and ambled over to the bar to fill them.

"Yes," said Ian. "They're going to send someone over to interview us shortly."

"How is your mother doing?" Aunt Winnie asked Ian. "How did she take the news? Is there anything we can do for you?"

Ian stared at his pint of beer as he answered. "Thank you, but I don't know what can be done, really. Mom wasn't feeling well earlier this evening, so I gave her a sleeping pill and sat with her," he said, not meeting our eyes. "She's sleeping now. I tried to tell her about . . . what happened, but I don't think she understood me, let alone heard me."

My mind was having trouble grasping why Ian would give Gail a sleeping pill when it was obvious that she was already looped on some kind of prescription drug. Ian's next words clarified my confusion. "When the police got in touch with me, I told them that they would have to wait until tomorrow to interview her. She's in no state to talk to anyone tonight."

John returned from the bar and placed a glass of white wine in front of me and a scotch and soda in front of Aunt Winnie. "Damned terrible business," he said as he resumed his seat. "I understand the police are interviewing Cora. Do they really think she had anything to do with it?"

Valerie gave an incredulous snort. "I can't think of anyone *more* likely. I mean, the woman practically threatened him every chance she got. Surely you noticed that, John?"

John acknowledged Valerie's statement with a reluctant nod. "I grant you that she may seem the obvious choice, but I've known Cora a long time. She's passionate, yes, but I never considered her to be violent."

Valerie looked away, unconvinced. "Well, the police seem to think otherwise," she said.

My cell phone rang then, and I glanced down at the display. It was Izzy. I excused myself from the table to take the call. However, given the small size of the bar, I suspected that every word I said would be clearly overheard.

"Izzy?" I said. "What's going on? How's your mother?"

"She's a complete and utter mess," Izzy said with a sigh. "I've never seen her so out of it. She must have really put away the wine tonight. She has a terrible headache—no big surprise there—and she can barely remember anything."

"What are the police saying?"

"They're releasing her for tonight, thank God, but of course we're not allowed to go anywhere anytime soon. I'm taking her back to the hotel now. Where are you?"

"I'm at the hotel in the bar—" I began, but before I could finish, she cut me off.

"That sounds perfect," she said. "I definitely could use a drink and a friend to talk to. Let me get Mama to bed, and I'll be right over."

"Okay, but—"

"I'll see you in a few," Izzy said before hanging up.

I stared at the phone in my hand, annoyed that Izzy had disconnected before I could tell her that Ian and Valerie were with us. I called her back, but she didn't pick up. Aware that everyone was waiting for me at the table and no doubt listening to every word I said anyway, I gave a mental shrug and let it go. I suspected that Izzy would be able to hold her own against Ian and Valerie just fine.

I settled back in my chair and reached for my glass of wine. "How's Izzy?" Aunt Winnie asked.

"She's okay, I guess," I said. "The police have released Cora for now. Izzy is taking her back to their hotel and putting her to bed, and then she's coming over here."

Ian's eyes widened at this, and some of the color drained from his face. Next to him, Valerie stiffened. "Here? She's coming here? But why?" she asked angrily.

"I think she wants to be with friends," I answered. "She hung up before I could tell her that you were here. I'm sorry."

"I can't believe this!" Valerie glared at me as if I were somehow to blame. "Of all the nerve! How dare she come here! We are in mourning!"

I bit my tongue, afraid that I might point out that most people don't mourn the recent murder of a family member in a hotel bar.

"For what it's worth, the police did release Cora. I don't imagine they would do that if they really thought she had something to do with your father-in-law's death," I said.

Valerie rolled her eyes. The effect, set against her already deadly pallor, was unnerving. "The police have released guilty people before," she replied as if speaking to an exceptionally slow child. "Besides, who else would want to hurt Richard? The very idea is absurd."

No one spoke. Everyone seemed suddenly thirsty for their drinks. I averted my eyes from Valerie's. I'd only just met Richard Baines, and I could think of at least three people who might have had reason to kill him. Two were sitting across from me and the third was supposedly sleeping off an illness upstairs.

The uncomfortable silence was broken by the arrival of Izzy. She had changed out of her Regency apparel and into faded skinny jeans and an oversized tangerine V-necked sweater. Thigh-high chocolate suede boots completed the look. It was the kind of outfit you would see in a catalog and want to buy but wouldn't because you knew you'd never be able to pull it off. Except Izzy pulled it off.

She spotted me and headed over, her long strides quickly covering the distance. When she was halfway to our table, her eyes registered Ian and Valerie, and her step faltered. It was only for a second and she quickly regained her composure, but I saw an uneasy expression creep into her normally confident eyes.

"Hello, Elizabeth. Hello, Ms. Reynolds," she said once at the table and then quickly turned to Ian. "Ian, I'm so sorry about your father. Please know that you have my every sympathy. I can't imagine what you must be going through. I . . . I hope you know that my mother—or *I*—didn't have anything to do with any of this. She can be something of a hothead at times, but she's not a murderer."

I wondered why Izzy felt the need to include herself in the denial, but then I spotted Valerie's peevish expression and understood. Ian glanced up at her, his manner both wary and embarrassed. He briefly met her eye, nodded, and then looked away. "I understand, Izzy," he said softly, his gaze fixed on the candle again. "It's a horrible situation, all around."

Even though Ian had averted his eyes from Izzy's, her gaze never left his face. "I hope I'm still welcome to join you?" she asked, her voice uncharacteristically small.

Ian glanced at Valerie before looking back to Izzy and nodding his consent. As for Valerie, she pressed her mouth into a hard, thin line and blew an angry snort out her nose. Izzy smiled timidly at Ian, ignored Valerie altogether, and pulled a chair up to the table.

"What would you like to drink?" I asked her.

"Anything with alcohol in it," Izzy responded. "What are you drinking?" Seeing the glass before me, she asked, "Is that Chardonnay?" At my nod, she said, "Good. I'll have a large one of those."

"I'll be right back," I said, pushing my chair away and standing up. "Can I refresh anyone else's drink while I'm up?"

Everyone demurred except Valerie. Pushing her still full glass of red wine across the table toward me, she said, "Could you take this back for me? I ordered a Zinfandel, which this is obviously not. I mean, look at it. It's red!"

"Sure," I said. "It's probably a red Zinfandel," I added as I picked up the offending glass of wine.

From Valerie's subsequent expression of disdain, you would have thought that I'd just sung my response. In pig Latin. "Zinfandels are *pink*," was all she said.

Aunt Winnie glanced at me, her eyes twinkling with laughter. I looked away, afraid of my own reaction. "I'll see what I can find," I promised.

I placed the order with the bartender, a young woman with long sandy-colored hair that was pulled back into a sleek ponytail. She wore a small white name tag that read MARY.

"Can I return this?" I asked, pushing the glass of wine across the wooden bar. "I think the lady was hoping for a pink Zinfandel."

Mary glanced over my shoulder at the table. A second later, her eyes narrowed with distaste. "Sure, you can return it," she said, "but we don't have any pink Zinfandel."

"Okay. What is your sweetest wine, then?" I asked.

She considered her stock a moment before replying. "I suppose that would be the Muscat. But I warn you, it's *really* sweet. It's almost a dessert wine."

"Perfect. We'll take a glass of that and a glass of Chardonnay."

When they were poured, Mary glanced at the table once again. "Look," she said, dropping her voice low, "just a heads-up, but you might want to tell your friend to tone it down a bit. This is a nice place, and the owners aren't going to tolerate her behavior if they catch her."

"Catch her?" I repeated in confusion. "Catch her doing what?"

Mary appeared to rethink her warning, because she ducked her head and said nothing. I was about to ask her what she meant again, when I heard Valerie's voice behind me. "Is there a problem?" she asked, shooting Mary a disdainful look. Mary busied herself by wiping down the already pristine counter.

"No," I said quickly, "no problem at all." I handed Valerie her wine and took Izzy's glass back to the table. Izzy thanked me and took a grateful mouthful. Valerie sniffed suspiciously at her glass before taking a tentative sip. Happily, she seemed to like it, as she took a slightly larger sip before setting the glass on the table. She, of course, said nothing to me, which was fine; I would have been all astonishment had she actually thanked me.

"So, how is your mother?" John asked now, scooting his chair closer to Izzy's.

Izzy regarded him a moment, her expression unreadable. "She's sleeping now. Thank you."

John rested his forearms on his knees and shook his head. "Damned odd business. I still don't understand how it all happened." Turning his head in my direction, he asked, "You were there when they found him, Elizabeth, and spent some time with the police. Did they say anything?"

Three sets of eyes lasered in on me. The fourth set, Aunt Winnie's, was focused on her glass of scotch, which she was drawing near her mouth to take a sip.

"I don't know that I know anything you don't," I said slowly. "I saw Professor Baines dancing with Alex, and then I saw her run out of the room. A minute later, she came back. Or so I thought," I amended. "Someone who was also dressed in an Elizabeth costume came back. Whoever that was ran up to Professor Baines, began to argue with him, and then pulled him out of the room. I didn't think anything of it until a few minutes later when Alex and Byron showed up, asking where Professor Baines was." I paused and took a sip of my wine.

John's brow crinkled into thin horizontal lines as he tried to process this. "So Alex wasn't with Richard?" he asked.

"Apparently not. She said that while she and Professor Baines were dancing, she suddenly felt ill and ran for the bathroom. On her way there, she bumped into Byron, and, seeing how sick she was, he waited for her to come out. When she did, the two of them went in search of Professor Baines so he could take Alex back to their room."

Valerie pulled her wineglass away from her mouth. "Alex was sick?" she asked.

"Yes," I answered. "She said it came on really suddenly. I gather she got quite sick in the bathroom. Frankly, I wonder if someone didn't slip her something. It's a bit convenient for her to get sick just as the killer lures Professor Baines out of the ballroom."

Valerie glanced uneasily at Ian but said nothing else.

"Anyway," I said, resuming my tale, "we went to look for him and . . ." I paused, not wanting to repeat the ugly details of the scene to Ian. "And then we . . . ," I began again.

"Found him," supplied Aunt Winnie. I shot her a grateful look.

John shook his head. "Bollocks. How awful. But why do the police think Cora had anything to do with it? Could have been anyone, really."

Izzy bestowed a small appreciative smile on John. "Thank you, John. I appreciate your kindness, but the sad fact is that Mama made no secret about her opposition to Richard's theories, and she was especially adamant that we somehow connive to prevent him from presenting his latest paper. Then, as far as I can piece together, she drank far too much at the ball, picked a fight with him in front of everyone, and then wandered off and promptly passed out in a remote area of the building where no one saw her." Izzy rubbed a hand over her face. "She really couldn't have done more to incriminate herself had she tried," she muttered.

"Didn't I hear something about a wig?" Valerie asked, her voice artificially innocent.

"Oh, yes. Thank you, Valerie," Izzy replied with a brittle smile. "Yes, there was a wig found next to . . . to Richard's body. It was the same kind of wig that went with the Elizabeth costume that both Mama and Alex wore this evening. Except Alex wasn't wearing one, and Mama seems to have lost hers." She sighed and drained her glass. "So you see, she's done a rather bang-up job of putting herself in the position of number-one suspect. Frankly, I don't know what I'm going to do."

Aunt Winnie leaned forward and took Izzy's hand. Holding it tightly, she said, "We will get to the bottom of this, Izzy. I promise you. Cora is an old friend of mine, and I am not without connections. I promise you that she will have every means of support I can provide. You both will."

Izzy's eyes welled up until they resembled shimmering sapphires. She even cried pretty. "Thank you, Ms. Reynolds," she said. "I don't know what I'd do without you and Elizabeth. I don't really have anyone else I can turn to."

"That's not true," I said. "What about your fiancé? I'm sure he'll help."

Inexplicably, Izzy's smile dimmed a little; however, she only said, "That's true."

Valerie set her now empty wineglass on the table with a decided thud. Her face having resumed its peevish countenance, she rose from her chair and said, "Well, I hate to break up this support party for dear *Izzy,* but Ian and I have funeral arrangements to attend to. Ian?"

Ian yanked his attention away from Izzy and focused on Valerie. Seeing her expression, which was rapidly morphing from peevish to thunderous, he jumped to his feet as well. "Of course," he said. "We should be going."

"Please let us know if we can do anything," said Aunt Winnie. Ian opened his mouth to respond, but Valerie cut him off.

"Oh, we wouldn't want to bother you, seeing how you're going to be spending so much time trying to help *Cora.* I imagine that will be a full-time job." She gave a huff, then turned and marched out of the bar. Ian managed a weak smile our way before he trailed after her.

Aunt Winnie watched their exit with a bemused expression. Turning back to us, she said, "You know, I do believe that Valerie belongs to that numerous class of females, whose society can raise no other emotion than surprise at there being any men in the world who could like them well enough to marry them."

Izzy, her eyes still on the door they just exited, said nothing.

CHAPTER 15

I do not pretend to set people right,
but I do see that they are often wrong.

—MANSFIELD PARK

So, DO YOU THINK THE POLICE really believe your mother killed Richard?" asked John a moment later.

Izzy didn't answer right away. She was still staring at the empty doorway. I nudged her, and she turned to John. "I'm sorry, what did you say?"

"I asked if you think the police are going to peg this on your mother," he said.

Izzy shrugged. "I have no idea. I know she didn't kill him, of course, but I'm not sure the police would agree. I mean, the case against her does look pretty bad. On paper, at least. I only hope that they will see reason and realize that she simply isn't capable of hurting someone, let alone killing him." Aiming a small smile my way, she added, "Perhaps I will have to engage your talents, Elizabeth, and ask you to investigate the matter for me."

John pulled his mouth away from his glass of beer and stared at me in confusion. "What are you talking about?" he asked.

"Nothing," I said quickly. "She's just kidding."

Izzy sat up straighter in her chair. "No, I'm not. Didn't you say that you were a detective?"

"No, I'm an editor. Well, I used to be an editor before I quit."

Izzy shook her head. "You know what I mean! Didn't you tell me that you'd been involved in murder investigations before and had actually helped the police find the killer?"

"Well, yes," I began, "but . . ."

"Are you serious?" John asked, his glass still hovering in front of his mouth, which was unfortunately still hanging open in apparent surprise. "You're a detective? But . . . but . . . you're a woman," he ended feebly.

"I'm not a detective," I said quickly, annoyed that I saw relief in his eyes as I did so. "Not officially, anyway," I added, just to tweak his antiquated views. "But I have helped the police out a few times in the past."

"Helped out, my ass," Aunt Winnie exclaimed loyally. "You saved my life!" Turning to John, she said, "A few years back, a man was murdered in my inn. The police thought I did it. If it wasn't for Elizabeth, I'd probably be in jail now. She figured out who the real killer was, risked her life to get proof, and . . ."

"Got my head bashed in," I finished helpfully.

"Well, yes," Aunt Winnie admitted, tipping her red head as if conceding a minor point, "there was that, too. But my point is, you found the real killer." Turning back to John, she continued. "And then, last year, Elizabeth was at a wedding where a guest was murdered, and she figured out who the real killer was then, too."

John turned and regarded me with a faintly horrified expression.

"And finally, just last month, Elizabeth helped the police solve a murder from eight years ago," Aunt Winnie concluded proudly.

"I'm beginning to think I'm underpaid," I joked.

John said nothing. He obviously disapproved of my involvement in police business, but as it might be just the thing for ending his interest in me, I didn't let it bother me.

"I'd be happy to pay you anything you think is fair if you can help Mama," said Izzy, jolting me out of my thoughts.

"What? No! I'm not a professional detective, Izzy. I've just been lucky, I guess. I've noticed things that turned out to be important. I'm sure the police will solve this on their own and without any involvement from me."

"But what if they don't?" Izzy cried, her eyes again filling with tears. "What if they charge Mama with Richard's murder! What am I going to do then?" Her voice rose to a squeaky pitch, as the stress of her mother's plight threatened to overpower her.

Aunt Winnie laid her hand on top of Izzy's. "We won't let that happen. I promise you. We will help you in any way we can." Shooting me a level look, she added, "And if Elizabeth won't investigate this, then I will."

"But . . . ," I began.

"However," continued Aunt Winnie, ignoring me completely, "it's late, and you should get to bed. We will talk to the police again in the morning and see if we can sort all this out. But for now, I really think that you should head back to your hotel and get some rest. We'll meet again first thing in the morning." Turning to John, she added, "John, might I ask you to walk Izzy back to her hotel? I think she should have an escort tonight."

John immediately stood up. "But of course. I wouldn't have it any other way." Extending his hand, he said, "Come on, Izzy. Let me walk you back. And don't worry about your mother. I'm sure it will all be straightened out very soon."

Izzy sighed and took his hand. Pulling herself to her feet, she aimed a watery smile our way and said, "Thank you. I really appreciate your help. I'll call you in the morning and let you know what our status is."

"I'm sure everything will be fine, Izzy," I said. "The police will get to the bottom of this."

"And if they don't, then we will," Aunt Winnie added firmly.

"OKAY, WHAT THE HELL was that all about?" I asked Aunt Winnie once Izzy and John had left the bar.

"What do you mean?" she asked as she signed the bar tab.

"I mean, why are you pimping out my services to Izzy like I'm some kind of detective for hire?"

Aunt Winnie regarded me, her expression solemn. "Cora may be a silly woman, but she is an old friend, and I will do anything I can to help her and Izzy."

"Yes, but . . ."

"And if I can make them feel better by telling them that you are an old hand with murder investigations and have had some success with them, then I will tell them that." She turned and walked toward the exit.

I trailed after her. "So all that was nothing more than a ploy to calm them down?"

"It worked, didn't it?" she asked with a smug smile.

"Well, yes," I admitted. "But what happens if the police really do focus in on Cora and then they actually expect *me* to find the real killer?"

Aunt Winnie scoffed. "I don't think you have to worry about that. I'm sure the police will quickly realize that Cora is nothing more than a harmless, if rather excitable, woman, and then they will move on."

"Well, I certainly hope so," I said as we climbed the wide staircase to our room. "Because I'd hate them to think I could really do anything, should they need it."

"I think you can rest safe tonight, my dear," she answered with a laugh. "You won't be needing to don your detective cap on this trip."

Of course, in the lingo of the land, what utter bollocks *that* turned out to be.

CHAPTER 16

*The power of doing anything with quickness is always
much prized by the possessor, and often without any
attention to the imperfection of the performance.*

—PRIDE AND PREJUDICE

HEY'VE TAKEN MAMA IN AGAIN," Izzy cried into my ear over the phone the next morning.

"But why?" I asked, still wiping the sleep from my eyes. From the bed next to me, Aunt Winnie cast a curious eye at me from underneath her pillow. "Izzy," I mouthed to her. She pushed back the comforter and swung her legs off the bed. Rising, she took the phone from me without a word and said, "Izzy? It's Winnie. What happened?"

I listened as Aunt Winnie asked Izzy for details. From her end of the conversation, I gathered that Cora had been brought down to the station about fifteen minutes ago for more questioning. I glanced at the clock. It was barely seven thirty.

"It's going to be okay, Izzy," promised Aunt Winnie. "I'll go to the station and see what I can find out. Don't worry. It will be fine. I'll call you when I know something."

Hanging up the phone, she turned to me, her eyes worried. "I don't like this, Elizabeth. The police should have figured out by now that Cora isn't the type of woman to kill someone. The fact that they brought her in again tells me that we may have a problem on our hands."

"What do you propose we do?" I asked, not really sure I wanted to hear the answer.

"Well, we're going to go down to the station and convince the police that they've got the wrong woman," she said as she yanked open her bureau drawer and pulled out a pair of cream-colored wool slacks and a navy blue sweater.

"And if that doesn't work?" I asked with some trepidation.

"Then it might be time to see about digging out that detective cap, after all," she answered before heading to the bathroom.

IT WAS PERHAPS fitting that the sky that morning was heavy with dark clouds, each spitting hard cold rain. By the time we arrived at the police station, a large cement structure that could serve as a model for unimaginative government buildings everywhere, the rain had progressed from spitting to outright pouring. Looking down at my wet feet, I wished for the second time on this trip that I had worn thick boots like Anne Elliot rather than my flimsy ballet flats.

As we entered the station, we saw to our relief that Cora was just being released. Our joy, however, was short-lived when we took a good look at her. Her face was blotchy, and her eyes were puffy slits of red. From the palpable tension radiating from her body, it was clear that while she might have been cleared to leave the station, she hadn't been cleared of suspicion. Standing next to her was Inspector Middlefield. She appeared tired as well, but in her case it was the look of someone who'd pulled an all-nighter studying but still didn't feel confident on the subject matter. That gave me some hope.

"Cora!" cried Aunt Winnie. "Are you all right?"

Cora nodded wearily. "I'm fine. Just very tired. I think I could sleep for a week."

Aunt Winnie turned on Inspector Middlefield. "You can't honestly believe that this woman had anything to do with Professor Baines's death. Yes, she found his theories vulgar—I think you'd be hard-pressed to find someone who didn't—but she would never harm him."

Inspector Middlefield sighed. "Ms. Reynolds, I'm sure Mrs. Beadle appreciates your loyalty, but the sad fact remains that she threatened Professor Baines on several occasions and cannot produce a valid alibi for a large portion of last night. I would be a sorry excuse for an inspector if I did not spend more than a little time investigating her story."

"Perhaps," countered Aunt Winnie, "but in the meantime, the real killer is still running about doing God knows what."

Inspector Middlefield produced a tired semblance of a smile. "It is not a perfect science, I grant you. However, we usually manage to get the job done." Turning to Cora, she said, "I will be in touch, Mrs. Beadle."

"I understand," Cora replied mournfully.

With a curt nod to us, Inspector Middlefield said, "Good day, ladies," and walked into a back office.

"Are you okay?" Aunt Winnie asked as we walked outside. "Do you want me to get you a lawyer?"

Cora shook her head. "Not yet. I don't want to appear guilty. I keep thinking that if I cooperate and answer their questions, they'll realize that I had nothing to do with this."

Aunt Winnie shook her head in disagreement. "Cora, while that sounds lovely, I really don't think good manners are going to be the determining factor here. We need to *prove* to them that you had nothing to do with Richard's murder."

Cora turned to me, her eyes now bright with hope. "Oh, that's right! I nearly forgot. Izzy told me that you were a detective of sorts. Do you really think that you can find the real killer? I'd be forever grateful for whatever you could do."

I opened my mouth, but it was Aunt Winnie who answered. "Of course she will, Cora. Don't give it another thought. We'll get you back to the hotel, and then Elizabeth and I will see what we can find out."

Cora enveloped me in a grateful hug before I could protest the absurdity of Aunt Winnie's proposal. I felt like the worst kind of imposter as Cora said, "Oh, you sweet, sweet child! I can't thank you enough! You know, I actually feel a little better knowing that you are out there trying to prove my innocence!"

Horrified, I stared at Aunt Winnie with agonized eyes, but she only winked at me.

It looked like supersleuth Elizabeth Parker was on another case.

God help us all.

* * *

AFTER WE GOT Cora settled at her hotel, Aunt Winnie and I argued over which session to attend: "Dueling Mr. Darcy" or "Dressing Mr. Darcy." It finally came down to a coin toss, which, naturally, she won. "And how exactly is that supposed to help us in our search for Richard's killer?" I groused, annoyed both at my loss and the fact that she had convinced Cora and Izzy that I would be able to solve all their problems by finding a killer.

"Now don't be grumpy. All I said was that we would *try*. And, don't forget, I'm going to help you!"

"Sure you are. Right after you learn how to dress Mr. Darcy."

"Well, of course!" she said with no trace of embarrassment. "There's no way in hell I'm not going to that class. And who knows, we might learn something important."

"Somehow, I don't see how learning if Darcy dressed to the right or left is going to be of material consequence in this case."

Aunt Winnie laughed. "Maybe not. But wouldn't it be delightful if it did?"

"DRESSING MR. DARCY" WAS, not surprisingly, packed. Woman of all ages—as well as a few men—crammed into the large conference room. I was beginning to despair of finding a seat, when Aunt Winnie spied two empty spots near the back. As we squeezed into the metal folding chairs, I was surprised to see Valerie and Gail in the row ahead of us. Well, I suppose it wasn't too surprising that Gail would carry on with her itinerary as planned, I amended, but shouldn't Valerie be playing the role of the grieving daughter-in-law? True, she was wearing a shapeless black dress made of some unidentifiable but definitely flammable material, which certainly suggested death inasmuch as most women wouldn't want to be caught dead in it, but other than that, her mood seemed almost cheerful. However, compared with Gail, her mood seemed somber indeed. Not only was Gail wearing a bright pink blazer and matching skirt, but her face appeared years younger than it had yesterday, and she was practically grinning from ear to ear as she listened to the lecture. Furthermore, her face no longer held that faintly vacant expression I'd noticed earlier in the week. Today she appeared alert and focused. It was apparent that Richard's untimely demise was just the tonic Gail needed to pull herself back together. I didn't fault her, exactly; from the sound of it, Richard had treated her pretty shabbily, but it did seem somewhat heartless to be in such obvious good spirits the day after the father of your only child was murdered.

As we learned about the items one might find in a proper Regency gentleman's closet—immaculate linen shirts with high collars, perfectly tied cravats, and exquisitely tailored dark coats—Valerie and Gail chatted softly about the magazine. Although they kept their voices low, it wasn't hard to overhear their whispered chatter. Especially as I was practically leaning forward in my seat to make sure I caught every word.

"This is going to save us," said Gail, with a sigh of contentment. "I've called the bank and transferred some of my own funds into the account until the money from the estate comes through. It should be enough to hold us. I know that Richard left the bulk of his money to Ian. I don't know how long these things take, but I imagine that within six months or so it should all be settled."

"That's wonderful," Valerie replied. "I hate to sound crass, but it really couldn't have come at a better time. I don't know what we would have done if the magazine folded. Little Zee just started nursery school last month. It's one of the best in the city." She paused and then, apropos of nothing, added, "Private, of course."

"Have you spoken to Ian about this?" asked Gail, her brow creasing in the first suggestion of concern I'd seen so far. "Is he on board with it all?"

Valerie waved away Gail's worry with an indifferent wave of her bony hand. "I talked with him briefly. He's focused on arranging for the funeral right now."

"Good. I'll talk to him as well, just to be sure," Gail said with a sigh. "Oh, Valerie, I can't pretend not to be excited about what this all means! Now we can sink some real money into the magazine and work on expanding our reader base. We can finally put some of our plans into action. Not all, of course, but some."

Valerie's thin, colorless lips pulled into a frown, and she said, "What do you mean, 'real money'? Ian and I have our own finances to deal with, too, you know. It can't all go to the magazine."

"What do you mean?" Gail asked, lowering her voice.

"What do you mean, what do I mean? Do you know how much private school costs? Little Zee deserves the best, and I'm not going to send him to some public school and have him sit next to God knows what."

Gail's expression cooled to a few degrees south of glacial as she stared at Valerie. Valerie, for once, seemed to notice someone else's feelings besides her own and said, "This is silly. There's no reason for us to argue. Especially as I think there might be more money available than we realize."

"What do you mean?" Gail asked, lowering her voice.

A self-satisfied smile formed on Valerie's face, and she leaned her head close to Gail's. "Well, it might not be perhaps entirely legal, but I . . ."

The woman to my left suddenly let out a loud "Shush!" and shot both Valerie and Gail a look of extreme annoyance. Valerie twisted in her seat, turning a baleful eye of her own toward the woman. It was a glare that would have stopped me in my tracks, but the woman to my left, a petite grandmotherly type with crimped coal-black hair and cold, sharklike eyes, was clearly made of stronger stuff.

"Do you mind?" she whispered with icy politeness. "Some of us are *trying* to listen to the lecture. If it is urgent that you have your conversation right now, perhaps you should take it *outside* where you can hold it in private." Her companion, a plump woman with an equally intense expression of irritation in her deep-set eyes, nodded her small gray head in vigorous agreement. I heard someone else nearby mutter, "Hear, hear!"

You don't mess with Janeites. Especially when Darcy is involved.

From the manner in which Valerie's small eyes rapidly narrowed further with contempt, it was evident that she did not care one iota about the women's complaints or her own rudeness. In fact, she gave every indication that she was about to escalate the situation by returning a verbal lob of her own. However, no sooner had she opened her mouth than she caught sight of me and Aunt Winnie. An odd expression crossed her peevish face, and she abruptly closed her mouth and turned around stiffly in her chair. From that point on, neither she nor Gail spoke.

While most of the attendees around us settled happily in their seats, eager to hear the rest of the lecture without further interruption, I was most exceedingly put out. For now I was left wondering just how much money was at stake and what Valerie had meant about there being more money than previously thought. What "not entirely legal" action was Valerie thinking of taking to gain more money, and perhaps even more important, did it have anything to do with Richard's death?

I snuck a glance at Aunt Winnie to see if she'd been following the conversation. From the exaggerated arch of her eyebrow as she met my eye, I gathered she had.

WHEN THE LECTURE ENDED, Valerie and Gail practically ran from the room, both studiously avoiding eye contact with me and Aunt Winnie.

"Did you catch all of that?" I asked as we snaked our way through the crowd and out into the hallway.

"Most of it, I think. Although I have to admit I did miss some parts. My hearing isn't what it used to be. I gather, though, that neither of them is exactly crying into her hankie over Richard's death."

"You could say that. In fact, you could say that Gail is doing better than ever. She actually looked alert and chipper today. I wonder if her need to self-medicate died with Richard."

"It would appear that many problems died with Richard Baines," Aunt Winnie replied. "The man certainly doesn't seem to be missed by his daughter-in-law or ex-wife. Although I suppose you can't fault Gail for not donning the widow's weeds. After all, he did leave her for another woman."

"Speaking of which, I wonder how Alex is dealing with all of this. I don't suppose that either Ian or Valerie are going out of their way to check on her."

As the crowd around us thinned out as the attendees made their way to the next session, I was surprised to see Byron ambling toward us. Based on his rumpled blazer, uncombed hair, and unshaven face, I gathered that he was still reeling from the shock of Richard's murder.

"Hello, Elizabeth. Hello, Mrs. Reynolds. How are you?" he asked in a dull voice.

"I think we should be asking that of you," Aunt Winnie answered. "Don't take this the wrong way, but you look terrible. Have you eaten?"

Byron shook his head. "No. I'm not hungry."

"You need to eat. Come and have a bite with us," said Aunt Winnie.

"No, really," he said with a polite smile, "I'm fine."

"The hell you are. You look like hell. Come with us. I insist." Her firm tone left no room for argument.

Byron managed a grateful smile. "Well, since you put it that way, I will. Thank you."

The morning's dark rain clouds had finally cleared, revealing patches of soft blue sky, and so we decided to walk to a nearby café, the Cork. There we were quickly shown to a table on the restaurant's spacious al fresco terrace. Decorated with oak sleepers, white

Italian planters, and lavender plant beds, the area was an oasis in the midst of Bath. Which, come to think of it, was a kind of oasis in itself, so I guess it was an oasis within an oasis.

Byron settled heavily into his chair and ordered a cup of coffee and a minute steak sandwich. From his almost robotic tone, I wondered if he was even aware of his actions.

"Is there any news?" I asked after I'd ordered a Diet Coke and a BLT.

Byron shook his head. "No. The police are still conducting their investigation. I gather that they are still very interested in your friend Cora. For what it's worth, I did tell that inspector that I really couldn't see her killing Richard."

Aunt Winnie smiled. "Thank you, Byron. That was kind of you. Do you have any idea, though, who might have wanted him dead?"

Byron ran a large hand through his already rumpled hair. "I don't know. I mean, I only worked for the guy. I don't really know what his personal relationships were like."

"Well, you said he seemed happy with Alex, right?" I asked.

"True. He did. But other than that . . ." He shrugged.

"Speaking of Alex," said Aunt Winnie, "how is she? Does she need anything?"

Byron raised stricken eyes to us. "Oh, God. I don't know. I didn't think to call her today," he said haltingly. "I guess I assumed that Ian and Valerie would be with her." He closed his eyes and shook his head. "But now that I really think about it, I doubt either one of them would call her. They weren't on the best of terms."

"Were you able to get in touch with Alex's sister?" I asked, after taking a sip of my soda.

"I left her a message. I don't know if she's called Alex back yet," Byron replied. "I should check on her. I just don't know what to say to her. I don't know her very well; most of my time was spent with Richard."

Our food arrived just then, and for a moment conversation was halted while we ate. Then Aunt Winnie asked, "So what do you do now, Byron? Are you going to stay for the rest of the festival?"

Byron finished chewing before he answered. "I don't know. I received a call from the group that invited Richard to present his paper. They still want to hear it. They asked if Alex would be interested in presenting it."

"Really?" I asked in surprise. "I would have thought the festival organizers would have held off on that."

"Oh, the festival didn't ask Richard to come," Byron clarified. "It was some literary society that focuses on hidden meanings in the classics. No, the festival organizers weren't huge fans of some of Richard's theories. I can't imagine any of them encouraging him to give a talk that basically turns the image of their beloved idol upside down."

"Oh. That makes more sense," I said. "So is she going to do it? Is she going to present the paper?"

"I haven't asked her yet. But I don't know what she'll want to do. She's not as well versed on Austen as Richard was. And given what's happened, I'm not sure if she should present it, but then again, I'm not thinking straight about any of this," he replied. "I'm not sure what the right thing to do is. From an academic standpoint, it might make sense, but from a personal one . . . I just don't know."

Aunt Winnie thoughtfully dipped an onion ring into the dish

of garlic mayo. "Have you spoken to Lindsay?" she asked before popping the morsel into her mouth. "What does she think should happen?"

"Oh, God," Byron said suddenly, dropping his sandwich onto the plate. "Lindsay! I completely forgot about her. I haven't seen her since last night. I don't even know if she knows what's happened."

"Well, I think someone should tell her," I said. "I got the impression that she was close to him."

Byron gave a rueful laugh. "Yes. So did I." He stared thoughtfully at his plate. "I wouldn't even know what to say to her."

"How about the basic facts?" offered Aunt Winnie, not unkindly. Seeing Byron's dazed face, however, she changed her tone. "Why don't Elizabeth and I come with you, Byron. Perhaps we can help."

Byron raised grateful eyes to Aunt Winnie. "Would you? I'd appreciate that. Lindsay is a nice girl, don't get me wrong, it's just that she's a bit . . ."

"Devoted?" I suggested.

Byron caught my meaning. "Yes," he said. "That's exactly what she is. She isn't going to take this well at all."

CHAPTER 17

All the privilege I claim for my own sex . . . is that of
loving longest, when existence or when hope is gone.
—PERSUASION

AFTER WE FINISHED LUNCH, we headed to Lindsay's hotel. Byron called her room from the lobby and asked permission to come up. I noticed, however, that he didn't mention that we were with him.

Lindsay answered his knock almost immediately. Her eyes and nose were both red, her face was pale, and her hair stuck out in at least four different directions. She was wearing black sweatpants and a blue-and-white baseball jersey emblazoned with the Austen quote YOU DO NOT KNOW WHAT I SUFFER.

I had a feeling that the sentiment was truer than she realized.

Seeing Aunt Winnie and me standing behind Byron, her expression changed from mild curiosity to outright alarm. "What's going on?" she asked, her voice scratchy.

"I'm afraid I have some news," Byron began. "May we come in?"

Lindsay hesitated a moment and then reluctantly nodded and stepped aside. "I'm not feeling very well," she said as we shuffled awkwardly into her room. "I think I've got some kind of stomach bug."

The room was small but, as they say, well-appointed. In one corner, there was a small maple writing desk and a coordinating delicate needlepoint chair; opposite that sat two twin beds, one of which was unused, its dark blue chenille bedspread still straight and flat. The desk held the remnants of a half-eaten meal: a few crackers, a bowl of soup, and a soda. The chair was piled high with papers. Lindsay pushed the pile onto the floor and offered it to Aunt Winnie. I perched on the unused bed, placing my purse on the floor in front of me. Byron sat next to me, while Lindsay sat on the bed opposite us.

"So what's the news?" she asked. "Is there something wrong with the paper?"

"No, the paper's fine. The reason I'm here is because of Richard. Professor Baines," said Byron.

There was no mistaking the panic in Lindsay's eyes, and I remembered their not-so-private fight last night. "What about Richard? What does he want? What did he say?" she asked, her voice a squeak.

Byron sighed and lowered his voice. "So you haven't heard, then?"

"Heard what?" she demanded. "What did he say?"

"He didn't say anything, Lindsay. I'm afraid that, well, I'm sorry to have to tell you this, but he's dead. Someone killed him last night at the ball."

Her eyes wide with apparent shock, Lindsay leaned back as if to distance herself from the news. "He's . . . he's dead? No! That can't be!"

Byron nodded. "I'm afraid it is."

Lindsay's breath came out in short quick pants. "Oh, my God! I can't believe it! Oh, my God—no! What am I . . . oh, my God!" With a strangled gasp, she wrapped her arms around her waist and closed her eyes against a rush of tears.

No one spoke. Frankly, I didn't know what to say. That she was genuinely upset was clear. But I don't believe Miss Manners ever addressed the issue of consoling a student who so clearly adored her professor.

Her married professor.

Her dead, married professor.

Aunt Winnie stood and walked the short distance to where Lindsay sat. Putting her hand on Lindsay's shoulder, she said, "I know, dear. It's an awful thing to have happen."

Lindsay gave a muted sniff and then nodded her head.

"Let me get you a glass of water," I said, standing up and heading to the bathroom. As I grabbed a glass from the bathroom shelf, I noticed the small bottle. A quick glance confirmed my suspicion. After filling the glass with water, I emerged from the bathroom. Handing the glass to Lindsay, I said, "Drink a little."

Lindsay did as she was told, and I resumed my seat on the bed next to Byron. After taking a few more sips, Lindsay raised her head and asked the question we all wanted answered. "Who killed him?" Looking at us with a dazed expression, she then went one further. "Was it Alex?"

Byron appeared surprised by this. "The police don't know who it was. Why would you think it was Alex?" he asked, leaning forward.

Lindsay opened her mouth but then shook her head and closed

it. "I don't know. I guess, I just thought that maybe . . ." She paused. "I don't know. Forget it."

Byron shook his head. "No, go on. If you know something, you need to tell us. The police need all the information they can get to solve this. Right now they are looking at Cora Beadle—the one who was so adamant against Richard's theory—but I'm not sure they're right. "

But Lindsay refused to elaborate on her suspicion about Alex. "I don't have any proof—I don't know what I'm saying, really. I guess I just thought that lots of times it's the spouse that is the murderer."

"That's true," Byron said slowly, as if he were mentally revisiting this idea. After a minute he shook his head. "But in this case, I don't think she could have done it." He quickly explained the odd scene of the second Elizabeth who fought with Richard and then dragged him from the room. "Alex was getting sick in one of the bathrooms at the time," he said. "I happened to run into her right before that and waited for her outside." His brow creased in concentration. "I suppose she might have been lying, but I don't see how. She went in the bathroom and didn't come out for a good ten minutes."

"Was there only one exit?" asked Aunt Winnie.

Byron nodded. "Yes. And no one else came in or out, so I don't see how she could have gotten past me—twice—without my noticing."

Lindsay nodded, but from her faraway expression, I doubted she had heard much of what he'd said. "Is . . . is his family still here?" she asked suddenly.

"Yes, they are," Byron answered. "Why? Do you need to talk to them?"

Lindsay looked down at her lap. "No," she said as she focused on picking at her cuticles. "I just wondered, that's all." A thought appeared to occur to her, and she suddenly sat up a bit straighter and stared at Byron. "What's going to happen to his paper?" she asked. "Is it still going to be presented?"

Byron shrugged. "Well, now that you mention it, the society did call me. They still want it to be presented at the meeting tomorrow night. They want either Alex or me to read it."

Lindsay leaned forward, her eyes the most focused I'd seen them since we'd arrived. "That paper must be presented! It must!"

Her theatrical reaction reminded me of her obvious distress during last night's ball and Richard's subsequent accusation that she was being "melodramatic." I chose my next words carefully. "I happened to see you talking to Richard last night. It seemed like you were trying to talk to him about something important. Did it have something to do with the paper?"

Lindsay's face flushed, and her eyes shifted away from mine. "Oh. That. That was nothing."

"It didn't seem like nothing," I replied. "In fact, you seemed pretty upset."

Lindsay's mouth twisted. "Did I? I don't remember that."

"What was your conversation about, then?"

Lindsay's eyes slid away from mine. "If you must know," she said, addressing the nightstand, "I was trying to warn him about that Cora woman. Frankly, she seemed like she was becoming unhinged. Richard didn't take her seriously. Perhaps he should have."

"After your conversation with Richard, you left. Where did you go?" I asked.

"I went to . . . I went back to my room. Here," said Lindsay.

"Did you go back to the ball?" I pressed.

"No. I went to sleep."

"Did you talk to Richard again?"

Lindsay's face crumpled a bit at my question. "No," she answered, her voice small. "I didn't. The last time I saw him or spoke to him was at the ball."

One of the piles of paper on the floor next to Aunt Winnie toppled over and she bent down to right the mess. "Oh, don't bother with that," said Lindsay, glancing in her direction. I took advantage of her distraction to nudge my purse under the bed a bit with my foot. Aunt Winnie saw the movement. Byron and Lindsay did not.

"It's no problem," answered Aunt Winnie, as she stacked the papers back up. "But you should get some rest, Lindsay," she said, suddenly getting to her feet. "You aren't feeling well, and no doubt we've upset you with this terrible news."

Byron and I got up as well. Lindsay remained seated on the bed. She suddenly looked very small and vulnerable.

"Call me if you need anything," Byron said as we moved toward the door. "I'll let you know if I hear anything."

Lindsay nodded at the floor. She did not look at any of us.

CHAPTER 18

It is very often nothing but our own vanity that deceives us.
Women fancy admiration means more than it does.
—PRIDE AND PREJUDICE

So what do you think of Lindsay's idea about Alex having had something to do with Richard's death?" I asked Byron as we headed down the stairs to the hotel lobby.

Byron shook his head. "I don't know. We aren't what you might call friends. But I really do think she loved Richard. And she did seem sick when she went in that bathroom. I just don't see how she could have gotten out without my noticing."

I thought about that. I figured it wouldn't hurt to take a look at the bathroom myself. After all, Byron hadn't actually gone into it. Maybe there was another exit that he didn't know about.

As we entered the lobby, I slapped my thigh in a show of aggravation. "Oh, crap! I left my purse up in Lindsay's room. I've got to go back up."

"Oh, sure . . . ," said Byron, as he turned back toward the stairs, but I cut him off.

"You don't need to come with me," I said to him. "You should go and get some rest. You've been through enough."

Byron managed a ghost of a smile. "Not as much as some," he said ruefully. "But I guess I better go and check in with Alex and see how she's doing. I have no idea what she's going to want to do about the paper. Frankly, I can't see her caring one way or the other."

"Lindsay seemed pretty adamant that it still be presented," I said. "Wouldn't Alex feel the same way?"

Byron shook his head. "Not necessarily. Alex loved Richard, and Richard loved Austen. Now that he's gone, I doubt she's really going to care."

"But he thought it was an amazing find," I said in some surprise. "I mean, I've got to be honest with you, I thought it was utter crap, but he clearly thought this was going to be the highlight of his career. Wouldn't she want to see it presented if for no other reason than to give him his glory?"

Byron sighed. "She might. You just never know with Alex. Like I said, we're not that close. I don't pretend to understand how her mind works. Your guess is as good as mine." Turning to Aunt Winnie, he said, "Thanks for coming with me to tell Lindsay. She's a nice kid, and I know she was fond of Richard."

"Not a problem," replied Aunt Winnie. "I'm sure we'll see you around later."

Byron nodded and headed for the hotel exit. Once he was gone, Aunt Winnie turned back to me, hands on her hips. "So, I see you decided to go with the old accidentally-leaving-your-purse excuse, huh?"

"Okay, so it's not the best excuse, I grant you, but it's all I could come up with," I said as I headed back to the stairs.

"Oh, don't get me wrong. You did it very nicely. But my question is, why do we need to talk to Lindsay again? Do you think she might have seen Alex?" Aunt Winnie asked as she followed me.

"I don't know, actually. She might have seen something, but that's not why I want to talk to her."

"I see. And are you going to share this information with me, or are you going to go all Poirot on me?"

I let my mouth curl up into a smug smile. "Weren't you the one who was touting my detective skills last night and trying to convince me to actually become one? Well, if I'm to do so, I need to act the part. And you know as well as I do that the really great detectives never tell their associates what they are thinking. Perhaps if you'd use your little gray cells, you wouldn't need to ask."

"I am not your associate. I am your great-aunt, and as such I am not above slapping you upside your smug little face," she jokingly retorted. At least, I think she was joking.

I still didn't elaborate, but I made sure to stay out of reach.

We made our way down the hall and to Lindsay's room. I gave a quick rap on the door and stepped back. Within seconds, Lindsay opened the door, clearly surprised to see us again.

I affected my most innocent smile while Aunt Winnie tried to affect an expression that suggested that she knew what the hell was going on. I'm pretty sure we both failed. "I'm so sorry, Lindsay," I said, "but I seem to have left my purse in your room."

Lindsay stepped back from the door but kept her hand on the doorknob. "Oh, sure," she said. "Come on in."

I walked over to the bed and scooped up the purse from where I'd shoved it. "Got it," I said, hoisting the strap over my shoulder.

Lindsay smiled politely. The door remained open and her hand stayed on the doorknob.

I looked back at her, my expression curious. In a matter-of-fact voice, I said, "So tell me, Lindsay. How far along are you?"

Lindsay's face did not change. In fact, the only indication that she heard my question was that the door suddenly slammed shut.

HER EYES LOCKED ONTO MINE, and she said, "What the hell are you talking about?"

I took a deep breath. "Lindsay, I'm sorry, but I've been around my pregnant sister enough these past few months to know the signs of pregnancy. You don't have the stomach flu. You have morning sickness."

Lindsay shook her head back and forth in adamant denial. "No. No, you're wrong. It is the flu. I'm not pregnant. I'm just . . . sick."

"Then why is there a bottle of prenatal vitamins in your bathroom?" I asked.

Aunt Winnie shot me a look of admiration. Lindsay did not. "You searched through my things?" she asked indignantly. "Who does that? Who the hell do you think you are?"

"I didn't search through your things," I answered. "I happened to notice the bottle when I got you that glass of water."

Lindsay glared at me. "I don't have to talk to you. In fact, I'd like you to leave."

I tried another tack. "Lindsay, it was pretty obvious how you felt about Richard. You aren't the first girl to sleep with her professor.

Did he know about the baby? Is that what your fight with him was about?"

Lindsay pulled her shoulders back and stuck her chin out. "This is none of your business."

"Technically, you're right. It's not my business. But the police are focusing on Cora as a suspect, and I think they're wrong. I'm trying to find out who really killed Richard. As you're carrying his child, I would think that you'd be curious about that point as well."

Lindsay regarded me in silence. "I'm not a slut," she finally said, her voice defiant. "I cared for him."

"I didn't say you were," I replied. "And I believe that you did care about him. Did he know about the baby?"

Lindsay didn't answer right away. Her eyes dropped to the carpet. After a long moment, she turned and sat on the bed. Looking up at me, she said, "Yes. I told him at the ball. I . . . I didn't fool myself into thinking he'd be ecstatic, but I thought he'd at least . . ." Her voice trailed off.

"You thought he'd at least react differently from how he did?" I suggested.

Lindsay gave a painful nod.

"What was his reaction?"

Lindsay closed her eyes. "He told me to get rid of it."

"He was uniformly charming, wasn't he?" Aunt Winnie said to no one in particular.

Lindsay's eyes flew open, and she glared at Aunt Winnie. "He didn't mean it! He was just taken aback, and focused on the paper. I'm sure that once he thought about it, he would have felt differently."

"And if he didn't?" Aunt Winnie asked.

Lindsay shook her head, as if to deny the possibility. "He would have. I don't know how to explain it without it sounding like a cliché, but we really cared for each other. I understood and appreciated his work—and he valued my contributions. We made a good team."

"Are you saying that you thought he'd leave Alex for you?" I asked in surprise.

"I don't know what he would have done," Lindsay replied. "But we would have worked it out. Once he delivered the paper, we would have worked it out."

"Why is it so important to you that the paper still be delivered?" I asked.

Lindsay regarded me in surprise. "Are you kidding? That paper will make him famous—immortal, even. All his earlier work will be republished and reviewed. Books will be written about him and his groundbreaking theories."

I regarded her with equal surprise. She was either a true believer or had a really bad case of baby mush brain. Either way, she had my pity if she honestly thought that Richard's paper was going to result in an influx of cash.

"What are you going to do now?" I asked.

"Have the baby, of course," Lindsay replied without hesitation.

"Do you have family around who can help you?" asked Aunt Winnie.

Lindsay shook her head. "No. My parents would never support me with this. They barely tolerate the idea of my life now. I'm the first girl in my family to go to college, let alone grad school. It's not exactly seen as a point of family pride." She sighed. "My parents aren't evil people, but they have this antiquated idea that women shouldn't be, as they so quaintly put it, 'overly educated.' According to them, a woman's place is serving her husband and children. In that order." She looked down at the carpet again. "That's their world, and I worked really hard to get away from it." She ran her hand through her short hair, a faint smile on her lips. "Richard was unlike any man I'd ever met before. He was sophisticated, intelligent, and charming. He knew so much about so many things— and not just literature. He knew about wine, food, travel, music, and poetry. The world he lived in was so different from the one I grew up in that at times I felt as if I was from a different planet. I don't want to go back to it. Ever."

I briefly wondered if Lindsay's desire to get away from that now alien world had something to do with her pregnancy. Had the pull of Richard's sophisticated world led her to get pregnant on purpose? Could she really have deluded herself into thinking Richard would leave Alex for her? I indulged in a mental sigh. Of course she could have. A thousand other women had done the same—why should Lindsay be an exception? "Did Alex know about you and Richard?" I asked.

Lindsay considered the question. "I don't know. She might have. But if she did, Richard never told me. We kept our relationship pretty secret."

I doubted that. Most cheating spouses think they are keeping it pretty secret and still end up getting caught. If Alex did know about Richard's relationship with Lindsay, would she have killed him? It made sense on a certain animalistic level, but somehow that just didn't seem Alex's style despite her claim to having a jealous temper.

"Are you going to tell her now?" I asked.

Lindsay regarded me, her expression inscrutable. "I guess I'll have to," she said after a minute. "I mean, I'll need money to raise the baby."

The ugly idea that Lindsay's pregnancy had been planned popped back into my head. But rather than Lindsay's hoping that Richard would leave Alex for her because of the baby, I now wondered if Lindsay could have gotten pregnant merely to ensure her financial future. After all, Richard had been a very wealthy man, and his child would be entitled to some of that wealth. And if that was the case, then it didn't really matter if Richard was dead. In fact, from a legal standpoint, it might be easier if he was.

My gray cells certainly weren't providing much in the way of illumination. I sighed. I had a sinking suspicion that my little gray cells were more charcoal than anything else.

CHAPTER 19

$$\sim\!\!\infty\!\!\sim$$

*I had a very pleasant evening, . . . though you will probably
find out that there was no particular reason for it.*

—LETTERS OF JANE AUSTEN

"ELL, THAT WAS INTERESTING," said Aunt Winnie
after we left Lindsay's room.

"If by 'interesting' you mean completely screwed up, then I
would concur," I replied, as I walked along the hallway toward the
stairs. "Do you think she might have gotten pregnant on purpose?"

"It's a definite possibility," Aunt Winnie said. "I think the poor
thing was besotted with both Richard and his 'sophisticated' world.
Seriously, how hard is it to get into that grad school anyway?"

"I wonder which was stronger, the desire to join Richard's world
or the desire to leave hers for good."

"Does it really matter?" Aunt Winnie asked, as we descended
the stairs to the lobby.

I considered the question. "No. Probably not. Do you think we
should tell Inspector Middlefield that Lindsay is pregnant?"

Aunt Winnie paused on the staircase and turned to me, her expression troubled. "I don't know. On the one hand, it's private and
none of our business."

"And on the other hand, she and Richard fought about it before he died," I added.

Aunt Winnie chewed on her lower lip while she debated the issue. Then, with a firm nod that sent more than a few of her red curls bobbing, she came to a decision. "We should tell the inspector," she said. "I think it's important. I don't think Lindsay had anything to do with Richard's death. I don't think she's a saint, mind you, but I don't think she killed him."

"Okay. For the record, I agree with you about telling the inspector. But I feel like a fink letting Lindsay's secret out of the bag."

"You shouldn't feel like a fink," she said, as she resumed her descent down the stairs. "If anyone should feel like a fink, it's Richard Baines. I thought he was an ass before, but the fact that he slept with one of his students—a student as vulnerable and unworldly as Lindsay—is criminal. The man was an ass on all levels."

"You'll get no argument from me on that," I said.

As I trailed along after her, I had a sudden thought. "What if Lindsay's secret wasn't a secret? An affair is one thing. A baby is another."

Aunt Winnie turned to me, her eyebrows raised high and her eyes hopeful. "Then I can think of at least one person who would be most displeased."

"Alex?"

Aunt Winnie nodded. "Alex."

"I think we should take a look at that bathroom. Maybe Byron was wrong. Maybe there is another way in and out of it. Maybe we can help Cora after all."

* * *

THERE WAS NO OTHER exit out of the bathroom, not even a window. It was just as Byron said: only one way in and one way out. The right side was lined with stalls, and the left was lined with sinks. Aunt Winnie and I even took turns standing guard outside and trying to sneak past the other, but unless Byron blindfolded himself and stuck plugs into his ears as he waited for Alex, there was simply no way that she could have passed by him unnoticed. It was a most vexing discovery.

We had just arrived back at our hotel, when we ran into John in the lobby. However, from the way he leaped out of his chair and rushed over to us, I suspected that it wasn't a chance meeting.

"Hello there," he said. "I was hoping I'd see you. I thought we could all go to the memorial this evening together."

"Memorial?" I asked. "What memorial?"

John affected an exaggerated expression of surprise. "Why, the memorial for Richard," he said, a shade louder than necessary. "Surely you've heard about it. Valerie arranged it. Everyone is going to be there."

He made it sound like the event of the century.

"Oh, I don't think so," I said, just as Aunt Winnie chimed in with, "Of course we'll be there. Where and what time?"

John smiled in obvious satisfaction. "It's at a local restaurant. Meet me in the lobby at five, and I'll take you. After all, I promised you a ride in my car, didn't I?"

"That you did, John," Aunt Winnie replied with a smile of her own. "That you did."

* * *

AS PLANNED, WE MET JOHN at five in the lobby. He was wearing his usual tweed jacket but in deference of the somber occasion had opted for a crisp pair of jeans rather than his ratty ones. I suppose it had something to do with that famous British sense of decorum. He grinned when he saw us and loudly called out, "The Jaguar is just out front. I had it brought round. It's a lovely night for a drive. Shall we go?"

Several startled heads turned our way, and I gave an embarrassed nod before following John out to the street. There, as promised, was a bright green Jaguar with the top down. John paused in front of it and stroked the leather interior in a manner that made me feel as if I was intruding on an intimate moment. "She's a damned beauty, isn't she?" he asked. "Bloody gorgeous lines. Paid a pretty penny for her, but she was worth it. Once I saw her, I just threw down my money and bought her. I'm not one to waste time haggling when I want something."

He paused, and I wondered if he was waiting for us to add our compliments. I've never been much of a car person; I usually run out of interest after asking, "What color is it?" And since I already knew that it was green, I was at a loss. I muttered something inane about its "lines," which seemed to do the trick. John beamed at me and nodded.

"Damn right. After all, it's a Jaguar! It's the best car on the road! I should know. I'm quite the car expert. All my friends are constantly coming to me for advice about cars. And I give it to them, you know. I'm not one to hold back. I think that if you have a special knowledge or talent, you should share it."

"I'm sure they appreciate that," I said as John swung open the passenger door for Aunt Winnie. Once she was settled, he did the same for me. As I slid into the backseat, I buckled my seat belt and asked, "So where is the restaurant we're going to? Is it far?"

John gunned the engine. "No. It's just around the corner, actually. But I thought it might be nice to give you a tour of Bath before we go. I did promise you one, after all. And I am a man who keeps his promises."

I gave an inward groan as the car lurched out into the street, immediately causing several other drivers to blast their horns in angry protest. John waved to them as if they were merely saying hello. I ducked lower in the bucket seat.

Bath is not a city that lends itself well to speeding. The streets are narrow and crowded with cars and pedestrians. That said, John did his level best to "give us a taste of what this baby can do."

I did my level best not to scream and instead hurriedly made my peace with my God.

"So what do you think about this business with Richard?" John yelled to us over the roar of the engine.

"It's very sad," I yelled back.

"Yes, but who do you think did it?" he pressed. "Didn't you say you were a detective of sorts? What have you found out?"

"I never said I was an actual detective," I countered. "I've just been able to help out the police a few times in the past. Please don't think I'm passing myself off as some kind of expert."

"She's just being modest, John," Aunt Winnie said with a mischievous grin. "We've found out quite a lot, actually."

John glanced sharply at Aunt Winnie. "Really? That is interesting. What have you found out?"

"Oh, I don't think we should say," said Aunt Winnie. "I wouldn't want to compromise anything."

John nodded as if he completely understood, but his face registered unease. "Of course, I can appreciate the need for secrecy. But you can trust me. I am discretion itself. Just ask any of my friends. They will tell you, 'John Ragget is the soul of discretion.' Do you think his death has something to do with the paper? Because, frankly, I don't."

"Really?" I asked, suddenly interested in the conversation. "You don't think his death had anything to do with his theories on Jane Austen?"

John gave an adamant shake of his head. "I don't. Not at all."

"Why?" I asked.

John gave a shrug. "Call it instinct. I've got a gift for it. Ask any of my friends. I think that Richard's death is unrelated to his work. If you ask me, his death was most likely the result of a drug problem."

"A drug problem?" Aunt Winnie repeated in a dubious tone. "Why do you think that?"

"Again, call it instinct. But Richard Baines never stopped moving. He was everywhere, doing everything. He was a very rich man, too. Men like that tend to dabble in drugs. They like the rush, the feel of power. Frankly, I've suspected for years now that the man was nursing an addiction of sorts."

"Wait," I said, trying to puzzle out John's logic. "You think that Richard Baines had a drug problem, which resulted in someone dressing as Elizabeth Bennet and stabbing him during the Jane Austen Masked Ball?"

John nodded. "Oh, absolutely. If I were you, I'd focus on that

angle rather than one revolving around his theories on Jane Austen. I think you'll find I'm right."

I didn't answer. I stared at the back of his head, lost in thought.
While John hadn't exactly established himself as an accurate source
of information so far, this claim seemed beyond even his usual em-
bellishments. Could John be trying to divert my attention from the
paper and Richard's theories as the reason behind his death, with a
ridiculous claim that drug abuse played a role? He could, I decided.
But the question was, why?

WHEN JOHN FINALLY pulled up in front of the restaurant, I saw
that it was a mere two streets over from our hotel. The ride had
taken us a good fifteen minutes longer than walking would have.
Somehow, though, I wasn't all that surprised. I had the distinct impression that John would drive his car across the street if he could
find a reason.

After giving the valet detailed and specific instructions for the
care and keeping of his car (which so bordered on the absurd that
they might as well have included, "Rub it with a diaper" and "Don't
make eye contact with it"), we made our way into the restaurant. A
large crowd was already gathered in the back room. On a table near
the entrance sat a large framed picture of Richard. He stared out at
us with a smug, self-satisfied smile that seemed all the more in-
opportune given his current condition.

In her role as hostess, Valerie came over to greet us. While the rest
of us were wearing the most somber clothes we could find under
the circumstances, Valerie's outfit was tailor-made for a memorial
service. Honestly, it was almost as if she'd packed anticipating death.

I wondered about that for a moment before pushing the thought away as ridiculous. If Valerie had really planned to kill Richard, she'd hardly pack a bunch of black clothes in morbid preparation for the event.

"Hello, John! How good of you to come!" she said as she enveloped him into a huge showy hug.

"But of course, Valerie. Where else would I be? Damned terrible business, damned terrible. Please let me know if there's anything I can do," John answered. "Have the police made any progress?"

Valerie gave a mournful shake of her head. Nary a blond curl moved. "No. Sadly, there's been no news. I don't know why—it all seems rather obvious who did it."

Then turning to us, as if she'd just noticed our presence, she said in a faintly surprised tone that wouldn't have fooled a six-year-old, "Why, Elizabeth and Ms. Reynolds. I didn't expect to see you here. I would have thought that you had other priorities."

I gathered that we weren't going to get a hug, either.

Aunt Winnie afforded her a smile. "Oh, no. Of course not. This is our priority."

Valerie narrowed her eyes as she tried to discern Aunt Winnie's meaning, while I opted for a pleasantly neutral smile, a tactic I usually opted for when Aunt Winnie made ironic statements.

Luckily, Ian noticed us and came over, thereby easing some of the tension. Greeting us with much more warmth than Valerie—which wasn't that difficult—Ian led us to a table laden with food and drinks. "Please help yourself," he said. Turning to face us, he added, "And thank you for coming. I realize you didn't know my father very well, and it's awkward that your friend is under suspi-

cion, but I want you to know that I really appreciate your being
here."

His words were so obviously sincere that I found myself riddled
with well-deserved guilt for being here at all. I hadn't liked his father, and I'd found his theories absurd. I was not here out of respect
for him and his family—although I genuinely liked Ian. I was here
for one reason only—to find out anything that might help Cora.

"I can't do this," I muttered to Aunt Winnie as Ian moved away.
"We shouldn't be here. This is wrong. This is a private event, and
we are here for all the wrong reasons. Let's pay our respects and
leave."

Aunt Winnie paused in the process of heaping a scoop of chicken
salad onto her plate. Regarding me with a serious expression, she
said, "Elizabeth, you are a nice girl. And your instincts do you credit.
Yes, we are barging in, but our reasons for doing so are not wrong.
We are here to help a woman who, I think, has intentionally been
set up as the fall guy for a murder. Someone went to a lot of trouble
to frame Cora, and I want to know who. We are not gate-crashing;
this memorial is as much for Valerie's ego as it is for Richard's
memory. It's not private, it's open to one and all who want to come.
Look around you; half of the people here are from the festival. If
people were truly mourning his death, then I'd stay away. But
they're not. They are largely here for the same reason you and I
are: curiosity. However, ours is altruistic, whereas theirs is largely
ghoulish."

I didn't respond right away. I still felt like an interloper and
wanted to leave. I was not a detective, and therefore I had no reason
to be here. But then I thought of Cora and felt some of my resolve

fading. As annoying as she had been in her opposition to Richard and his theories, she was a nice woman who probably had been set up to take the blame for Richard's murder. And if I could help her, then I should.

I let out a sigh of acceptance. Aunt Winnie heard it and smiled at me. "Good girl," she said, putting a scoop of chicken salad on my plate. "I knew you'd do the right thing."

Plates in hand, we milled about the room looking for a suitable group to join. Aunt Winnie was right; most of the memorial attendees were from the festival and most likely had never met Richard Baines other than in passing. Seeing this, some of my guilt began to ebb, and I allowed myself to take a bite of the chicken salad.

Spying Lindsay in deep conversation with Valerie, Aunt Winnie moved to where they stood. I reluctantly followed. Lindsay appeared much the same as she had earlier, under the weather/pregnant. She wore a dark gray wool skirt with a cream-colored sweater set and clutched a crumpled tissue in her hand. Her panicked expression as she noticed our approach led me to believe that she had not yet shared with Valerie the joyful news that little Zee was going to acquire a cousin.

"Hello," Lindsay said to us. "Valerie and I were just talking about Richard's paper. We are both agreed that it must be delivered."

"Is there a reason it wouldn't be?" Aunt Winnie asked innocently.

"None at all," Valerie replied archly. "However, the decision does not reside with us. It is up to Alex to decide." Both Valerie and Lindsay glanced irritably at Alex, who was standing on the other side of the room. Still wearing the dazed expression of one who's had a shock, she was listening with glassy eyes to John as he expressed his sympathies.

Aunt Winnie allowed her eyes to open wide. Leaning in a bit, she lowered her voice to the pitch of a confidential murmur. "Don't tell me you think that Alex might prevent the paper from being delivered? Why would she want to do that?"

Valerie pursed her lips and gave a snort of dissatisfaction. "Well, that is the question, isn't it? Going on with the presentation of that paper would be the best thing for . . ." Valerie stopped herself just in time from saying "us" and instead remembered to say "Richard's memory." Lindsay nodded in agreement. "However, Alex is the one who has been asked to make the decision," Valerie added, throwing another dark look in Alex's direction.

"Yes, but why wouldn't she want the paper to be delivered? Didn't she agree with Richard's theories?" Aunt Winnie asked.

"I'd be surprised if Alex even bothered to read it," answered Valerie. "She didn't care about Austen or Richard's theories. It's too bad. It would have been wonderful for Richard if he had a wife who could actually *help* him advance his career, someone who understood his work. Someone who was a *true* soul mate."

Lindsay quickly ducked her head, but not before I saw the swift flush of crimson that stained her checks at hearing Valerie's "hope." I had a sudden vision of Valerie's reaction to learning that Lindsay was not only carrying Richard's child but also had been quite ready to step into the role of "true soul mate." It was all but identical to the scene from *Sense and Sensibility,* when Lucy Steele confides to Fanny Dashwood of her engagement to Edward Ferrars and is roundly beaten about the head and shoulders for her effort. Afraid that my own face might be expressing more than I wished, I quickly busied myself with my chicken salad.

Aunt Winnie pressed on. "Well, this is surprising," she said, her voice still conspiratorial. "I really got the feeling that Alex supported Richard's work. Do you think that there could be something wrong with the paper? Could that be why Alex is hesitating to present it?"

Lindsay's head shot back up. "There is nothing wrong with that paper. It is perfect."

"Then what could be her reason?" I asked.

Valerie lifted her shoulder in a half shrug. "Well, it's not actually definite that she's not going to present the paper. She hasn't told us one way or the other."

"Perhaps she's been preoccupied with the fact that her husband was murdered," Aunt Winnie offered sweetly, and I was again forced to examine my chicken salad. It was just as I'd left it—largely unremarkable. Which, I've noticed, is pretty standard for chicken salad.

"Perhaps," Valerie agreed with a tight-lipped smile. "Well, we'll just have to wait and see." Giving Aunt Winnie and me a dismissive nod, she turned her attention back to Lindsay and said, "Lindsay, there's someone I'd like you to meet." Without another glance in our direction, she pulled Lindsay away to another part of the room. As I watched them go, I wondered at the reason behind Valerie's interest in Lindsay. Was it because of their mutual interest in seeing Richard's paper shared with the uneducated masses, or was it something else?

"Come on," Aunt Winnie said. "Ian is talking with Gail. I think we should convey our sympathies."

"But we just did that!" I protested.

Aunt Winnie shot me an exasperated look. "Are you going to get into the spirit of this or not? We are here to learn what we can, which means we need to talk to people."

"You're right. I'm sorry. Lead the way."

Aunt Winnie briskly crossed the room to where Ian and Gail stood talking. Although Gail had changed out of her pink suit into a more somber navy blue one, there was no escaping the quiet sense of happiness that emanated from her. I didn't think it was done deliberately; rather, it was akin to seeing someone who was clearly in excellent health. If your skin glows, well, it glows. And if you are content with your situation, then you are content. Gail was obviously content.

Seeing our approach, Ian nudged his mother and nodded our way. Gail stopped whatever it was she was saying and aimed a polite smile in our direction.

"Mother," Ian said, "I don't think you've met Winifred Reynolds and her niece, Elizabeth Parker."

"No, I don't believe we've formally met," agreed Gail as she extended her hand to Aunt Winnie. "I've seen you at the festival, of course."

"Yes, this is our first year here," said Aunt Winnie. "I just wanted to say that I didn't know Professor Baines very well, but I'm very sorry for your family's loss."

Gail dipped her head in acknowledgment. "Thank you. It's all so confusing. None of us know what to think, really." Then, suddenly seeming to place Aunt Winnie, Gail asked, "You're friends with Cora, aren't you?"

Aunt Winnie nodded. "Yes. I used to work with Cora's late husband. I haven't seen her in years, actually. We bumped into each other quite by chance."

"Cora is a dear soul," said Gail. "She's been one of my magazine's biggest supporters."

Despite the fact that she'd never laid eyes on an issue, Aunt Winnie glibly added, "Oh, I've been meaning to compliment you on that, by the way. It's such a wonderful magazine, and so much more insightful than its counterparts."

Gail's face lit up in a genuine smile. I suppose most people are predisposed to believe compliments about their work, and Gail proved no exception. I was happy that Aunt Winnie possessed the talent of flattering with delicacy, for Gail suddenly seemed much more receptive to our company.

"Why, thank you," she said. "I'm rather fond of it myself. In many ways, it's my baby—after Ian, of course," she added, gently patting Ian's arm. Ian produced a strained smile.

"Cora speaks very highly of it," said Aunt Winnie. "And that is high praise indeed, as you know. Cora takes the subject of Jane Austen very seriously."

Gail nodded. Then, with a furtive glance to make sure our conversation wasn't being overheard, Gail dropped her voice. "Speaking of Cora, I understand that there is some question about her involvement in Richard's death. I don't for a second believe that she had anything to do with it. Cora didn't like Richard's theories, nor did I, for that matter, but I know her well enough to know that she'd never resort to violence."

"I agree," said Aunt Winnie, lowering her voice as well. "The whole situation is very sad. I just hope the police find the answer. Have they told you anything?"

Gail shook her head. "No, they've told me nothing, really. I imagine that they've been more forthcoming with the current Mrs. Baines," she added with a dark look in Alex's direction. Ian shifted uncomfortably.

"At least you were both spared not to have been there," Aunt Winnie continued with a glance at Ian, her voice one of an old confidante. "That would have been too horrible."

Ian nodded quickly in agreement. "Yes, that's right. Neither one of us was at the Guildhall when it occurred. Mom wasn't feeling well, so I'd escorted her back to her room and stayed with her there. I saw the lights from the police cars from her room. Remember?" Gail's forehead crinkled, and she turned confused eyes to Ian. He ignored her and continued to address me, saying, "I'd just left her when I ran into you in the lobby."

"I remember," I said. "Valerie was with us."

"Yes, that's right," he agreed with unnecessary firmness. Gail resumed her earlier placid expression, either having sorted out her confusion or having decided to address it later.

"We were just talking to her," I said. "She mentioned that there was some uncertainty regarding whether Professor Baines's paper would still be delivered. Why is that?"

At my mention of the paper, Gail's lips pinched together in a small, tight ball, not terribly unlike a shriveled prune. But whether this reaction was involuntary or designed to prevent herself from speaking, I couldn't tell. Ian produced a kind of strangled cough and said, "Well, yes, that is true. I think Alex has some reservations about the propriety of going forward with it as planned."

"Propriety, my ass," Gail interjected. "She just wants to see how much she can get if she sells it." While Ian sputtered ineffectively in an attempt to shush his mother, she continued on. "Everyone thinks Richard was killed because of what's in that stupid paper. That paper is now gold. Alex figures that she can make a pretty penny selling it. I can just see the headlines: 'Read the Paper That Was Worth Killing For.' It's disgusting. Had he just read it, it would no doubt have been dismissed as utter rubbish. But now . . ." She waved her hands in an expression of fatalistic frustration.

"Mom!" hissed Ian.

Gail sighed and shrugged her shoulders in acquiescence. "Sorry. Forget I said that."

"No, it's all right," said Aunt Winnie. "For what it's worth, I quite agree with you. I'm horrified at Professor Baines's death, but that doesn't mean that I want to see his paper suddenly given more credence than it should." Glancing at Ian, she added, "Sorry, Ian. No offense."

"None taken. I know that Dad's theories weren't for everyone," Ian said in the weary tone of one who has said those words too many times before.

A petite woman with waist-length jet-black hair that was pulled off her angular face with a gold beaded headband sidled up to us.

"Gail?" she asked tentatively. "I'm Marsha Zucker. I don't know if you remember me, but we met last year . . ."

Gail smiled and extended her hand. "Marsha! Of course, I remember you. How nice to see you again. Have you met my son, Ian?"

Aunt Winnie and I stepped back to allow Marsha her turn to offer her sympathies (or lack thereof) to Gail and Ian. Giving Ian a small wave good-bye, Aunt Winnie and I moved toward one of the room's many tables. We had just taken a seat at the only unoccupied one when we were joined by Byron and Alex. Both looked exhausted.

"Hello, Elizabeth," said Byron as he slid into a seat opposite me. "Hello, Ms. Reynolds. It's nice to see you again."

At the sound of our names, Alex's head snapped up in apparent recognition of who we were. "Oh, hello," she said, offering us a perplexed smile. "I'm sorry. I didn't recognize you at first."

"I imagine we look a little different out of our Regency garb," I offered.

Alex nodded. "And I'm a little overwhelmed with everything," she said, rubbing a hand over her eyes. After a quick glance over at the refreshments table, Alex said, "Byron, would you please get me a cup of coffee? I'd go, but Gail is over there with Valerie. I don't have the energy to deal with their crap right now. Honestly, I don't see why they wanted to do this in the first place. If you ask me, it's in bad taste. I feel like we've made ourselves into another exhibit at the festival."

Byron, as well as Aunt Winnie and I, glanced over at the refreshment table. As Alex said, Gail was standing next to it, plate in hand,

and deep in conversation with Valerie and Lindsay. I didn't blame Alex for not wanting to venture over. No doubt they were all discussing the fate of Richard's paper.

"Sure," said Byron, getting to his feet. Turning to us, he said, "Can I get either of you anything?"

"No, thanks," Aunt Winnie and I said in unison. Byron nodded and moved away.

"I don't think I ever properly expressed my condolences to you," said Aunt Winnie to Alex after Byron left the table. "I obviously didn't know your husband very well, but I'm so sorry for your loss."

Alex bit her lip and gave a nod of her head, the small gesture sending a section of silky hair tumbling over her shoulder. With a quick movement, she raised a hand to tuck the errant strands back behind her ear. "Thank you," she said.

"Have the police made any progress?" I asked.

Alex shook her head. She regarded us with a wary expression. "Not really. They're still looking at your friend, Cora."

"I know you don't know either of us from a hole in the wall," offered Aunt Winnie, "but I can tell you that I've known Cora for a very long time. She's not a violent person. I firmly believe that she did not do this."

Alex regarded us in silence, her expression unreadable. Byron returned with a cup filled with steaming caramel-colored liquid that I assumed was coffee. He placed it in front of Alex. She thanked him and took a grateful sip.

"So I understand that the presentation of Richard's paper is on hold. Is that right?" Aunt Winnie asked, her expression deceptively innocent.

Alex's face pulled into a dark frown. She sat back in her chair and folded her arms across her chest. "Good God. Is that really all you people care about? That damn paper? My husband is dead. Murdered. And yet the first thing out of any of your mouths is a question about the status of his paper. As hard as this might be for you to believe, I really haven't given it much thought."

Byron stared awkwardly at his lap, while Aunt Winnie nodded with enthusiastic approval. "I have to say, I'm glad to hear you say that. I quite agree with you," she said.

Alex leaned forward, her arms on the table. "Excuse me? You *agree* with me? You're the one who asked me about the paper in the first place!"

"Yes, but only because I wanted to make sure that you weren't going to present the paper," Aunt Winnie replied. "I'm glad to know that you're not. I think it's the best way to find Richard's killer. Because despite how it looks, Cora Beadle did not kill your husband. I want to find out who did."

Alex's only response was to gawk at her in confusion. I couldn't blame her. It was all I could do not to join in.

Byron now leaned forward as well. "Wait, why do you think that delaying the publication of the paper will help find Richard's killer?"

"Because," answered Aunt Winnie, "it might force him or her to try and destroy it. If Richard was killed because of that paper, then whoever did this will try and stop it from ever being presented."

"So you want to use the paper to set a trap?" asked Byron.

Aunt Winnie nodded. I picked at my salad. She was driving this train; I had no idea where she was going or where it was scheduled to stop. I figured I might as well grab a bite while I could. "That's exactly it," Aunt Winnie said.

Byron glanced questioningly at Alex. She raised her shoulders in a noncommittal shrug. "I don't know if that's a good idea," he said slowly. "I tend to think it might make more sense to let the police handle it. Alex? What do you think?"

Alex closed her eyes and gave a weary sigh. "I don't know what to think anymore."

Just then, there was an amplified cough, and a voice said, "Um . . . excuse me? If I could have your attention, please."

We all looked up at the source and saw Ian standing awkwardly at a microphone. "I'd like to take a few minutes to thank you all for coming out tonight," he said, after clearing his throat again. "As you know, my father loved Jane Austen's work, and this festival was very dear to him. It means a lot to us that you came here tonight." Ian paused, clearly not comfortable speaking in front of a crowd. "I would just like to say," he continued, "that I hope this terrible occurrence does not negatively affect this festival or future ones. I know that my father would not have wanted that." He paused again.

Valerie swiftly approached Ian or, more accurately, she swiftly approached the microphone. With a less than gentle hip check, she pushed him out of the way and quickly took his place. With a serene smile, she gazed out at the room. Seeing her tiny, pale frame and weird smile, I had the sudden, and frankly uncomfortable, sensation that I was watching a scene from an updated version of *Carrie,* specifically, the one when Sissy Spacek smiles out at her classmates—right before her telekinesis goes haywire and she kills everyone. I instinctively glanced over to the room's doors to assure myself that they were still standing open.

"This is obviously very difficult for my husband—for all of us, " Valerie began, "but I want to add my sincere thanks that you all came out tonight to pay your respects, not only for Professor Baines the man but also to his amazing body of work."

From across the table, I heard Alex mutter, "Oh, God." Byron shot her a quick look of annoyance but said nothing.

"However, before I do that," Valerie said, "I wanted to take a moment to sing a quick verse of one of Professor Baines's favorite songs. Not only was it his favorite, but I think it captured his spirit quite well."

Valerie closed her eyes and delicately cleared her throat directly into the microphone. The amplified sound left the audience with the unfortunate impression of a tuberculosis patient's final stran-gled cough. However, this was still preferable to what came next, as Valerie bleated out the lyrics to the first stanza of "My Way" in elevated octaves normally associated with amorous chipmunks. Aunt Winnie shot me a look of horrified amusement. I shot one right back at her.

Once finished with her musical tribute, Valerie dipped her head to the nonexistent applause and said, "Professor Baines devoted his career not only to studying Jane Austen and her novels but also to sharing his amazing discoveries and revelations with the literary establishment. He unveiled aspects of Austen's work that no one ever detected before." There was a quiet murmuring among many of the attendees when this was said. I wondered if they were mur-murings of agreement or derision. Valerie continued on. "As many of you know, Professor Baines was planning on presenting a ground-breaking paper this week, one that would forever change the way both Jane Austen and her body of work would be viewed." Alex stiffened in her chair, her eyes narrowed with dark suspicion. "Even though Professor Baines has cruelly been denied the opportunity to present this paper himself, I would like to ask everyone here to take a moment to demonstrate our support of his work and support for this piece of work in particular." Valerie paused and seemed to look directly at Alex. "Professor Baines was taken away too soon. But I hope you'll support me in seeing that his excellent work is neither lost nor forgotten."

With that, Valerie raised her hands and began to clap. After an awkward pause, the rest of the room followed along. It was like watching lemmings clap, if lemmings had hands, that is.

"Alex?" Valerie called out into the microphone. "Would you like to come up here and say a few words?"

There was a rippling sound of heads turning our way, as the crowd tried to see both Alex and her response. They were just in time to miss it, Alex having replaced the furious scowl that covered her face with a more composed expression. Her eyes, however, still glittered with anger. Slowly getting to her feet, Alex said, "Thank you all for coming . . ."

"They can't hear you back there, Alex, dear," Valerie purred into the microphone. "You'd better come up here to talk."

There was a brief pause, during which I was sure that Alex was debating either leaving the room or cramming the microphone down Valerie's throat. She did neither. Instead, she pasted a brittle smile onto her face and quickly strode up to the microphone. Taking it from Valerie, she turned to the small crowd before her. "As you know, this has been a very horrible couple of days for me and Richard's family. I want you to know that I appreciate your sympathy and support in coming out tonight to honor Richard's memory. Thank you very much."

Turning the microphone back over to Valerie, Alex made to leave. Valerie stopped her short with her next announcement. "Thank you, Alex," she said, "but before you go, I wondered if you could tell us when Professor Baines's paper will be delivered. I know that many of us here tonight, myself included, want to make sure that his work is heard."

Alex froze and regarded Valerie with an expression that left no room for doubt as to her feelings of disgust and contempt. Walking slowly back to the microphone, Alex seemed to come to a decision. Squaring her shoulders, she faced the room, a determined gaze in her eyes. "But of course," she said. "I can think of no reason that Richard's paper should not be delivered as planned. He would have wanted it no other way."

"Well, I expect he'd have preferred not to be dead when it was delivered," Aunt Winnie muttered to me under her breath, while I smothered a wholly inappropriate smile. I quickly glanced at Byron to make sure he hadn't heard and was relieved to see that his attention was focused on Alex. I also noticed that he did not appear happy at her announcement, despite the general round of applause that greeted it.

I nudged him gently. "You don't agree with her, do you?"

Byron pulled his attention away from Alex and regarded me, his mouth pinched in concern. Finally, he shook his head. "No, I don't. I don't know what the hell is going on here, but I have to be honest. If Richard was killed because of his paper, I don't want to use it as bait. After all, I was second only to Richard in putting it together, and speaking from a purely selfish standpoint, I'd rather not be used as bait, either."

I looked back to where Valerie and Alex stood just in time to see Alex turn on her heel and head for the doors. After a moment's hesitation, Lindsay called out after her. If Alex heard, she didn't let on and continued out of the room. Lindsay bit her lip and paused, as if debating whether she should follow. Dear God, I thought. She wasn't really going to spring the news of her pregnancy on Alex now, was she?

Apparently not, I was relieved to note, as she turned back and headed into the room. I was, however, surprised to see that instead of rejoining Valerie, she was now walking our way, her stride determined.

"Byron," Lindsay said, once she drew near, "can I talk to you?" From the way she gnawed at her lower lip, I saw that something was bothering her. Either that or she had mistaken her mouth for an hors d'oeuvre.

"Is something wrong?" Byron asked, apparently coming to a similar conclusion.

"I don't know. It might be. It depends," Lindsay said, with a nervousness that was hard to miss.

"Is it about the paper?" Byron asked, lowering his voice.

Lindsay glanced uneasily in my direction, while I attempted to exude a harmless, yet trustworthy persona. Apparently, it's a trait I need to work on, as Lindsay said, "Umm . . . yeah, it is. But I don't want to talk about it here. Can I talk to you later? In private?" she added with another sideways glance my way.

"Sure," said Byron, his expression perplexed. "When do you want to talk?"

"Can I come to your room after this is over?"

"Sure, that sounds fine. I'll be there."

"There you are, Lindsay," a shrill voice sang out. "We'd wondered where you got to." Lindsay gave a startled jump, and pressed a steadying hand against her stomach, before turning around to face the owner of the voice—Valerie. Next to her stood John and Gail, the latter's head tilted and studying Lindsay as if she were preparing to sketch her portrait. "Is everything all right?" Valerie asked Lindsay. "You ran off in such a hurry, I thought you might not be feeling well."

"Oh, no, I'm fine," Lindsay replied, her voice a squeak. "I just was talking to Byron."

"Yes, so I see. How are you, Byron?" Valerie asked, her eyes now sliding in his direction. "I imagine you are pleased that Alex decided to go ahead with the paper's presentation."

"I am," Byron replied. "But I only hope that its presentation doesn't detract from the focus to find Professor Baines's killer."

Valerie glanced at Lindsay a moment. "I'm sure it won't," she said.

Gail, her head still slightly tilted to one side as she gazed at Lindsay, said nothing.

CHAPTER 20

Let me only have the company of the people I love,
let me only be where I like and with whom I like, and the
devil take the rest, say I.

—NORTHANGER ABBEY

I THOUGHT VALERIE SANG VERY ILL tonight," observed Aunt Winnie sometime later as we were making our way back to our hotel.

"Yes," I agreed. "Poor Valerie. But she is determined to do it."

Having politely extricated ourselves from having to endure another ride in John's Little Car of Horrors, we strolled along the streets of Bath, in no particular hurry. The night was lovely, with just enough warmth left in the air to prevent us from feeling as if we were imitating the ideal of the "hearty Englishman." More important, it allowed us to talk without fear of being overheard.

"So tell me," said Aunt Winnie as we turned down a street lined with crisp white buildings and perfectly aligned trees. "What did you think of the memorial?"

"Oh, I expect you know what I think. In fact, I expect your thoughts on the matter are remarkably similar," I said.

"That depends," she answered. "Do your thoughts contain the words *vulgar, hysterical,* and *painful?*"

"Throw in *absurd,* and I believe that we have a match."

Aunt Winnie laughed loudly. A woman who was walking a small white poodle across the street looked up in surprise. Giving the leash a quick tug, she hurried along. "Then we need to discuss it no more," Aunt Winnie said lightly. Dropping her voice to a more serious tone, she added, "Except I don't know what to make about Richard's paper. Do you think it was the reason behind his death?"

"I don't know," I answered, shoving my hands into my coat's pockets. "It certainly seemed to be a lightning rod of sorts for lots of people."

"That's for sure. However, I feel as if I'm missing something. Granted, the paper was sure to make a sensation—the ridiculous generally does. But would it really have skyrocketed Richard to literary stardom?"

I considered the question. It was one that I'd pondered myself as well. I knew little about the world of literary analysis and even lit-tler about the world of Richard Baines. Many people seemed to be of the opinion that this paper was valuable, but whether that value was monetary or intellectual depended on who you talked to. I wondered how Richard himself saw it. Granted, he had been a very wealthy man, but that wealth came from his father, not from his career as an English professor. Was the goal of this paper to be able to legitimately add to that wealth, or was he solely interested in boosting his reputation as a Jane Austen (ahem) expert? And did it even matter what *his* goal had been? He might have been killed either for the potential money associated with the paper or to prevent its release. Then again, the man might have been killed merely for being a pompous, two-timing jackass. I sighed. When you stopped to think about it, there were several reasons someone might want to kill Richard Baines. It was very vexing, I thought, although, I suppose, more so for him than me.

"Elizabeth?" said Aunt Winnie. "Are you listening to me?"

"Hmmm? Oh, sorry. I was just wondering why Richard was killed. I have cleverly narrowed the list down to three, maybe four reasons. Six at the very most."

"Clever girl. Now tell me what you think about the paper. I honestly can't see it suddenly becoming the darling of the academic community," she said. "It's laughable at best. At its worst, it's the result of an addled brain prone to conspiracy theories and hidden messages."

"Then in either case, it wouldn't be a big moneymaker," I observed.

"Oh, I wouldn't say that," Aunt Winnie said, with a firm shake of her head. "Far stupider things have made money in this world. I believe the Chia Pet is making a comeback."

"I was always particular to the Chia Head," I replied.

"See what I mean? Therefore, just because *we* think it's a pile of gibberish doesn't mean that someone else doesn't see sunshine and flowers."

"And cold hard cash," I added.

Aunt Winnie nodded in agreement, her red curls bobbing as if to second the motion. "Exactly."

Aunt Winnie's cell phone rang just then, a note-for-note match to the one that Laura Linney's character has in *Love Actually*. I wondered if that was a ringtone I could download.

"Hello? What? I can't . . . oh, hello, Izzy. Yes. How are you?" Aunt Winnie said, as she held the phone up to her ear. "Yes. Really? But . . . oh, I see. Sure, that sounds fine. We'll see you there." Clicking off the phone, she stuffed it back into her pocket and said, "That was Izzy. She and Cora want to meet us for a drink at our hotel."

I stopped in my tracks, somewhat amazed. "At *our* hotel? But why?" I asked. "Surely they must realize by now that Valerie and Ian, not to mention Gail, are staying at our hotel as well? Izzy's coming the other night could be excused as an oversight, but to come again? What could they be thinking?"

"I wondered at that myself at first, but then Izzy explained that the bar in their hotel is crammed full from a local wedding's after-party. She assumed that the memorial would still be going on and so there'd be little chance of seeing any of them at our hotel."

"I'm pretty sure that there are plenty of bars or restaurants where there would be *no* chance of seeing them," I said.

"Oh, I quite agree. Izzy had a reason for that as well. Apparently, many of the more convenient bars in the area are frequented by various festival attendees," Aunt Winnie said.

"She's certainly thought this one out, hasn't she?"

"She certainly has. My guess is that Izzy is clearly banking on that little chance that she will indeed run into Ian, Valerie, Gail, or all three. The question I wonder about is which one does she want to see, and why?"

We continued our stroll back to the hotel in meditative silence. Despite Izzy's fervent proclamations that we were kindred spirits, I really didn't know her all that well. She was enjoyable to talk to, but that didn't mean she was nice or trustworthy. After all, there were plenty of people in life who could be perfectly pleasant just before they stabbed you (or someone else) in the back. Dorothy Parker was one. So was Hemingway. Actually, I took that back. I rather had the impression that Hemingway was nasty to you either way.

I forced my thoughts back to Izzy. What was her reason for wanting to come to our hotel? She'd been paying an inordinate amount of attention to Ian since the festival began, but was that merely because she was genetically programmed to flirt with any man in a ten-foot radius, or was there more to it? Could she be flirting with Ian for another reason—perhaps to annoy Valerie? I considered this a more likely scenario. Granted, Ian was nice, but Izzy was engaged. I had known Izzy and Valerie for only a few days, but I could state with almost certainty that there was more than a healthy dislike between them. My mind trailed off momentarily as I attempted to discern the difference between a healthy dislike and an unhealthy one. When did dislike become unhealthy? When knives were employed?

Of course, there was another person Izzy could be interested in seeing, and that was Gail. But again, why? I wondered if any of Izzy's odd behavior stemmed from Richard's paper, or if it was completely unrelated. An ugly thought popped into my brain. Richard had been unfaithful in his marriage to Alex at least once. Izzy was a professional flirt. Could there have been something between them? Could that be the motive for Izzy's interest in seeing the family? But again, even if Izzy had had an affair with Richard, why would she want to tell his family? It made no sense. Actually, none of the events over the last few days made sense. I said as much to Aunt Winnie.

"You're wrong," she replied, shaking her head. "It makes sense to someone. We just need to figure out who. Once we know that, we'll be able to figure out the rest."

"Oh, well, if that's all we need to do, then it'll be a snap." I snapped my fingers to illustrate the sentiment, adding, "Thanks, I feel much better."

Aunt Winnie regarded me with the charged silence that is usually a precursor to snark. Sure enough, within seconds, she asked with deceptive politeness, "Elizabeth, dear, do you know why donkeys don't go to school?"

"No, but do tell," I replied with equal politeness.

"Because nobody likes a smart-ass."

I pretended to consider the answer. "So you prefer a dumb-ass? Really? I think I'm going to have to respectfully disagree with you on this one. Dumb-asses are annoying."

"Elizabeth?"

"Yes, Aunt Winnie?"

"Shut up."

I laughed. "Yes, Aunt Winnie."

WE HAD JUST SETTLED ourselves at a table at the hotel bar when Cora and Izzy arrived. Once again, Izzy looked stunning in a snug-fitting blue cashmere jersey dress and cream-colored suede boots. The stress of the last few days had left no mark on her face; if anything, she looked even more stunning than when I first met her. She practically glowed. By comparison, Cora looked far less polished.

Her green wrap dress was not only wrinkled but did nothing for her sallow complexion. Her hair, which was of a triangular shape to begin with, now resembled something the ancient Egyptians might have built. Whether this was due to the humidity, neglect, or design wasn't clear.

"So how was it?" Izzy asked us as she slid into a chair next to me. "Was it weird?"

"Weird isn't the word," I said after brief consideration. "Valerie sang the first verse of 'My Way' as a kind of tribute to Richard."

Izzy's mouth formed into a crimson O.

"She did not," Cora said, her eyes wide.

"Oh, yes, she did," I replied. "If it had been a fight, they would have stopped it."

"What else happened?" Izzy asked. "Did they talk about his death at all?"

I shook my head. "Not really. Everything focused more on his past accomplishments. A lot of talk focused on his paper and whether or not it should still be presented. Valerie basically strong-armed Alex into agreeing to deliver it."

Cora sighed. "I wish to God I never heard about that stupid paper. I wish to God that I hadn't picked a fight with Richard. And I wish to God he wasn't dead. I'm heartily ashamed of myself."

Aunt Winnie leaned over and patted her hand. "I know, honey. But just because you fought with someone who was subsequently killed doesn't mean that you're a bad person. Richard Baines annoyed a lot of people in his short life. Had he lived, I'm sure he'd have gone on to annoy even more."

"Aunt Winnie!" I exclaimed with some surprise.

She waved away my protestations with a flick of her wrist. "Oh, please, let's not pretend. The man was a pompous ass, not to mention a philandering ass. I'm sure he was an ass in other ways, too, I just don't know what they are right now. I'm not saying that he deserved to die," she amended, seeing my appalled expression, "far from it. But I'm not going to suddenly sugarcoat his life."

Izzy leaned forward. "What do you mean 'philandering'?" she asked, her expression curious. "Do you mean his affair with Alex?"

Ignoring—or not seeing—my warning expression, Aunt Winnie continued, "I most certainly do not. I have found out additional information about Richard that I think you—and the police—need to know. There are other reasons—reasons other than that damn paper of his—that might be behind his death."

"Such as?" Izzy asked.

I tried once more to stop Aunt Winnie with a pleading look, but to no avail. "I am referring to his affair with Lindsay—the soon-to-be mother of his child," she said.

Izzy's face was a portrait of shock. She slumped against the back of her chair, her breath coming out in a long, thin hiss. "His child?" she whispered, her eyes wide.

Cora's reaction was no less dramatic. "What?" she cried out, her voice shrill and indignant, and immediately gaining the attention of the bar's few other patrons. Seeing their startled reactions, she lowered her voice and said, "Are you serious? Lindsay is pregnant with Richard's child? But how did you find this out?"

"She told us," I said.

"Well, actually, she told Elizabeth after Elizabeth confronted her with it," Aunt Winnie added proudly. "Elizabeth saw a bottle of prenatal vitamins in her bathroom and guessed the truth."

Izzy continued to stare wordlessly at me. Cora shook her head in disgust. "That poor girl. Now what is she going to do? Is she going to tell the family?"

"I think she is," I said. "I got the impression that she was banking on getting money from the estate so she could support the baby."

"Poor Alex!" Cora said with real sympathy. "Say what you like about the woman, but to lose her husband like this and then have to find out that he was having an affair! It's horrible."

"I have to tell you, I think the one who is going to be the most upset is Valerie," I said. "I wouldn't be surprised if she hasn't calculated Richard's net worth down to the last penny. Another heir set to queue up in line for their fair slice of the pie is the last thing Valerie will want to hear about."

Izzy scoffed in agreement. "That's for sure. I can only imagine the look on her face when she hears of it." Izzy paused in apparent contemplation of the anticipated expression. "On the other hand, now that I think of it, it might be hard to discern the difference given her usual peevish expression."

Cora frowned. "Izzy! That's not nice!"

Izzy rolled her eyes in response. "No, Mama, it's not. But then neither is Valerie."

"Does anyone want a drink?" I offered quickly, seeing Cora's expression darken with annoyance. "My treat."

The diversion worked, and I made my way over to the bar. I had just placed the orders when I noticed Gail and Ian enter. Although they passed close by, they didn't notice me. Gail was apparently in the middle of a conversation with Ian, as I heard her say, "But you couldn't have been!"

Ian responded curtly, saying, "Mother, please. I told you to drop it. It doesn't have anything to do with it." Then spotting Izzy and Cora, he muttered, "Oh, dear God."

Gail followed his gaze and added her own expression of dismay. "Christ, this is going to be awkward." Pasting a polite smile on her face, Gail moved toward the table, Ian following slowly in her wake. I lingered at the bar until they arrived at the table before bringing the drinks over.

"Hello, Gail. Hello, Ian," I said as I approached the table and dispensed the drinks. "The service tonight was lovely."

Ian responded with a wan smile. "Thanks, Elizabeth. It was all Valerie's doing, really."

"Is she with you?" I asked, glancing around.

Ian nodded. "Yes, but I think she had to make a phone call," he said vaguely, his eyes straying to Cora and Izzy.

Silence followed. It was terribly awkward, and I wondered again why Izzy had wanted to come. I glanced at her now. She sat with a properly mournful expression on her face that didn't fool me for one minute. Cora quickly jumped up and moved around the table to give Gail a hug. "I'm so sorry about all of this, Gail," she said, as she awkwardly wrapped her arms around Gail. "I hope you know that I didn't have anything to do with any of it."

While Gail gave Cora a reassuring pat on the back, I noticed that her face was still guarded. "Don't worry, dear," she nevertheless said. "I know that it will all be straightened out soon."

Cora stepped back and, unfortunately, directly into me, spilling my glass of wine down the front of my dress.

"Oh, Elizabeth!" Cora cried in dismay. "I'm such a klutz! I'm so sorry!"

"It's okay, Cora," I said as I grabbed one of the cocktail napkins from the table and began dabbing at the large wet stain. The napkin immediately reverted to pulp and stuck to my dress in small white clumps. "If you'll excuse me for a moment," I said, "I'm just going to go to the ladies' room."

I made my way across the bar area into a small lavatory. As I pushed open the door, I heard a voice coming from one of the stalls. "That's right," it said. "That's perfect. Now, do you know what I'm going to do?"

I paused in confusion. While I recognized the voice as Valerie's, it was as if she was trying to disguise it. The result was a low-pitched, halting, breathy sound. It was not unlike listening to Marilyn Monroe—if she was having an asthma attack, that is.

Hearing me, Valerie suddenly whispered, "I've got to go. I'll call you back."

I grabbed a handful of paper towels and attempted to dry my dress, while Valerie remained in the stall. After a few minutes, it became clear that Valerie had no intention of exiting the stall while I was there; either that, or she was in the clutches of some sort of gastrointestinal distress. In either case, I had no desire to hang about—although perhaps more so, if it was for the latter reason—and so I returned to the table after securing a replacement drink at the bar. Not surprisingly, the conversation was on the apparent plan to present Richard's paper.

"Honestly, I don't see why it matters so much," Gail was saying to Ian, as I slid into my chair. "Yes, I suppose that it will get a large turnout, although I imagine mostly from ghoulish souls who will want to see if there is to be more drama. But what's the point? It's not as if you can sell tickets to the reading."

At this, Ian shifted awkwardly in his seat and focused on tracing the embossed crest on his beer stein with his forefinger. "Well, it's funny you should say that," he began, "but Valerie actually was able to arrange something with the organizers—"

Gail cut him off. Leaning forward with an abruptness usually associated with a prodding from a hot poker, she said in the steely I-am-displeased voice employed by all mothers, "Are you kidding me? You are going to actually charge people money to hear that paper? Money that will no doubt end up lining Alex's silk pockets? What on earth are you thinking?"

Ian's face flushed and his shoulders hunched up toward his ears, and I had a sudden image of him as a little boy, squirming in embarrassment after being caught with his hand in the cookie jar. Ian opened his mouth to defend himself, but it was Valerie, who had finally arrived, who responded in a cool voice, "Gail, don't be silly. The proceeds from the event will be split between us and Alex. Trust me, I wouldn't have bothered to set it up if it was only going to benefit Alex."

Ian said nothing and instead watched his mother, trying to gauge her reaction to this news. Gail rhythmically tapped her middle finger on the table in a manner both contemplative and irritated. Valerie watched her, unconcerned. "How much are you charging?" Gail finally asked.

"Twenty pounds," Valerie answered.

"Twenty pounds!" Gail replied, shocked. "But that's absurd! No one in their right mind is going to shell out that kind of money to hear Jane Austen's life reduced to smutty innuendo."

Valerie produced a catlike smile. "They already have fifty people signed up." She practically purred with satisfaction.

"They do?" replied Gail. "But how? Alex only gave the go-ahead on the paper not thirty minutes ago."

Valerie's self-satisfied smile only increased. I half expected her to start grooming herself with the back of her hand. "I spoke with the organizers earlier today and told them I was pretty sure that I could convince Alex to present the paper as planned. They realized, as did I, that there might be increased interest in the paper now. Of course, I have also arranged to have copies of the latest issue of *Austen Forever* on sale in the back."

Ian stared at Valerie. From the way his lips pressed together and the muscles along his jawline bunched, I suspected that he found her casual avarice as reprehensible as I did. But then again, what did I know? After all, he'd married her. Maybe he had a thing for cold-blooded, grasping women. Maybe she made him feel alive, much in the same way that a corpse did for regular folks.

Gail's reaction to Valerie was easier to read. She disliked the idea of promoting Richard's paper, even if indirectly. However, she was not so disinterested that she was going to walk away from a chance to make some money. "I see," she said after a moment's hesitation. "Well, I will leave that to you, then. I don't think it would be appropriate for me to attend the presentation."

Valerie gave a curt nod. "I agree. Ian and I will be happy to man the table, as it were. Won't we, Ian?" She looked to Ian for confirmation and then seemed to notice Izzy's and Cora's presence. I wondered if Valerie had some kind of undiagnosed affliction that affected her vision. She certainly seemed to notice things and people only when they were shoved right in front of her face.

Her mouth twisted in displeasure. "Cora, Izzy," Valerie said. "What a surprise. I certainly didn't expect to see you here. But then, now that I stop to think about it, I don't know why I would be surprised. You two seem to always be here. I wonder why that is?"

Cora flushed at Valerie's words, but Izzy did not. Instead, she regarded Valerie with an expression of such lofty condescension that even Lady Catherine would have been impressed.

"My mother and I joined our friends for a drink," Izzy said. "I really don't understand what aspect of that is confusing for you, Valerie."

Valerie pulled her thin shoulders back and regarded Izzy with an icy stare. "Oh, I don't know," she said in a glacial voice to match the stare. "Perhaps I thought that a woman with any breeding might realize that, given the rather damning circumstances surrounding my father-in-law's death, it might be prudent for you and your mother to remain at your own hotel."

A coy smile spread over Izzy's face. "Perhaps you haven't had the advantage of moving in society enough," she said, her tone faintly sympathetic. "There are many very accomplished young ladies among *our* acquaintance who would see no problem with an innocent woman visiting a friend at her hotel."

Valerie's eyes narrowed to angry slits, and her skin turned a mottled red. "You know what you are, Izzy Beadle? You're nothing but a man-crazy b—"

Ian jumped out of his chair just in time to stop Valerie from completing her thought, which was a wise move. In a fight between Valerie and Izzy, my money would be on Izzy. As Ian hustled Valerie out of the bar, Gail turned to Izzy. "You have an extraordinary ability to discompose my daughter-in-law, Miss Beadle," she said.

Without missing a beat, Izzy shot back, "And she has an extraordinary ability to piss me off, ma'am, for which I find it hard to forgive."

Gail's expression did not change, but I could have sworn that I saw the faintest sparkle of laughter in her eyes.

"Gail, I'm sorry," sputtered Cora, shooting Izzy a quelling look. "Izzy didn't mean to be rude. She's just trying to defend me."

Gail only nodded, then rose from her chair. "Her loyalty does her credit," she said. "Well, ladies, it's been a long day. I'm going to head up to my room. I'm sure I will see you all again later." With a polite nod, she turned and left the bar.

As soon as she was out of earshot, Cora rounded on Izzy. "What is your problem? Why do you feel compelled to attack Valerie at every turn?"

Izzy glared at Cora. "Are you kidding me? I was defending you! She practically accused you of murder, and here you are defending her!"

"I am not defending her," Cora said. "But please don't use her suspicions about me as an excuse for your nastiness to her. You have never liked her and have never bothered to disguise that fact. Richard's murder and the police's suspicion about me have nothing to do with that animosity." Izzy opened her mouth to defend herself, but Cora cut her off. "Gail is my friend. And as such, I will not let you bad-mouth her daughter-in-law in public or in private."

Izzy's mouth twisted into an angry pucker. Folding her arms across her chest, she exhaled a heavy, dramatic sigh and muttered, "Yes, we wouldn't want to upset Valerie, now would we?"

Cora glared at her. "No, as a matter of fact, we wouldn't."

"Why?" demanded Izzy. "Would you please tell me why in the name of God you feel it necessary to try and placate a woman as worthless as Valerie Baines?"

Cora held her ground for all of three seconds before her shoulders collapsed. With a heavy sigh, she said, "Because she knows about the money."

CHAPTER 21

Everything is to be got with money.

—MANSFIELD PARK

ONEY? WHAT MONEY?" demanded Izzy.
Cora stared at the floor, unable to meet Izzy's gaze. "The money from the Jane Austen Society. I was in charge of it. I don't know what happened to it exactly, but about three thousand dollars of it went missing."

Izzy stared at her mother, dumbfounded. "Are you telling me that you embezzled money from the society?"

"Of course I didn't embezzle it!" Cora shot back indignantly. "I just don't know—precisely—what happened to it."

"Wait. You just lost three thousand dollars? How did that happen?" Izzy asked. "Dear God, I know you can be absentminded at times, but how does a person lose three thousand dollars?" Aunt Winnie and I were curious to hear her answer as well.

Cora sighed. "I don't know how it happened. For last year's festival, Gail asked me to participate in a giveaway. All Jane Austen members were eligible to participate, even if they weren't able to attend the festival. They bought an advance ticket and then were entered into a drawing for various prizes. The proceeds went to both the magazine and the societies that participated. Somehow, though, a large portion of my money went missing."

Izzy leaned forward. "What do you mean, it went missing? How?"

Cora looked up, her expression both embarrassed and baffled. "That's just it. I don't understand how it went missing. I had the check with all the tickets and papers and then . . . it was gone."

"So someone stole it, then?" asked Aunt Winnie.

Cora shook her head. "No. I delivered all the paperwork myself. Valerie called me soon after to ask where the check was. That's when I realized that I must have lost it. I felt terrible and, of course, offered to replace the money. Valerie was understandably upset, but she was fair about it. Of course, I didn't have three thousand dollars that I could just hand over, so I paid back what I could. For the remaining balance, Valerie deducted it from the money I got for my monthly articles to *Forever Austen.* As a favor to me, Valerie said that she wouldn't mention it to Gail."

Izzy leaned back in her chair and regarded Cora with a look of utter astonishment. "So you're telling me that you've been writing articles for *Forever Austen*—for free—for this past year, and have been kowtowing to Valerie as well, because you lost the check?"

Cora nodded. "I know you don't like Valerie, but really, she could have made it very difficult for me. I might have lost my position in the Jane Austen Society."

"Tell me, Cora," asked Aunt Winnie, "did anyone ever cash the check?"

Cora lifted her hands in a helpless gesture. "I don't know. Probably. It was a cashier's check."

No one spoke. I glanced at Aunt Winnie. She gave a minuscule shake of her head. Izzy let out a heavy sigh. Cora resumed her study of the carpet. "You all must think me an idiot," she said after a moment.

"Oh, I think you're an idiot, all right," replied Izzy, getting to her feet, "but not for the reasons you think. I'll bet you dollars to doughnuts that Valerie took that check herself and convinced you that you'd lost it. You really are Uncle Billy, and she's Mr. Potter! I can't believe you allowed yourself to be conned like this!"

Cora gaped at Izzy in astonishment. "Izzy! You can't be serious! Why on earth would Valerie steal that check? It doesn't make any sense!"

Izzy shut her eyes in frustration. "Of course it does, Mama. This is Valerie we're talking about. She's a money-grubbing bottom-feeder with the morals of one of Wickham's baser cousins. She played you, clear and simple. Dear God, I thought I hated her before—but now I really want to strangle her!"

"Izzy!" cried Cora, getting to her feet as well. "I'll not have you speak that way—"

"I think she might have a point, Cora," interrupted Aunt Winnie. "I hate to say it, but the story does sound like a con of sorts."

Cora turned to Aunt Winnie, her face now displaying fresh embarrassment. "You really think she lied to me about the check? But why?"

"Who knows?" said Aunt Winnie. "But the whole thing sounds a bit suspicious, especially the part about her not telling Gail. Do you really believe that Gail would have tried to discredit you to the society? Does that sound like her? I thought you two were friends."

Cora stared at Aunt Winnie in silence for several seconds. "Oh, I've been quite the old fool, haven't I?" she said. Tears welled up in her eyes. "At least Harold wasn't here to see this. He used to get so mad at me at times. 'How can you be so naïve?' he'd yell. Well, he'd certainly have reason to yell this time."

Izzy moved to Cora and pulled her into her arms. Holding her now weeping mother close, she murmured, "Now, Mama. Don't be silly. Daddy loved you, in spite of your naïveté. Actually, I think that might be part of your charm. It's Valerie who should feel ashamed, not you. Oh, I'm going to have quite a little chat with her. I think I'm rather going to enjoy it, actually."

Cora's eyes grew wide, and she pulled back from Valerie. "Oh, please don't say anything, Izzy. Don't! Promise me you won't say anything!"

Izzy stared uncomprehendingly at Cora. "But why not? She scammed you! You can't let this go—you aren't actually thinking about letting this go, are you?"

Cora violently shook her head, her expression suddenly fearful. "But I can't prove anything. It would be her word against mine." Her voice rose in consternation. "What if Gail believes Valerie? Do you realize how horrible I would look?"

Izzy sighed. "Settle down, Mama. Settle down," she said soothingly. "We'll figure it out. Later. For now, why don't we go back to our hotel? I think you need to go to bed."

Cora nodded in agreement before bowing her head. "I'm sorry, Izzy. I should have told you before."

A fond expression replaced Izzy's exasperated one as she stared at the top of Cora's lowered head. "It's all right, Mama," she said, softly. "It's not your fault. We'll set it right."

Taking Cora's arm, Izzy steered her toward the exit. "Elizabeth, Winnie," she said, "we're going to head back to our hotel now. I'll call you in the morning."

"Good night, Izzy. Good night, Cora," I said.

"We'll talk to you in the morning," added Aunt Winnie.

With a backward glance, Izzy rolled her eyes expressively in my direction, and left.

CHAPTER 22

Money can only give happiness where there
is nothing else to give it.

—SENSE AND SENSIBILITY

TURNED TO AUNT WINNIE. "Do you believe that? Do you really think that Valerie stole the money and then tried to blame Cora? Why would she do that?"

"Honestly, I have no idea," said Aunt Winnie. "I mean, it's obvious that Valerie likes money, but would she really steal it?" She picked up her glass of wine and took a sip. I did the same.

"Well, I don't see what can be done about that now," I said. "I mean, Cora is right. There is no proof, and Valerie could just pretend that she was trying to help Cora pay back the debt in the least painful way."

"Yes. The least painful way, which, oddly enough, still netted Valerie a few thousand dollars and a free monthly column for the magazine," Aunt Winnie pointed out.

I took another sip and stared thoughtfully at the table. "I wonder if Gail has any idea."

Aunt Winnie considered the question. "I rather suspect she doesn't, but I'm not sure if it's connected to Richard's death."

"It may not be, but then again, we may find out that it is." I drained the rest of my glass. Placing it on the table, I pushed back my chair to stand up. As I did, the chair leg hit something. Looking down, I saw that it was Gail's purse.

"Gail left her purse," I said, stating the obvious as I picked up the item in question. "I think I should return it."

Aunt Winnie raised her eyebrows in mock surprise. "Of course you do." With a sigh, she finished her drink and stood up as well. "It would appear that the Fates would like us to chat with Gail about Valerie, after all."

I grinned at her. "My thoughts exactly. And after all, who are we, as mere mortals, to argue with the Fates?"

Aunt Winnie shook her head. "Who indeed?"

GAIL ANSWERED MY KNOCK almost immediately, leaving me wondering if she'd been expecting a visitor. The quick expression of confused disappointment that crossed her face at finding Aunt Winnie and me on the other side of her door only increased this suspicion.

"Oh, hello," Gail said, opening the door a bit wider. "Is something wrong?"

"Oh, nothing at all," I said, pasting a friendly smile on my face. "You forgot your purse." I held up the bulky item in question.

"Oh," said Gail, "so I did. Thank you for returning it."

She took the purse from my outstretched hand and seemed about to say good night when Aunt Winnie said, "Forgive me for asking this, Gail, but were you aware that Cora is under the impression that she somehow lost three thousand dollars of the society's money last year and has been working it off under Valerie's terms?"

From the manner in which Gail's face and her still outstretched hand froze as she gaped at Aunt Winnie in bewilderment, I gathered she did not.

"I see that you did not," Aunt Winnie continued blithely. "I know that it's late, but do you have a quick moment? I think you should be made aware of this."

Gail nodded dumbly at us. Then, finding her voice, she said, "I think I should, too. Won't you come in?"

Gail's room was very similar to the one Aunt Winnie and I shared. It had the same high ceiling, comfortable furniture in muted colors, and a view of the courtyard out back. I sat down in the desk chair while Aunt Winnie settled into the wingback chair. Gail cinched her robe a bit more tightly around her waist and perched on the edge of her bed. "So what has Valerie done now?" she asked wearily.

Aunt Winnie arched an eyebrow. "You don't seem surprised."

Gail shook her head, a grim smile on her lips. "No, I'm not. I know my daughter-in-law very well, better sometimes than I think my son does. But what is this about Cora and missing money?"

"According to Cora," said Aunt Winnie, "she delivered a cashier's check for some raffle event last year, but Valerie called her soon after to tell her that it wasn't in the paperwork. Cora was upset, of course, and offered to pay what she could to replace the loss. Valerie agreed to not tell the society—or you—if Cora paid what she could and worked off the rest by not accepting payment for her monthly articles."

Gail closed her eyes as if she was in pain. "I see," was all she said.

"Cora doesn't know that I'm here, of course," continued Aunt Winnie. "In fact, she'd be horrified to find out that I was. But despite the fact that she's prone to bouts of absentmindedness, she's just not that careless. Cora is a good woman. She respects you and values your friendship. She's horribly embarrassed and upset by all this."

Gail stared at her hands. "I'm sure she is." Looking back up, she added, "I, of course, knew nothing about any of this. This past year I . . . haven't quite been myself," she said, glancing back down at her hands. "I've been trying to deal with some personal issues, and as a result Valerie took over most of the finances for the magazine. Although despite my . . . inattention, I've nevertheless suspected for some time now that . . ." Gail waved her hand as if to erase away the rest of the sentence. "All I can tell you," she continued a moment later, "is that while Valerie handles most of the day-to-day finances, I still oversee everything. And I can tell you that I've been approving Cora's usual fee for her articles."

"So," I said, "Valerie could either be funneling that money to replace the supposedly lost money from last year, or . . ."

"Or she could be funneling it into her own account," finished Gail with a sigh. "I'll have a chat with her in the morning. However, I think I already know what I'm going to learn. Please tell Cora that I will take care of this and that I'm very sorry."

Aunt Winnie nodded and stood up. I followed her lead. "Thank you for seeing us," I said. "Cora's had a rough time of it this week—as I'm sure you have, too," I added hastily, mentally kicking myself for my thoughtless gaffe.

But Gail only shook her head at my apology. "Please. It's no secret that Richard and I ended on bad terms, and I'd be lying if I said that time had lessened those feelings. I hope you don't think me terrible, but his death does not trouble me as much as what you've just told me."

Aunt Winnie nodded. "I'm not judging. I'm just here to help an old friend."

"I'll see that it's taken care of," said Gail. "Thank you for telling me. And thank you for my purse."

We said our good nights and went back out into the hallway. As we started toward our own room, I asked, "Did you notice Gail's windows?"

"I don't believe I did," replied Aunt Winnie. "But apparently you did. Tell me."

"They face the back courtyard," I said.

"And?"

"I just thought it was odd, is all."

"Of course you did. Who wouldn't?" came her assured reply.

I said no more and we continued walking. After a few moments, she stopped, turned to me, and put her hands on her hips. "You're actually going to drag this out, aren't you?"

I smiled. "Well, it is kind of fun."

"It won't be when I smack you upside your smug little head," she retorted. "Tell me."

"It's just that Gail's room looks out back . . ."

"Yes, yes, we've established that," Aunt Winnie prompted.

"And when we returned from the ball, we ran into Ian in the lobby. He said he'd been in Gail's room the entire time. But he also said that he'd seen the police cars and ambulance go by."

Aunt Winnie raised her eyebrows in admiration. "So he did. Nice catch, Elizabeth."

I dipped my head modestly. "Thank you. I thought so, too."

"So whose room was Ian in, I wonder?" Aunt Winnie asked as we resumed our walk to our room.

"One thing at a time, my dear Watson. One thing at a time," I responded, and then jumped out of her reach before she could hit me.

I almost made it.

SLEEP PROVED ELUSIVE. I kept thinking about Ian's lie. Did it have anything to do with the murder? Could Ian have drugged his mother and then slipped out and headed back to the ball to kill his father? Granted, while Ian did benefit from Richard's death, he also struck me as a nonviolent, almost passive person. The fact that Valerie was still alive and well was perhaps the strongest testament to this fact. As much as I tried to puzzle out how it might have been Ian, I couldn't. The figure who had rushed into the ballroom wearing the Elizabeth Bennet costume simply couldn't have been Ian. He was too tall and broad in the shoulders for me to mistake him for a woman.

But if he hadn't gone back to the ball, where had he gone? And why was he lying about it?

I was just starting to fall asleep when another thought occurred. If Ian wasn't with Gail, then that meant that Gail was also alone and without an alibi. And she definitely would have fit into the costume that I'd seen. Could Gail have snuck back out to the ball? And if so, did Ian know about it? Or did he help her do it?

CHAPTER 23

*[She] will never be easy till she has exposed herself
in some place.*

——PRIDE AND PREJUDICE

*A*T BREAKFAST THE NEXT MORNING, Aunt Winnie and I sat in companionable silence as we ate our poached eggs and buttered toast and drank our tea. At the table next to us sat Gail and Ian, similarly occupied. As it should be in the morning, we'd exchanged brief pleasantries but no conversation of real substance.

However, just because we weren't engaged in conversation didn't mean I wasn't acutely focused on them and their conversation. We all have talents in this life, and the ability to eavesdrop unobserved is mine.

Gail's face was haggard, and she watched Ian with an expression that vacillated between pity and frustration. If Ian noticed his mother's scrutiny, he didn't let on and instead concentrated on his breakfast.

After a moment, Gail said in an almost casual tone, "Where is Valerie this morning? I thought she was going to join us."

Ian raised his head, and I saw a fleeting expression of dread flash in his eyes. "Oh, she had an errand to run. She said she'd meet us later," came his bland response. He then immediately took a sip of his coffee, almost as if he hoped to ward off further conversation. From the way Gail's mouth tightened, I suspected that it was a futile hope.

"Really?" said Gail, her tone dipping a few degrees with each syllable. "Well, that's odd, because I specifically called her last night to tell her that I needed to speak with her—first thing this morning. I thought she understood that. She certainly told me she did." By the time she finished speaking, even I was chilly.

Ian gripped his coffee cup in his hands—probably for warmth—and glanced uneasily at Gail before averting his eyes to his plate of half-eaten eggs. "I don't know what to tell you, Mom. She didn't say anything to me about meeting you. She made a few calls this morning and then rushed out saying there was something she had to do."

Gail raised her eyebrows. "And you didn't ask where she was going or what she was doing?"

Ian delayed answering by taking another sip of coffee. "Oh, you know how Valerie is, Mom. When she gets a notion in her head, there's no stopping her. Questions only annoy her."

"Notion? What notion did she get in her head?" Gail pressed.

Ian raised the cup again, only to discover that his delaying tactic was now empty. With a mournful look, he put the cup down and glanced longingly at the coffee urn on the sideboard. "Ian," Gail snapped, "what notion did Valerie get in her head?"

Ian jumped slightly. "Mom, I told you. I don't know. She said something about needing to have a little chat with someone and ran out."

Gail exhaled noisily through her nose. Ian leaped from his chair.

"I'm going to get some more coffee. Would you like some?" he asked.

When Gail shook her head, Ian immediately scurried over to the buffet and therefore missed Gail mutter "that little bitch" under her breath.

I, however, did not.

It's one of the perks of being a practiced eavesdropper.

GAIL AND IAN left soon after, while Aunt Winnie and I lingered over our tea, quietly discussing what Ian's lie could mean. Like me, Aunt Winnie had trouble seeing Ian as the murderer. "That man is a born doormat," she said.

"True," I said. "But sometimes doormats snap."

Aunt Winnie took a sip of tea before answering. "Yes, but when they do, it's usually in a sudden violent outburst. They don't don a dress and storm into a Regency ballroom."

I sighed. "I guess you're right. But what about Gail? She could have done it."

Aunt Winnie put down her cup and stared at me with a thoughtful expression. "Yes. I guess in theory she could have," she said slowly. "But she seemed pretty blotto when Ian hustled her out of the ballroom that night. I suppose she might have been acting, but if she was, then she's missed a successful career on the stage."

I nodded. "That's kind of what I thought, too. But that still doesn't answer where Ian was and why he lied about it."

"No, you're right, it doesn't." Aunt Winnie glanced at her watch. "Oh, we'd better scoot. The morning sessions are about to begin."

We quickly finished our tea and headed over to the morning sessions. We looked for Izzy and Cora, but not seeing them, headed for "Regency Skin Care: Keeping Your Bloom."

Like "Dressing Mr. Darcy," this session was packed. However, unlike that session, neither Gail nor Valerie was in attendance. In fact, no one we knew was there. At the time, I felt relieved not to have to deal with any additional drama; however, later it would prove to be a problem for those needing an alibi.

For the next hour, Aunt Winnie and I happily sat back to learn about some of the more popular beauty lotions available to the fashionable lady of the era, such as Gowland's Lotion and Milk of Roses. Gowland's Lotion was not for everyday use but to combat sudden skin eruptions, such as pimples, sunburn, and "scrophula." Unfortunately, it contained both lead and mercury, and therefore was by no means safe. However, one assumes that it was a risk that Sir Walter Elliot would think worth taking. Milk of Roses also promised to create "a complexion delicately fair and beautiful" by removing "redness, sunburn and freckles." As it mainly contained rosewater and almond oil, products found in many of today's healing lotions, it was a far safer choice.

In case the lotions didn't provide the sought-after effect, there were plenty of cosmetics available to do the trick. There was a powder foundation (which, unfortunately, also contained lead), as well as rouge and lip salve (equivalent to today's lip gloss). There was even a modern-day equivalent to mascara and eyeliner. The black paste was created by mixing soot with a little oil and was then applied to the eyebrows and eyelashes. However, because its application required a delicate, practiced technique and was, therefore, probably more noticeable, it was considered quite wanton. One assumes that Lydia Bennet would have become a frequent user.

When the session ended, Aunt Winnie and I headed out into the main hallway to study the itinerary to decide on our next session. We were debating between "A Regency Wedding" and "From China to Chintz," when Byron, clearly agitated, ran up to us.

"Have you seen Ian or Valerie?" he asked, his breath coming in small pants.

"No," I said. "Why, what's wrong?"

Byron ran his hand through his hair and glanced around before answering. "It's the paper," he finally said, his voice almost frantic. "Richard's paper. It's gone! Someone stole it!"

"Stole it!" I gasped. "But how?"

Byron shook his head, perplexed. "They broke into my hotel room," he said. "I got a call this morning from Valerie. She asked me to meet her at a nearby café. She said she had a proposal to talk to me about. When I got there, she wasn't there, so I waited a bit. I tried to call her, but there was no answer. After a while, I went back to my room, only to find that someone had broken into it and taken the paper!"

I stared at Byron in confusion. "But they can't have gotten the only copy—I mean, wasn't it on a computer?"

"No, that's just it. Richard hated computers. He had this stupid paranoia that his work could somehow be hacked. He would write everything out in longhand and then give it to me to be typed. He even insisted that it only be typed on this super-thick paper he special-ordered from London, because he believed that it would be harder for people to copy if they somehow got hold of it. He was especially paranoid about this paper. Once a change was made, I'd have to type up a new version and burn the old version. There was only one copy of the damn thing, and now it's gone!"

"You've got to be kidding," said Aunt Winnie. "Who in the name of God doesn't use a computer these days? It doesn't make any sense!"

Byron's agitation only increased. "Yes, I know. Trust me, I tried to tell him that myself on several occasions. But the fact remains that he didn't listen to me. He only kept one version of the paper, and now it's gone!"

Around us, some of the other festival attendees stared at Byron in concern. He lowered his voice and said, "I just need to locate Ian or Valerie and find out what is going on."

"Do you think that Valerie called you to get you out of your room?" asked Aunt Winnie.

Byron nodded but then paused, as if to reconsider the question. "I did, actually. But now that I think of it, it could have been anyone. I mean, I don't know Valerie all that well and the voice sounded a bit thick. She—whoever called—said she had a cold, so I didn't think anything of it."

"Could it have been Alex?" I asked.

Byron shook his head. "No. As it happened, Alex was with me when I received the call. She had stopped by to give me a list of phone numbers she wanted me to call back home—associates of Richard's. She wanted me to tell them what had happened."

"Did you tell her that you were meeting Valerie?" I asked.

Byron shifted his feet awkwardly and looked down before answering. "No, I didn't. With Richard dead, I'm out of a job. I wondered if the proposal Valerie wanted to discuss with me was a job opportunity with the magazine. However, it didn't seem very tactful to tell Alex that I wanted to work for Gail, so I said nothing."

I glanced at Aunt Winnie. Her brows were pulled together in puzzlement. "I think you should call Inspector Middlefield," I said. "This might be important."

"Well, of course it's important," snapped Byron. "The damn paper is missing! Do you have any idea how much that thing is worth?" He paused and added in a calmer voice, "I'm sorry, Elizabeth. I'm just on edge. I get what you're saying. You think this might have something to do with Richard's death, don't you?"

I shrugged. "I don't know. It might. In any case, I think you should call the police."

Byron sighed. "This whole thing is just completely crazy. I don't get it. But you're right, I should let Inspector Middlefield know what's going on. In the meantime, if you see Ian or Valerie, can you tell them that I need to talk to them?"

"Sure," I said. "But do you want me to mention the paper?"

Byron had just turned to go. Hearing my question, he now turned back to face me. "I don't know," he said slowly. "But maybe, to be on the safe side, it might be best not to mention it if you see them. Let me talk to Inspector Middlefield first."

I nodded. "Okay. Good luck."

Giving me a half wave, Byron quickly headed down the lengthy corridor. His long strides covered the distance in no time, and soon he was out of view. I turned to Aunt Winnie, once again wishing that I possessed the ability to raise one eyebrow. If there ever was an appropriate time to do so, it was now.

"Can you believe this?" I asked. "Someone actually stole that ridiculous paper!"

"There's so much about all this that I can't believe already," said Aunt Winnie, "I don't see why one more thing should matter. I wonder if Valerie did have something to do with it."

"It wouldn't surprise me," I said. "When it comes to matters of money, she seems quite adept at turning a blind eye to pesky little details like morality."

Aunt Winnie nodded her agreement as she scanned the morning's itinerary. "Well, what do you want to do? Do you want to search for Valerie and Ian, or do you want to attend 'A Regency Wedding'? It starts in ten minutes."

I glanced around at the other attendees, happily moving along the corridor on their way to the next session. A few men and women dressed in Regency garb glided by. From the men's blue dress coats with gilt buttons, white waistcoats, and dark gray breeches, and the women's delicate white gowns and white lacy caps, I deduced that they were part of the Regency wedding presentation. The Janeite in me won out over the Nancy Drew. I wanted to attend the session. I didn't want to deal with stolen papers and dead bodies—at least for a little while. I said as much to Aunt Winnie and she nodded her approval. "Good," she said, stuffing the itinerary back into her purse, "because that's where I was going. I'd have hated for you to miss it."

"You're all heart," I said good-naturedly. "Now, where are we going?"

"I think it's up here on the right," she answered.

We ambled along the corridor and then turned the corner to find a closed door. "Is this the room?" I asked, looking around.

"I think so." Aunt Winnie pushed open the door. We entered the meeting room which, although set up for a lecture, was now empty, save for one attendee sitting in the front row.

Aunt Winnie pulled out her itinerary again and studied it. "Room 5A. Isn't this 5A?"

I glanced at the plaque over the door. "According to the sign this is the Green Room."

"Well, that's not helpful." Calling to the woman up front, Aunt Winnie said, "Excuse me? Do you know if this is room 5A? We're looking for the session on Regency weddings? Are you here for that as well?"

The woman didn't answer. In fact, she didn't move. Based on her slumped posture, I guessed she was napping.

"I think she's asleep," I whispered to Aunt Winnie. "Let's go find 5A. This can't be it."

But Aunt Winnie peered suspiciously at the woman and slowly moved toward her. I followed, suddenly uneasy. The woman, who was wearing a black shawl and matching hat, did not stir. When she was within inches, Aunt Winnie reached out and gently touched her shoulder. The light movement tipped the woman over, and she fell in an ungainly heap onto the floor.

Horrified, I found myself looking down at Valerie's bloated, purplish face.

No one would think she was one of the living dead ever again.

CHAPTER 24

Only think of Mrs. Holder's being dead! Poor woman,
she has done the only thing in the world she could possibly
do to make one cease to abuse her.

—LETTERS OF JANE AUSTEN

ONCE AGAIN I WAS SITTING in front of Inspector Middlefield and reflecting that the reality of an English murder investigation is far different from its fictional counterpart. Frankly, the fact that I'd even *had* this thought made me stop for a moment and question my sanity. Maybe my friends were right; maybe I did watch too much *Masterpiece Theatre*.

I was sitting at a table in one of the smaller conference rooms. Inspector Middlefield sat across from me. From the various placards that sat on the white cotton tablecloth, I gathered that the room had initially been set up for a session on social customs in Regency England. I was seated next to one that read: "High Tea vs. Low Tea." Inspector Middlefield sat next to "Card Games: Whist, Commerce, and Loo."

"So, it seems you found another body, Ms. Parker," Inspector Middlefield said to me. She didn't sound particularly sympathetic.

"I did," I answered.

Inspector Middlefield leaned back in her chair and regarded me with an expression I couldn't quite interpret. However, that's not to say that I didn't get the general gist of it. The piercing stare and grim face were something of a tell.

"That's two bodies you've managed to stumble across since you arrived here. Not the usual sights for the typical tourist who comes to Bath," she observed. "And yet you don't seem particularly upset."

Sadly, there was some truth to what she said. I hadn't screamed, burst into tears, or fainted at finding Valerie's body. Instead, with almost robotic calm, I grabbed a hotel employee and told him to call the police. Could the fact that—unfortunately—this wasn't the first dead body I'd seen have something to do with my relative calm? Was I becoming jaded to murder? If that was the case—and I dearly hoped it wasn't—I nevertheless wasn't going to share this with Inspector Middlefield. I suspected that if I did, it would result in an expression on her face that would be far easier to interpret.

I closed my eyes. The gruesome image of Valerie's purple face immediately swam before my eyes, and I felt the bile rise in my throat. My eyes flew back open, happy to be once again staring at Inspector Middlefield's dour face. No, I concluded, I was not immune to the horror of it all. Instead, it was as if a part of my brain had shut down. The result was that I felt as if I was watching the latest chapter of this deadly drama happen to someone else. I made a mental note to Google signs of shock once my interview with the inspector was over.

"I think I might be in shock," I said now. "I'm kind of numb."

Inspector Middlefield's glacial stare thawed a fraction upon hearing this. Not a lot, mind you. The polar bears were still safe.

But it was a start. "Well, I wouldn't be surprised," she said. Turning to one of her sergeants, she added, "Lewis, would you go and get a cup of tea for Ms. Parker?

Sergeant Lewis, a reed-thin man with a shock of bushy red hair, nodded and quickly left the room. "So why were you and your aunt in the room where the body was discovered?" Inspector Middlefield asked.

"We were looking for the session on Regency weddings," I said. "Aunt Winnie thought this was the room. We saw Valerie sitting . . ." I swallowed and took a deep breath. "We didn't know it was her. We thought it was another conference attendee. It was only when we walked over to her to ask if she knew where the wedding session was that we realized it was Valerie." I closed my eyes, but Valerie's face appeared, grotesque and swollen. Once again, I yanked my eyes back open. The detachment that my brain had created seemed to be breaking down.

Sergeant Lewis returned with the cup of tea, which I accepted with a grateful smile. Handing me a plate with a few creamers and several sugar packets stacked on it, he said, "I didn't know how you took it, so I brought you extra."

I thanked him and began adding cream and, taking Inspector Middlefield's advice, more sugar than usual. As I gave the tea a quick stir, I had the sensation that an important memory was on the edge of my subconscious trying to push its way into the light. I frowned at the cup of tea, trying to coax the memory out, but it slid back into darkness and was gone.

"When was the last time that you saw Mrs. Baines?" Inspector Middlefield asked me after I took a sip of the sweet tea.

"Last night at the bar in our hotel."

"Who else was there?" she asked, as she jotted this information down in her notebook.

"Well, Aunt Winnie and I were in the bar. Cora and Izzy joined us. A few minutes later, Gail, Valerie, and Ian came into the bar."

Inspector Middlefield glanced up from her notebook, her gaze laserlike. "An interesting group," she said. "Not one that I'd imagine would socialize together given the current track of the investigation."

I acknowledged her statement with a small nod. "It wasn't intentional. Izzy and Cora were joining us for a drink. We didn't think Gail and Ian and Valerie would be there. We thought they'd still be at the memorial service that Valerie had set up."

Inspector Middlefield nodded. "Ah, yes. I heard about that. I would be curious to hear your thoughts on that as well later. But first let's finish with this. Did the Baines family join you?"

"Yes, they did."

"What did you all talk about?"

I took a sip of the tea. "Valerie brought up Richard's paper. At the memorial, she sort of bullied Alex into agreeing to allow it to be presented. She told us that she'd apparently made arrangements, and they were going to charge twenty pounds a person for admission."

Inspector Middlefield arched an eyebrow at this. "Really?" she said. "What was the reaction to that?"

"I think Ian already knew about it. Gail, however, didn't. She was upset at first; I think that she was angry at the thought of Alex benefiting financially from the paper. But then Valerie explained that the proceeds would be split between Alex and Ian."

"And did that seem to appease Gail?" Inspector Middlefield asked.

I thought back to the conversation. "Yes. I think it did."

Inspector Middlefield tapped her pen against her notebook. "But now, of course, this paper has been stolen. The only copy, I understand."

"That's what I was told."

Inspector Middlefield stared at her notebook, her expression thoughtful. I got the impression that she was debating whether to tell me something. Her next words confirmed this. "I'm debating whether I should tell you something," she said.

See?

"What would you say if I told you that a scrap of that missing paper was found in the dead woman's hands?" She watched my reaction closely.

I'm sure my surprise was quite evident. "In Valerie's hands?" I repeated. "Are you sure?"

She nodded. "Fairly sure. Apparently, Professor Baines only used a specific type of paper." I nodded, remembering what Byron had told me. Inspector Middlefield went on, "It's a very heavy paper stock and not one that's commonly used."

"Byron told me that someone sounding like Valerie called him this morning and asked to meet him. When she didn't show up, he returned to his hotel room and found that someone had broken in and stolen the paper," I said.

"Yes, I know that. What do you make of it, though?"

I thought about it. While I could see Valerie stealing the paper if she thought she could sell it for more money than what she stood to make from the ticket sales, it didn't quite make sense. For one thing, just last night she was excited about the presentation. What could have changed in only a few hours? But there was something else that bothered me. "Why would Valerie die with paper—even if it was only a scrap—in her hand? I'm not a medical expert, but it appeared to me as if she was strangled. Wouldn't she have fought back? How could she fight back with it in her hand?" I asked.

A ghost of a smile appeared on Inspector Middlefield's lips. "That's an excellent question," she said. "It doesn't make sense. In fact, it makes me think that someone wants me to think that Valerie stole the paper and fought to the death to keep it. I have to be honest—I don't understand the fuss over this paper."

I shrugged sympathetically. "Nor do I. But it certainly stirred up a lot of emotions in others."

"Like Cora Beadle," Inspector Middlefield observed.

"Yes," I agreed somewhat hesitantly. "She hated the idea of the paper. But I don't believe she would have killed to prevent its presentation."

Inspector Middlefield stared at her notebook again, her face thoughtful. "How was Gail with Cora last night?" she asked after a moment.

"It was awkward, but Gail and Cora are friends. I don't think Gail really believes that Cora had anything to do with Richard's murder," I said.

"I rather had the impression that Valerie felt otherwise," said Inspector Middlefield.

"I would agree with you there. In fact, I thought Valerie was rude to Cora last night, but Cora didn't let it get to her." I forced myself not to add more. I didn't think it would help Cora's case if Inspector Middlefield found out that Valerie had essentially been blackmailing Cora. However, I didn't want to hide evidence, either. My head gave a sudden throb. I took another sip of tea.

"I gather that Izzy took offense at Valerie's behavior," said Inspector Middlefield.

I took my time swallowing. Inspector Middlefield had clearly already talked to someone else. But who? And just how much did she know? I certainly didn't want to withhold evidence, but I didn't want to screw things up for someone else, either. "Yes," I finally answered, "she did. I didn't really blame her. She defended her mother. I'd probably have done the same thing."

"What happened then?" she asked.

"Ian could see that Valerie was going to escalate the situation and so he basically hustled her out of the bar. Gail stayed a few minutes, and then she left as well. I don't think she was angry at either Izzy or Cora."

Inspector Middlefield nodded, still watching me closely. "So was that it? Everyone went to bed after that?"

I took a deep breath. My Irish Catholic conscience screamed at me to do the right thing and tell the inspector everything I'd learned. My gut told me I was in danger of potentially harming innocent lives.

"Ms. Parker? Is there something you are not telling me?"

I put the cup of tea down. "Yes. I suppose there are one or two things," I said. And then in a low voice I began to tell what I'd learned.

CHAPTER 25

*How horrible it is to have so many people killed! And what
a blessing that one cares for none of them!*
—LETTERS OF JANE AUSTEN

WENTY MINUTES LATER I had finished telling Inspector
Middlefield what I'd learned: everything from Lindsay's
pregnancy to Valerie's blackmail of Cora to Ian's lie about his
whereabouts during the Regency Masked Ball.

It was a full three minutes before Inspector Middlefield was
able to find her voice to respond.

Frankly, I would have been fine if it was longer.

"Are you kidding me?" she finally asked, her voice the personification of some hard metal on the periodic table.

I assumed the question was rhetorical but still found myself
answering. "Um, no. Not really. No."

My response was met with a steely glare to match the voice. "The
mind truly boggles. Who the hell do you think you are? You Americans really are unbelievable! This 'going rogue' spirit may sell
across the pond, but over here, let me tell you, it's bloody annoying!"

"I wasn't trying to interfere," I began but then realized that was
a lie. Oh, dear God. Had I just pulled a Sarah Palin? I shuddered

in disgust. "Well, maybe I was," I amended. "But I just wanted to help Cora. I don't believe that she had anything to do with Richard's death. I only wanted to help."

Inspector Middlefield's mouth twisted into a taunting smirk. "Really? And how is this helping? You didn't come to me with any of this information. You kept it to yourself. What were you going to do—track down the killer and out him in a room full of other suspects? Tell me, was there a plate of watercress tea sandwiches being served when this happened? Were you all drinking sherry? I also suppose that once you cleverly outed the killer, he would meekly bow to your superior detective skills, quietly confess, and then allow himself to be arrested! Let me remind you that this is real, Ms. Parker. This is not some bloody period drama on Channel 3!"

My face flushed with well-deserved embarrassment. She was absolutely right, of course. Years of watching civilized murderers tracked and unmasked by equally civil detectives all from the safety of my couch had clearly warped my thought process. Somewhere over the past few years, I had assumed the mantle of amateur sleuth. Granted, it wasn't without merit. I did seem to have a knack for finding things out, but I wasn't helping anyone by keeping those tidbits to myself. "I'm really very sorry," I said. "I didn't mean any harm."

Inspector Middlefield closed her eyes and let out a weary sigh. "I could have you locked up—you know that, right? I could charge you with about eight different offenses."

"I am sorry," I repeated.

Inspector Middlefield tapped her notebook in frustration. "Right. Well, I'm not. Going to lock you up, that is. Whether I like it or not, you have provided me with some valuable information. But from now on, I must insist that you stay out of this investigation. And if you do happen to *innocently* stumble across information"— she paused to glare at me as she said this last part—"then you will call me immediately."

I nodded my agreement. "Of course I will."

She paused, as if uncertain how to proceed. "There were several— well, more than several—a surprising number of incoming calls logged on Valerie's phone. She did receive calls from Ian, Gail, Byron, and Cora this morning, but it would seem that the vast majority came from New York; however, they are all different numbers. We are working on identifying them, but it's still early."

"Do you think that these calls might have been from the killer?" I asked, leaning a bit forward in my chair. "Could Valerie have been working with this unknown person all along to get hold of Richard's paper and then sell it? If so, does that mean Valerie might have been involved in his death? Could Valerie have been the woman in the Elizabeth Bennet costume who rushed Richard outside?" As my questions tumbled out one on top of the other, I felt a faint sense of hope that Valerie's frequent caller was the killer. I liked that scenario much better than one in which the killer was someone I knew.

Inspector Middlefield held up her hand and shot me a quelling glance. I closed my mouth and tried to affect an expression of casual interest, rather than one suggesting unhinged meddler. I leaned back against my chair in what I hoped was a nonchalant manner.

"I am saying no such thing," she said. "I just wondered—seeming as you've been conducting your own investigation—if you'd noticed anything odd about her incoming calls."

I thought about the question. "She did seem to always have her phone with her," I said after a minute, "but I guess that's not too surprising, as she has a young child back home. However, I did overhear one of her calls last night." I quickly told her about Valerie's odd conversation in the bathroom.

Inspector Middlefield listened intently. "So are you sure she said, 'Now, do you know what I'm going to do?'"

I nodded. "Yes."

Inspector Middlefield frowned. "Any idea what she was talking about?"

I shook my head. "Sorry, I don't. It was just the way that she was talking that struck me more than anything else. I mean, it wasn't her usual voice. It was lower, somehow. And once she realized that someone else was in the bathroom, she got off the phone."

Inspector Middlefield closed her notebook and stood up. Fixing me with a dark look, she said, "Okay. Well, thank you for letting me know what you've found out. But please believe that I'm serious about your staying out of this investigation. Unless I ask for your help, consider it not needed."

I'd like to think I left the interview with poise, but I'm pretty sure that any unbiased witness would have used the term *slunk*.

AUNT WINNIE WAS waiting for me when I came out of the interview. She took one look at my face and said, "Are you okay, sweetie? What happened?"

I sank into one of the nearby chairs. "No, I'm not okay. I feel like a jackass. I told Inspector Middlefield everything we've learned. She was pretty angry. And you know what? I don't blame her. I'm not a detective. I've no right investigating this murder—especially as I didn't tell the police what I learned. I'm nothing more than a meddling phony."

Aunt Winnie sat in the chair next to me and put a comforting hand on my leg. Giving me a reassuring smile, she said, "Honey, you are not a meddling phony. You are a sweet girl who tried to help a woman who was scared and afraid of being arrested for a murder she didn't commit."

I tried to return her smile, but I couldn't. "No, I'm not. I'm trying to be something I'm not; namely, a clever detective. I appreciate your trying to make me feel better, but it's no good. I'm not a detective, and I need to stop pretending that I am."

Aunt Winnie scoffed. "That's a load of bullshit. You've been amazing in helping the police in the past—and you've done it again this time, whether they want to admit it or not. Yes, you didn't tell them what you'd learned, but that doesn't make you a meddling phony. I know you. You just didn't want to say anything until you knew it was relevant. You kept quiet because you didn't want to hurt anyone."

I stared at my lap. I wanted to believe her, but I just didn't know anymore. Ever since I'd lost my job and my apartment, I felt like I was at loose ends. All around me, friends and family were moving forward with their lives. My best friend, Bridget, was newly married. My older sister, Kit, was expecting her second child. And what was I doing? Playing Miss Marple.

Before I could explain this to Aunt Winnie, Izzy ran up with Cora in tow. "Is it true?" Izzy asked breathlessly. "Did someone really kill Valerie?"

Her face was pale, her eyes large with fright. Cora simply looked dazed. "It's true," I said in a low voice. "Aunt Winnie and I found her. She'd been strangled. But that's not all. Someone broke into Byron's hotel room this morning and stole Richard's paper. Part of it was found in Valerie's hand."

Izzy's hand flew up to her mouth. "Oh, my God. You poor things! Poor Valerie! I didn't like her, but she didn't deserve this." The memory of Izzy last night saying that she could cheerfully strangle Valerie popped into my head. I quickly looked away before my face transmitted my thoughts. However, I wasn't fast enough for Izzy not to notice. "Elizabeth?" she asked, squatting down in front of me and grabbing my hands in hers. "I hope you don't think I had anything to do with this. I was mad at Valerie for what she'd done to Mama, but I swear to you, I wouldn't kill her!"

I tried to read her expression. She certainly looked sincere, but what the hell did I know? Despite her declaration that we were "soul mates" and destined to be "friends forever," I had met her only a few days ago. I really didn't know her at all.

"How is Ian taking it?" Cora asked.

I shook my head. "I don't know. I haven't seen him since breakfast."

"So, do the police think that Valerie stole the paper?" Izzy asked.

I shrugged. "I don't know. Byron said he got a phone call this morning from someone claiming to be Valerie. She asked to meet him to discuss a job with the magazine. Valerie never showed up, and when Byron went back to his room, he found that the paper was gone."

"Was it the only copy?" asked Cora. "I know that Richard was weird about computers."

I nodded, wondering how well known Richard's aversion to computers had been. "Yes," I said. "It was the only copy. Either Valerie made the call to get Byron out of the room, stole the paper, tried to sell it to someone, and then was killed for her efforts . . ."

". . . or someone is trying to make it seem that way," Aunt Winnie finished.

Something that Inspector Middlefield said suddenly resonated in my mind. "Cora?" I asked. "Why did you call Valerie this morning?"

Cora flushed crimson at my question and looked down at the carpet in confusion. "Um, well, I don't think that I . . . ," she began, but I cut her off.

"The police have Valerie's phone, Cora," I said. "They've already checked. They know you called her."

Izzy whirled around and stared at Cora with all the indignant fury of a mother finding her child sneaking out of the house. "You didn't! Oh, my God! You did!" she cried. "You actually called her! I told you not to. I told you that I would take care of it, but did you listen to me? No! Of course not! And now you're probably back in the police's crosshairs!"

Surprisingly, Cora did not crumple under Izzy's withering glare. Squaring her shoulders, she lifted her chin a few millimeters and said, "Yes, I called her. I wanted to find out if it was true—if she'd really scammed me into thinking that I'd lost the society's money. How was I to know that she was going to be killed? And how dare you talk to me like that? I am your mother, not some half-wit child."

Izzy took a deep breath and then two more for good measure. "I'm sorry, Mama. You're right. I shouldn't have yelled. I'm just scared that the police are going to renew their interest in you."

"Well, you two have been together this morning, haven't you?" I asked. "Once Inspector Middlefield learns that, she'll have to look elsewhere for the killer."

My question was met with an uneasy silence. Both Izzy and Cora exchanged anguished glances. "Well, no, actually, we weren't," began Izzy. "I went out this morning to get some shampoo and . . ."

"I was gone when she got back to the room. I'd gone out for a walk," finished Cora.

"Oh, you have got to be kidding," said Aunt Winnie, her expression incredulous.

Cora produced a ghost of a smile. "I'm afraid not. Looks like I've done it again, haven't I? There's been another murder, and once again I don't have an alibi."

CHAPTER 26

Have you never known the pleasure and triumph of a lucky
guess? I pity you. I thought you cleverer; for, depend upon
it, a lucky guess is never merely luck. There is always
some talent in it.

—EMMA

Y HEAD ACHED; throbbed, to be more precise. I was
minutes away from a full-blown migraine. I was back
in my room, where I had shut the curtains against the wholly inap-
propriately cheerful afternoon sun, in the hopes of taking a quick
nap, but every time I closed my eyes, the gruesome image of Valerie's swollen purple face swam up in front of me. I wanted desper-
ately to talk to Peter, to hear his voice, and to have him reassure me
that everything would be okay. I had left him a message about Valerie this morning, but since then my calls kept going straight to his
voice mail, at which point a mechanical voice politely informed me
that the mailbox was full.

Nursing a secret hope that he actually was on a plane coming to
see me rather than stuck in a meeting, I rolled off my bed in frustration. "I'm going downstairs to see if I can get a cup of coffee or

something. The caffeine might help," I said to Aunt Winnie, who was sitting on her bed scribbling into a notebook.

Peering at me in concern, she swung her legs off her bed and stood, saying, "I'll get it for you, honey. I know how bad your headaches are."

I shook my head—gently. "No, I want to go. Maybe walking will help. Lying down certainly isn't doing the trick."

"Are you sure?" she asked doubtfully.

"Yes. You stay here and work on your list." I indicated the notebook that was covered in her distinctive looping handwriting. Aunt Winnie was convinced that if she just wrote everything down about the murders, a solution would present itself. I was less optimistic. The only thing I ever gleaned after writing out the facts to a particular problem was that I have really lousy handwriting.

Aunt Winnie raised an eyebrow. "Don't mock me. You never know, it might prove helpful."

"I wish you luck with that," I said, as I gingerly made for the door. "I'll be back in a few minutes."

When I got downstairs, I saw that the lobby was deserted, so I poked my head into the bar in the hopes that someone was there. I was in luck. Mary, the bartender from the other night, was behind the bar restocking and kindly agreed to make me a cup of coffee.

As I perched on one of the red leather barstools, Mary busied herself with the coffeemaker. "I heard that woman you were here with the other night was killed," Mary said as she placed a white mug, a small pitcher of cream, and a tin of sugar in front of me.

"You heard right," I said.

"That's awful," Mary said, as she poured steaming coffee into my mug. "First that Professor Baines was killed and then her. It's not the kind of occurrence that generally happens in Bath. Was she a close friend of yours?"

I shook my head as I added a generous dollop of cream and several scoops of sugar. "No. I'd just met her," I said. "She was attending the conference. She was actually the daughter-in-law of Professor Baines."

Mary shook her head sympathetically and crossed her arms across her chest. "That poor family. It's mind-boggling. Have the police arrested anyone yet? Was it her husband, do you think?"

I paused, my mug halfway to my mouth. "No, they haven't arrested anyone. Why do you think it might be her husband?"

Mary flushed slightly and fiddled with the coffeemaker. "Oh, no reason, I guess. They just always say it's usually the spouse in these kinds of cases."

I put down my mug. "The other night, you said something about Valerie—the woman who died. You said something about her behavior and what might happen if the owners caught her. What did you mean?"

Mary wouldn't meet my eyes. "Honestly, I don't like to say. After all, the poor woman is dead," she said.

I reached across the bar and gently touched her arm. "If you know something, please tell me. It might help the police find her killer."

Mary didn't answer right away, seeming to debate the matter a little more in her head. After a few moments, she came to a decision and said haltingly, "Well, I heard her several times on her phone."

I nodded encouragingly. "And?"

Mary took a deep breath. "And, well, she seemed into phone sex."

I blinked, sure that I'd misheard. Perhaps my headache was now affecting my hearing. "I'm sorry. Did you say 'phone sex'?"

Mary nodded, embarrassed. "I did. She was really into it. I must have caught her at it at least five times. I don't know who she was talking to, but it was pretty gross."

"She was having phone sex with Ian?" I asked.

Mary shook her head. "No, it wasn't with him. She seemed to always do it in a bathroom. Privacy, I guess. Anyway, I ran into her husband a few times immediately after and he wasn't on the phone, so I don't think it was him. That's why I wondered if he might have killed her out of jealousy or something."

Whether from my headache or this bizarre bombshell, my brain was processing information at the speed of dark. Valerie was having an affair? And engaging in phone sex? An involuntary shudder rippled through my body at the images that thought produced. Now, while I am not a prude, I have never seen the appeal of phone sex. With the unfortunate image of Valerie purring God knows what kind of kinky suggestions into the phone to some stranger, it pretty much cemented that opinion.

I stared at my cup of coffee, still somewhat dazed. Frankly, it was hard to believe. But why would Mary lie? She had no reason to. The memory of Valerie's brief phone conversation I'd overheard in the bathroom last night suddenly took on a whole new meaning. My stomach gave a nauseous lurch, as the realization that Valerie's breathy question as to "what she was going to do" was most likely of a sexual nature.

It also meant that my hope that Richard's and Valerie's killer was an unknown accomplice from New York was doomed.

Honestly, I didn't know which realization was more upsetting.

I RETURNED TO the hotel room in a fog. Still clutching my cup of coffee, I sank down into the wooden chair at the desk. Aunt Winnie regarded me with an expression of mild alarm. "Elizabeth? Are you okay? Do you need me to call a doctor?" she asked, tossing aside her notebook.

I shook my head. "No, I'm okay. I think. I just had a rather interesting conversation with the bartender downstairs."

"And?" Aunt Winnie prompted.

"And, well, she overheard Valerie on the phone a few times," I said, before taking a sip of coffee.

"By all means, go ahead and take your time," Aunt Winnie groused.

I smiled. "Trust me, you should thank me. Remember the 'you' in this moment. You will never get back the innocence that you now enjoy." I paused. "Apparently, Valerie was rather fond of explicit phone sex. And she wasn't having it with Ian."

Aunt Winnie's face scrunched in disgust. "Are you serious?"

"According to Mary—she's the bartender—she caught Valerie at it on a number of occasions."

Aunt Winnie said, "Is she sure it was Valerie? Valerie Baines?

The woman whose own child was probably created in a burst of friendliness that would most likely never be repeated?"

I nodded. "That's the one."

Aunt Winnie let out a low whistle. "I guess it's true what they say about still waters running deep."

"Or kinky."

Aunt Winnie nodded in agreement. "Or kinky. I wonder if Ian knew."

"I wondered about that, too," I said. "Let me see that notebook of yours. I might have an idea."

IZZY CALLED US about an hour later to see if we wanted to meet her and Cora for lunch. "We've just finished talking with Inspector Middlefield," Izzy said. "Charming woman. I hope she chokes on her suspicions."

"I take it, then, that your mom is still a suspect?" I asked.

"That would be putting it mildly," she answered morosely. "I don't know what we're going to do."

I glanced at Aunt Winnie's open notebook on the bed, which now contained several pages of my own scribbled notes. "I think I might have some ideas on that. Why don't Aunt Winnie and I meet you and your mom at that café down the street from your hotel."

"The Pig and Fiddle?"

"That's the one. Let's meet there in about half an hour, and we can discuss it."

There was the briefest of pauses. "Can you tell me now?" she asked.

258 /3 Tracy Kiely

"I'd rather not get into it over the phone," I said, wondering why that would make a difference. But for some reason, it did. "I'll see you in thirty minutes."

"We'll be there," answered Izzy.

When Aunt Winnie and I arrived at the pub, Izzy and Cora were waiting for us. The coveted outdoor heated garden area was full, so we got a table in the main room, a cheerful area jammed full of various sporting memorabilia and comfy leather sofas.

"What do you know?" Izzy asked as we sat down. "Have you figured out who did it? Have you figured out a way to get Mama off the hook?"

I held up a quelling hand. "Wait. I don't know anything for sure, but I do have a couple of ideas."

Izzy leaned forward, resting her elbows on the wooden table. "Well? What are they?"

I glanced at Aunt Winnie. I had already discussed my suspicions with her. She nodded her head for me to continue. "Now, please keep in mind," I said, "that this is only an idea, and I really need you to promise not to repeat it."

"Sure, of course," answered Izzy.

I took a deep breath. "It's about Ian," I said.

"Ian!" Izzy and Cora repeated in astonishment.

"Shhh!" I ordered, nervously glancing around to see if anyone had overheard us. "Keep your voices down!"

"Sorry, but Ian? You must be crazy!" Izzy protested. "He wouldn't hurt a fly. He's a teddy bear!"

"That's what the neighbor of every killer says, right after, 'He was always so quiet and kept to himself,' " I retorted.

"You think Ian killed his father? For what? His money? I don't believe it," Izzy scoffed.

"People have killed for far less. And I'm not saying that Ian killed anybody. I'm just saying that I've discovered a few things that are odd."

"Like what?" Izzy asked, her color suddenly pale.

"Well, as strange as this may sound, I think Valerie was having an affair," I said.

Both Cora's and Izzy's eyes grew wide with astonishment at this. "Valerie? You've got to be joking!" said Cora.

I quickly told them what Mary had told me. Cora stared back at me, clearly horrified. Izzy's expression was dubious.

"Are you sure? I really have a hard time believing Valerie was that . . . adventurous. I mean, Ian told me . . ." She paused.

"Ian told you what?" I asked.

"Nothing. It's not important," she said quickly. "In any case, I still don't see how any of this implicates Ian."

"I realize that. What does implicate him is the fact that he lied to the police."

Izzy's eyebrows pulled together. "When? When did he lie to the police?"

"He lied about being in Gail's room the night of Richard's murder. He told me that he'd seen the ambulance from her window, but Gail's room doesn't look out onto the street."

Izzy suddenly reached across the table and grabbed my hands tightly. They were very cold and very strong. "Did you tell the police that?" she asked in a low voice.

I stared back at her in confusion. "Well, yes, I did. Why?"

Izzy cringed and closed her eyes. She gripped my hands even tighter. I winced and tried to pull them back. "Because I know where Ian was that night," she said, her voice small.

"You do?" A sick suspicion suddenly settled in the pit of my stomach. "Where?"

Taking a deep breath, she said, "He was in his room. With me."

CHAPTER 27

They were very accomplished and very ignorant . . . and the object of all was to captivate some man of much better fortune than their own.

—SANDITION

"WHAT?" CRIED CORA in the universal tone of motherly outrage. "You were *where?*"

Not to be outdone, Izzy raised her blond head in the universal pose of adolescent defiance. "You heard me, Mama. I'm not repeating it."

"But Izzy, you don't mean that you . . . that you . . . ." Cora broke off, unable to complete the thought.

"Slept with him? Actually, I do mean that."

"But what about Allen? Do I have to remind you that you are engaged?"

Izzy rolled her eyes. "Of course not, Mama. But you know that I've had feelings for Ian for a long time now." From Cora's dumbfounded expression, I gathered that Cora had no idea whatsoever of this tidbit. Izzy continued, unconcerned. "While I'm very fond of Allen, I know now that he isn't The One. Ian is. And on this trip, well, we grew closer. I can't go back to Allen now. It wouldn't be fair."

"Fair!" Cora yelled. "How can you possibly pretend to be in a moral position to judge what's fair?"

Several heads turned our way. "I think it might be a good idea to either leave or lower your voices," I said, suddenly wondering what the hell I'd been thinking in suggesting that we have this meeting in a public place.

Cora glanced around and lowered her voice accordingly. "I can't believe you, Izzy. I really can't. To betray Allen like this is terrible! What kind of girl are you?"

Izzy raised her head and stared unblinking into her mother's eyes. "I'm the kind of girl who goes after what she wants. I wanted Ian, and I got him. Allen is a nice man, but he's not in the same league as Ian. I'm sure he'll understand when I tell him."

Cora blinked. "But Ian's married!"

Izzy shrugged. "*Unhappily* married."

"And now he's not either," offered Aunt Winnie.

Izzy flushed. "I realize what you must think of me, but I'm not going to apologize for what I've done. That said, I had nothing to do with Valerie's death, or Richard's, for that matter. And I promise you, neither did Ian."

Cora stared at Izzy in horror and pressed her hand to her mouth. "I think I'm going to be sick," she moaned. "Izzy, you have no idea what you've done!"

Izzy stuck out her chin in apparent indifference, but her chin wobbled a bit, and she was having trouble meeting her mother's agonized expression. "Well, I think you're a bunch of hypocrites!" she finally said. "You just told me yourself that Valerie was apparently having an affair. Ian was lonely and unhappy. I did nothing wrong!"

I glanced over at Aunt Winnie. She rolled her eyes in disgust. I quite agreed. Turning back to Izzy, I said, "You have to tell the police, Izzy. You have to tell them that you were with Ian, because I've told them that he couldn't have been with Gail when Richard was killed."

Izzy reluctantly nodded. "I will. Of course, I will." Reaching out, she impulsively grabbed my hand again. "But please don't you be mad at me, Elizabeth! You would have done the same, you know you would have."

I gently, but firmly, pulled my hand away. "No, Izzy. I wouldn't have. You went after a married man—a married man with a small child—simply because he was a better prospect than your fiancé. I think what you did was pretty despicable, actually."

Izzy looked as if I'd slapped her.

The image of Valerie's face rose in front of me again, and I suddenly found myself wishing that I had.

THE REST OF LUNCH WAS A STRAINED AFFAIR. There was very little conversation, and no one seemed to have much of an appetite. Once it was over, we quickly parted ways, with Izzy promising that she would call Inspector Middlefield. She also kept hinting that once I thought about everything from her point of view, my anger at her would fade, and we'd be friends once again.

Out of respect for Cora's obvious distress, I said nothing, even though I was sorely tempted to tell Izzy that I thought she made Lydia Bennet look like a prude.

As Aunt Winnie and I walked back to our hotel, I said, "I've got to tell you, this festival is nothing like I thought it would be."

Aunt Winnie shook her head in disbelief. "I know. In a weird way, it's a little funny. Not funny ha-ha, mind you, but funny weird. Baines saw sex and intrigue in Austen's novels, and yet it seems like all the sex and intrigue was actually going on around him."

"I thought it was weird the way Izzy kept flirting with Ian," I said, "but I thought she was doing it to tweak Valerie, not because she actually liked Ian! Of course, I don't think for one minute she really likes him. I think she only likes his money."

"I guess I shouldn't be that surprised when I stop to think about it," said Aunt Winnie. "Izzy is a very pretty girl, and, as Cora herself said, she usually gets what she wants when she puts her mind to it. Given Valerie's rather unfortunate personality, and Ian's own weak will, it couldn't have been hard for Izzy to seduce him. Especially as it seems that Valerie was fooling around herself."

"My head is spinning from all this," I admitted. "Izzy seduces Ian on the night that Richard is killed. Is it a coincidence, or does it have something to do with his murder? I mean, Ian inherits a lot from Richard's death."

"And now Valerie has been deftly removed from the scene," added Aunt Winnie.

"Of course, Izzy could be lying about their being together," I mused.

"How do you mean?" Aunt Winnie asked. "Why would she do that?"

"Well, if she says that she's with Ian, and he backs her up, then she has an alibi. Which means that . . ."

"...she couldn't have killed Richard," finished Aunt Winnie. "Interesting theory. Just one question."

"Really? Just one?"

"For now. Why would Izzy want to kill Richard?"

I paused. "She might be tempted if she thought she was in line to become the second Mrs. Ian Baines."

NOTHING MUCH MORE was said after that. I think we were both caught up in trying to puzzle out what this latest development meant. When we got to the hotel, I was dismayed to see John in the lounge area. He leaped to his feet when he spotted us. "Elizabeth!" he called out to me, as he hustled his slight frame across the lobby to where we stood. "Can you believe this? Valerie Baines! Dead! It's bloody awful. What have the police told you?"

I stared at him in confusion. "Why would the police tell me anything?"

"Well, you are working for them, aren't you? I'm sure you told me that you were."

"I never said any such thing," I protested, but John would have none of it. He continued to ask, pry, hint, and repeat all that he'd heard in connection with Valerie's murder, most of it woefully wrong. I gave up trying to correct him as that only seemed to prolong the conversation, and so I stood in silence waiting for him to run out of air. As I did so, I glanced down to the far end of the lobby and saw Gail and Lindsay exit the bar. Deep in conversation, they didn't seem to notice our presence. Gail spoke soothingly to Lindsay, who was weeping into a napkin. I couldn't hear what they were saying, but the body language seemed to indicate that Gail was trying to convince a reluctant Lindsay of something. After a minute, Gail reached into her purse and pressed what appeared to be a check into Lindsay's hands. After a moment's hesitation, Lindsay put the check in her pocket. Gail said something else, and Lindsay nodded, before leaving by the side exit.

Right then, Gail looked up and caught me staring at her. Without a word, she turned and went up the stairs. But I'd seen her face. She was scared.

CHAPTER 28

*[She] consoled herself for the loss of her husband by
considering that she could do very well without him.*

—MANSFIELD PARK

FTER I'D EXTRICATED MYSELF from John—no small
task in and of itself—I headed up to Gail's room with
Aunt Winnie. Silence met my knock, but I wasn't buying it. I rapped
my knuckles a tad harder against the wooden door. "Gail," I called
out. "I know you're in there. Please. I'd like to talk to you."

The silence was replaced with a faint shuffling sound followed
by the lock sliding open. Gail opened the door and regarded me
with a weary expression. Her face was haggard, and her eyes were
red. And a shade glassy, I amended, after closer inspection. I wondered if Valerie's death had sent Gail back to her prescription-
induced emotional shield. "Elizabeth, this really isn't a good time,"
she said. "I have a lot to do. Ian and I have to make arrangements
for poor Valerie's funeral. There are a lot of tasks that we need to
attend to."

I nodded. "I am sorry, Gail. I really am. But I need to ask you
about the night that Richard died."

Gail's face betrayed no emotion. "Yes?"

"How long was Ian gone?"

Gail sighed and opened the door wider and stepped aside. "You might as well come in. This isn't a conversation that I want to have out in the hall."

Aunt Winnie and I stepped inside the room and sat down. Gail took a seat on her bed. "Why do you think that Ian was gone?" she asked with one last effort at motherly protection.

"Because I just had a conversation with the person he was with," I answered.

Gail's shoulders slumped in acknowledgment. "Oh. Well, I guess there's no use in saying otherwise. Yes, Ian left a few minutes after he brought me back here. I . . . wasn't feeling well," Gail said, her eyes sliding away from mine as she uttered the euphemism for *wasted*. "He put me to bed and then left."

"Did you stay here, then?" I asked.

Gail nodded. "Yes. I did. I think I dozed a bit."

"Do you know where Ian went?" I asked.

Gail looked away. "I have a general idea. He was with Izzy, wasn't he?"

"Yes. Did he tell you that?"

She shook her head. "No, but I could see that Izzy was pursuing him, and it was clear that Ian was flattered. I guess a mother just has a sense about these things when it comes to her children."

"Do you think that Valerie knew?" I asked.

"No," Gail answered quickly. "It would never occur to Valerie that Ian would cheat on her. Valerie ran things in that relationship, so to speak. She was rather single-minded in some ways."

"Do you think Ian was going to leave her?" I asked.

"Absolutely not!" Gail said firmly. "Look, I don't approve of what Ian did—that's the sort of behavior I put up with myself for years. But he wouldn't have broken up his family because of it. He wasn't going to end up like . . ." She suddenly closed her mouth and crossed her arms across her chest.

". . . his father?" I asked.

She gave a curt nod. "Yes. Richard cheated on me from day one. Hell, I think he even fooled around when we were on our honeymoon. He was incapable of keeping his pants on when there was a pretty girl to be had," she said bitterly. "Ian may be his only child by *name*—but I suspect that were one to poke around a bit, they'd find that Richard sired many more children 'on the wrong side of the sheets,' as they used to say. Poor things. I'm sure Richard never bothered with helping any of them."

"Is that why you were talking to Lindsay just now? Were you trying to help her?"

She didn't answer right away. "Yes," she said finally, "I was. I wondered about her. She was just the type of girl he went for: young, naïve, and inexperienced. He'd swoop in like the wealthy, sophisticated charmer and keep them dangling from a string for a while until he grew bored. He was in all manner of ways a rat bastard. I called Lindsay today and asked her, well, I asked her if she needed any help."

"That was very kind of you," said Aunt Winnie.

Gail produced a rueful smile. "Is it? I don't think so. I knew the kind of man Richard Baines was for years and never said a word. I watched him seduce and lie and cheat. And I held my tongue because I was too proud to admit it. I suppose I feel a bit like Darcy did about Wickham. Had I made his worthless character known and all that. I figure the least I can do is help Lindsay. Call it a symbolic attempt at restitution."

"Well, I'm sure she appreciates it," I said. "I wonder what Alex's reaction will be."

Gail smirked. "You'd have to ask her, of course, but I would imagine that she is not going to be happy when she finds out what goes around, comes around."

I didn't say anything, but I rather wondered if Gail's generosity toward Lindsay stemmed more from the whole "the enemy of my enemy is my friend" adage than any real desire for restitution.

I suspected it did.

I also wondered if she had really stayed in her room as she claimed.

BACK IN OUR ROOM, I said to Aunt Winnie, "So what did you make of Gail?"

Kicking off her shoes, she plopped down on her bed and stretched out her legs. "I don't know," she admitted. "I can't decide if I like her or think she's a phony. I didn't get the impression that she was broken up about Valerie death."

I flopped on my bed as well. "Me neither. But to be fair—"

Aunt Winnie stopped me. "Valerie was the mother of her grandchild. Gail may not have liked her, but to not mind seeing her dead is something entirely different."

"True. But I wonder if some of her lack of emotion could be pharmaceutical in nature rather than something more sinister. Her eyes were glassy again."

"I noticed that, too. Honestly, Elizabeth, I don't know what to think. Neither Richard nor Valerie was very nice, but I don't even think I know *why* they were killed. Was Valerie killed because of the paper or because of her affair? And are they somehow connected?"

I sighed. "I don't know. But speaking of which, I'd better call Inspector Middlefield and tell her about Valerie. I promised to tell her if I learned anything new."

I dialed the number and soon was speaking to Inspector Middlefield. She did not sound pleased to hear from me, but a promise is a promise. I quickly told her what Mary had relayed to me. There was brief silence, and then I heard the faintest of curses. "You really do seem to have a knack for finding things out, don't you?" she said.

"I'm sorry? I don't understand."

"We know about the calls, as well—we just learned about them. However, there's one little detail that you are missing."

"Really? What?"

Inspector Middlefield hesitated. Then she told me.

I felt a bit like Mr. Bennet when he learned about Lydia's elopement—I could not speak for a full ten minutes.

CHAPTER 29

Facts are such horrid things!

—LADY SUSAN

FTER HANGING UP with Inspector Middlefield, I looked at Aunt Winnie. "Well? What did she say?" she asked. "What's the big news?"

"It appears that Valerie wasn't having an affair after all. She had taken a job as a phone sex operator."

Aunt Winnie regarded me pop-eyed. "Bullshit," she said.

The absurdity of the situation hit me, and I began to giggle. "Well, this is a wretched beginning indeed. I am sure nobody else will believe me, if you do not. Yet, indeed, I am in earnest. I speak nothing but the truth."

"You're serious, then? Valerie was a phone sex operator? Valerie? I can't believe it!" Then she began to laugh. Hard. So did I. Soon we were both gasping for air, with tears streaming down our faces.

"We're going to hell," I said a few minutes later. "You realize that, don't you? The poor woman is dead."

"I know, I know," said Aunt Winnie, wiping the tears from her face. "It's not funny. Well, it is, but we shouldn't laugh."

"I wonder if Ian knew," I said.

"Who knows? It's not exactly something that I can see myself asking the poor man."

I lay back down on my bed and stared at the ceiling. "I keep thinking that I'm missing something in all of this. It's like someone threw a bunch of sand up into the air, and I'm having trouble seeing things clearly."

Aunt Winnie picked up her notebook and flipped it open to a new page. "Tell me about it," she said as she added this new bit of information to the rest.

I closed my eyes, listening to the scratches of her pen as it moved across the paper, as I tried to sort out what I knew about both Richard and Valerie. It seemed clear that in addition to being a delusional pseudo-academic who saw conspiracy theories at every turn, he was a two-timing bastard who'd made a secondary career at seducing naïve young women. His paper on Jane Austen was sure to annoy, even anger, certain Janeites, but would it have made a difference in how Austen and her works were viewed? Would it really be worth money? I wondered if it was Richard Baines the man rather than Richard Baines the scholar who had been murdered. But again, if it was the latter, why? Was it his money, or was it something more?

As for Valerie, I was equally confused. She hadn't been a particularly nice woman—she'd struck me as someone more concerned with money and status than people. The fact that she'd taken a job as a sex operator proved that. Had she stolen the paper and tried to sell it only to be killed for her greed? And if so, who was she trying to sell it to? Surely no one in the Baines family would want to buy the paper. Not any of the family that I'd met, I amended. A thread of a thought flashed. I was missing something, but the thought refused to form and instead faded back into the inky blackness of my subconscious.

At least I assumed it was inky blackness back there. I've never actually seen it.

AFTER AN HOUR or so—I think I dozed off—my headache was starting to recede, and I felt like taking a walk. As Aunt Winnie was just falling asleep herself, I told her that I was going to head over to the Guildhall.

"Why are you going there?" she asked.

"I don't know. I might get another cup of coffee and walk around. I just thought it might help me sort everything out."

"Do you want me to come with you?"

"No, you stay here. I doubt I'll find anything. I just want to look around, that's all."

Aunt Winnie yawned. "Okay. Well, be careful."

"You know me," I responded lightly.

Aunt Winnie pried open a sleepy eye. "Are you trying to scare me?" she asked.

"I'll be fine," I said with a laugh. "Have a nice nap. I'll be back before you know it."

"Hey, if you think of it, will you bring me back a coffee?" she asked. "The usual. Oh, and some toothpaste. I'm almost out."

"Sure thing," I said. I had just opened the door when I paused, wondering why I felt like whatever I was missing was important. I frowned, trying to think what it was but failed.

Downstairs, I was dismayed to find John in the lobby, lounging in one of the chairs by the front desk. Judging from his sprawled position and the book in his hand, I suspected that he was lying in wait for someone. Instinct told me that someone was me. His head was down, focused on the book, so I tried to slide toward the side exit without being seen, but of course he looked up at the last minute. "Elizabeth!" he cried with false surprise. "I didn't expect to see you here!"

"Really, John?" I asked, annoyed. "You're surprised to find me in my hotel?"

"Of course not," he said. "I just thought that you'd be out with the police. Helping."

I let out a heavy sigh of frustration. "For the last time. I am not working with the police. I am here as a tourist, that's it. Now, if you'll excuse me, I'm going to take a walk."

John's face fell at my abrupt response, and I felt a pang of guilt at my rude behavior. "A walk?" he said. "Where are you off to? I could use a bit of exercise myself. I'll join you." True to his words, he stood up and dropped the book on the chair.

My pang of guilt evaporated so quickly I was surprised there wasn't an accompanying sucking sound.

"I didn't have any place in mind," I lied. "I just wanted to take a walk. By myself," I added for good measure.

John was having none of it. He regarded me in utter astonishment. "By yourself?" he sputtered. "Are you barking mad? When there's a killer running around Bath? Absolutely not! I would never forgive myself if anything happened to you."

I sighed in resignation. I could argue with him, I thought, but what did it really matter if he tagged along? I would walk to the Guildhall, and then, once there, ditch him under some pretense.

"Fine," I huffed with very little grace, "you can come along."

John smiled at me. He had very big teeth.

THE SUN WAS just starting its descent when John and I walked outside. The temperature had dipped since I'd been out earlier, and I pulled my wool cardigan a little tighter to ward against the chill. John kept up a steady stream of conversation—mainly about how most of Richard's theories had originated with him. I gave an occasional murmur, but I wasn't really listening. I had heard most of it before.

We hadn't gone more than a few blocks when I spotted Byron coming out of a café, a take-away coffee in his hand. "Hi, Byron," I called out to him. He turned around startled, but then smiled when he saw me.

"Hello, Elizabeth. Hello, John," he called, crossing the street to where we stood. "How are you doing?" he asked me. "I heard about Valerie. It's horrible."

"I know," I said. "I don't understand any of it." I pointed at his coffee. "Did you get that inside?" I asked.

Byron glanced down at the cup. "Oh, yes. It's not bad. Why, did you want me to get you a cup?"

Giving him a brief smile, I said, "No, thank you, Byron, but your namesake would be proud. I'll be just a minute."

I ducked inside the café, leaving John and Byron standing outside. John did not look pleased. I did not care.

Minutes later, I rejoined them with a cup of coffee in tow. Taking a sip, I asked Byron, "Have you talked to the family yet?"

Byron nodded. "A little. Ian is devastated, of course. Alex is in shock. I'm trying to help, but frankly, I don't know what to do."

"Well, we don't want to detain you," said John curtly. "Elizabeth and I are taking a walk. I'm sure we'll see you later."

Byron glanced at John in some surprise and then back at me. I'm sure he saw my annoyance. "A walk?" he said thoughtfully. "That sounds nice. Do you mind if I join you?"

"No, not at all," I said, just as John said, "Well, actually . . ."

Byron, thankfully, ignored John and fell into step with us. "Where are we heading?" he asked.

"Oh, I don't know," I said casually. "I thought I'd just head downtown, nowhere in particular."

We walked in silence—an oddity given John's propensity to fill every void with stories of his superiority. Soon we came upon the Guildhall. I gave what I hoped was a little cry of surprise. "Oh, isn't this where they were holding the sword-fighting session, 'Dueling Mr. Darcy'?"

Byron nodded. "Yes. Of course, with Valerie's death, the organizers have suspended all the sessions."

I nodded. "Well, I think I'll go in and take a look anyway. They might still have all the props on display." Turning back to both of them, I said, "Thanks for walking with me. I'm sure I'll see you later."

"See you, Elizabeth," Byron said, giving me a half wave and

then heading down the street. Unfortunately, John stayed put and eyed me suspiciously.

"Are you sure you're not investigating?" he asked, finally breaking his silence.

"No, John. I'm not. Don't be silly," I said firmly. "I just want to take a look inside at the display. See you later."

Without giving him a chance to say anything further, I turned on my heel and headed into the Guildhall. I was sorry that I'd been rude, but I'd had it with John and his particular brand of obtuseness.

I pushed open the heavy doors. The large hall was now empty, but it was indeed still set up for fencing demonstrations. The left side of the room was covered with all sorts of swords and protective gear. I gave them a passing glance and then headed to the back hallway where we'd found Richard's body. I don't know exactly why I was drawn there, but I felt there was something I was missing and that it had to do with the hallway. Besides, wasn't there some wise old adage about "going back to the beginning"? Well, this was the beginning. I was here. Let the games begin.

I stood in the narrow hallway staring down at the floor where Richard's body had lain. Oddly enough, no previously unseen clue jumped out at me, waving its little clue arms, shouting, "Over here, Elizabeth! Look at meeee!"

Which was, frankly, kind of annoying.

I walked up and down the hall, opening various doors that led to other rooms. I did this twice. I took the back stairs to the upper level, but the door from the stairwell was locked. I slowly made my way back down the stairs and sat down. Opening my purse, I pulled out my phone and tried Peter again. Once again, it went to voice mail, and once again the mechanical voice told me that it was full. It was probably just as well. My frustration at not being able to reach him was so pronounced that had I been able to leave a message it probably would have been riddled with rather unladylike language.

I tossed my phone back into my purse and stared at my cup of coffee in frustration. The thing that made my frustration all the worse was that I didn't know what I was looking for; I just had a feeling that it was here. After several minutes, I resigned myself to the fact that going back to the beginning wasn't getting me anywhere—a fact, which shouldn't have surprised me, as that was advice from *The Princess Bride*. With a sigh of resignation, I took a sip of the coffee, remembering that I'd promised to get one for Aunt Winnie as well.

That's when the thing I felt like I'd missed earlier came knocking again. Thankfully, this time my brain was home.

Bit by bit, the pieces came together. Like one of those stupid sudoku puzzles that drive me nuts but that I can't seem to stay away from, each fact led to another until, finally, the pattern was complete.

But seeing the pattern and proving it were two different things. I quickly pulled out my camera and began to scroll through all the pictures I'd taken until I came to the ones of the Regency Ball. There was one of Izzy dancing with Ian. There was one of Cora talking to a group of women. Finally, I got to the one I was looking for, the one of Richard and Alex dancing what would prove to be their last dance. I stared at the picture for a minute, trying to see if the item I suspected wasn't there really wasn't there. I enlarged the photo and double-checked.

A faint thrill went through me as I realized what I was—or rather, *wasn't*—seeing.

It was Richard dancing, his hand raised high to hold Alex's. But there was no pinkie ring on his hand. When we'd found Richard's body, he was wearing the ring, but here—a mere few minutes before his death—he wasn't.

Above me, the air vent kicked on, sending a blast of warm air my way. I stared at it for a second and wondered. I saw that the screws supporting the metal cover were in but not secured. Standing up on my toes, I reached my hand up and slid my fingers under the cover. I was able to push it open just enough to squeeze my arm inside. My fingers groped blindly only for a second before hitting pay dirt. My heart pounding, I grabbed the wadded-up bundle of cloth and yanked it out.

I already knew what it was, but I shook it open anyway.

It was a duplicate Mr. Darcy costume, complete with Colin Firth face mask.

The pieces of the puzzle were all together. I understood everything now. Take that, sudoku.

CHAPTER 30

What is right to be done cannot be done too soon.

—EMMA

BUNDLED THE COSTUME back up and ran out of the hall-way and into the main room. However, the room was no longer empty. John now stood there.

"John! What are you doing here?" I yelped in surprise, pulling the costume close to my chest.

"I wanted to see if you were okay," he said. "It's not safe around here anymore."

"Oh. Well, I'm fine. Really. I was just going to head back to the hotel," I said.

"What are you holding?" he asked conversationally, taking a step toward me. "Is that a costume?"

I paused, unsure what to do. However, before I could respond, another figure suddenly appeared behind John. In a quick move-ment, he smashed something down on John's head. In horror, I watched as John collapsed to the marble floor without a sound, his body sprawled out like a limp rag doll.

"He's right, you know. It's not safe around here," said Byron, looking down with satisfaction at the metal handle of the fencing saber in his hand. "For once, that babbling idiot said something that was actually correct. He told me outside that you were investigating the murders. I had to make sure that you didn't succeed."

My heart slammed against my chest, and I forced myself to remember to breathe. "What do you think you're doing?" I said, taking a step backward.

"I'm tying up loose ends."

I inched toward the side wall, my eyes fixed on the saber. "It was you in the costume dancing with Alex when she pretended to get sick, wasn't it? You were in it together. This was never about Richard's paper, was it? It was about you two."

Byron pushed at John's inert form on the floor with his foot. Satisfied that John was unconscious, he stepped over him and moved toward me. With shaking fingers, I used the costume as a cover as I reached into my purse and groped for my phone. Blindly, I dialed Aunt Winnie's phone and hoped to God that she could hear me.

"You and Alex killed Richard, didn't you?" I nodded at the bundle in my arms. "You got a duplicate costume, and then what? Did you wait for him to come out into the hallway for a cigarette?" I asked, in a voice I realized was squeaky. I tried to lower it to a more normal tone. "You killed Richard and then returned to the ball, pretending to be him. Then Alex pretended to get sick and ran to the bathroom. But she didn't go to the bathroom, did she? She ran back into the room, wearing a mask and wig this time, and pulled you out into the hall."

I knew I was babbling, but I couldn't seem to stop. Byron kept coming toward me; I kept moving back toward the wall where the sabers were hanging. Surely some of those had to be real; after all,

Byron's certainly looked real. "Once in the hall, you got out of your costume and stuffed it into the vent," I said. "You took the knife that you killed Richard with and put it in the wig where it would be found by the police. Then you and Alex reappeared and pretended to look for Richard."

"What do you want? Applause?" Byron sneered. "I get it. You figured it all out. I killed Richard, hid his body under a pile of table linens, and then took his place. I even smeared a bit of food on my shoe to make it look like Alex had really thrown up."

"Weren't you taking a huge risk that you might get caught?" I asked as I retreated farther. "I mean, what if someone tried to talk to you when you were dressed as Richard?"

Byron shrugged. "It was a risk, but then Richard could be a rude son of a bitch at times. No one would be too surprised if he waved away a conversation."

I remembered how Cora had said that she'd tried to talk to Richard at the ball but he only laughed at her. Byron was right; when we'd heard that, no one assumed anything other than Richard was being an ass.

Byron continued. "Unfortunately, your prize for figuring this all out is that you have to die, too. Alex and I didn't go through all this trouble so we could get Richard's money and be together just so we'd have to stop now. Sorry and all that. You seem nice enough. But those are the breaks, I guess."

I edged closer to the wall. The swords were only inches away. "Is that what you said to Valerie when you killed her?" I asked. "What happened? Did she try to blackmail you when she realized that Alex couldn't have been in the bathroom like you claimed?"

"Of course she tried to blackmail us. She was a greedy, horrible woman. Valerie called Alex demanding money. Alex agreed to meet her, but first I ran around claiming that Richard's paper had been stolen. Then I met with Valerie. Briefly." The corners of his eyes crinkled in ghoulish amusement. My stomach lurched. "With everyone milling about in Regency garb," he continued, "it was easy to don an outfit myself and go unnoticed. I really doubt anyone is going to miss her—or Richard, for that matter. However, you probably will be missed, which is a pity."

He was now about a foot in front of me, and the display swords were right behind me. With a sudden movement, Byron raised his sword and lunged. I saw the silver blade slice the air inches from my chest. Blindly grabbing a sword from the wall, I dropped my purse and frantically leaped out of his range just in time to feel the blade ripple the air again—this time by my neck. With a horrible but heartfelt primal scream, I raised the sword up in front of me and commenced what I would later refer to as my foray into "batshit-crazy fencing."

I began to wildly parry and thrust, imitating every move I ever saw in any movie that featured a sword fight. Since I had come to the hall in the first place based on advice gleaned from *The Princess Bride,* I wondered if I could imitate Inigo Montoya's fencing moves.

That's about the time I realized that I was probably having some kind of panic-induced mental breakdown.

However, my frenzied moves appeared to take Byron off guard, and he jumped a few steps away from me. Still screaming and slashing away, I advanced, hoping that I could back him up far enough that I could make a break for the front door. For a minute or two, it actually seemed to work, but just when I thought that an escape was feasible, Byron steadied himself and resumed his attack.

"You can't do this!" I hysterically screamed at him as I managed to block one of his hits. "You won't get away with it!"

"Oh, I think I will," he said as the metal clang of our swords smacking against each other rang out. "I think it will be quite easy to pin this all on John."

My stomach sank at the realization that he was probably right. John could easily be made to take the fall for all of this—especially if my call to Aunt Winnie didn't go through. With a renewed energy born of hysterical fear, I charged at him. I would not lose this fight, I told myself, as Byron brought up his sword to block my hits. Neither of us spoke as our swords flashed and hit time and time again. I managed to slash his arm at one point but saw with sick disappointment that it didn't do more than rip his sleeve. My hit didn't even produce a lousy flesh wound.

With renewed energy, I charged again. I had just managed to back him toward the doorway, which was better than his backing me into the room, when I heard a familiar voice call out, "Elizabeth? Are you in here?"

"Peter?" I screamed in disbelief. "Peter! In here! Help!"

Within seconds, Peter came charging into the room. Surprised, Byron turned his attention away from me. It was all the time I needed. I lunged at him, both horrified and relieved as the tip of my sword sank deep into his upper right shoulder. Byron screamed in pain, just as Peter knocked him to the ground with a hard right cross to his face. Peter and I both jumped onto him and pinned Byron to the ground.

Looking at me, his face a mask of shock and worry, Peter said, "Jesus Christ! What the hell is going on? Are you all right?"

I smiled at him. "I am now."

CHAPTER 31

If I loved you less, I might be able to talk about it more.

—EMMA

STILL CAN'T BELIEVE you flew over here and didn't tell me!" I said to Peter much later. We were back in our hotel room, curled up together on my bed, each with a much needed glass of wine in hand. John had been treated for a concussion at the local hospital and released. Inspector Middlefield had taken both Byron and Alex into custody. While Inspector Middlefield thanked me for my help, she also asked me when I would be leaving Bath. Somehow I got the impression that "sooner rather than later" was what she was hoping to hear.

"Well, what did you expect?" Peter replied. "You found not one, but *two* dead bodies! As soon as I heard your last message, I got on the first plane I could. I tried to call you to tell you, but I couldn't get through."

"Thank God he got ahold of me when he got here," said Aunt Winnie. She sat on her bed, a large glass of wine in her hand as well. "Your call to me went to my voice mail. I was just listening to it when Peter got to the hotel. I hate to think of what might have happened to you if I hadn't told Peter where to find you," she said with a shudder.

"Hey!" I said, mildly offended. "I did stab the guy. I was holding him off."

"Elizabeth! He was trying to kill you!" Aunt Winnie countered with visible frustration.

I closed my eyes. "I know. I know. I'm trying to forget that part."

Aunt Winnie reached out and grabbed my hand, giving it a tight squeeze. "I still can't believe that it was Byron! He had me fooled. I really thought that he and Alex didn't like each other."

I nodded. "He had us all fooled. I didn't start to put it together until I remembered that he brought Alex a cup of coffee at the memorial. He'd already added sugar and cream to it. It dawned on me later, when I was talking to you about your coffee, that it was a fairly personal thing to do. It made me wonder what their relationship really was. Then I remembered that Valerie seemed to make most of her . . . uh . . . calls, from a bathroom. I wondered if the reason she'd been killed was that she'd tried to blackmail Alex because *she knew* Alex hadn't been in the bathroom getting sick that night. It would be entirely in Valerie's greedy nature to get money out of Alex—money that she didn't have to share with Gail and the magazine—rather than hand her over to the police."

Aunt Winnie nodded. "I certainly can see her doing that."

"Anyway," I continued, "I thought that if Alex hadn't been in the bathroom, then where had she been? When the masked Elizabeth came into the ballroom that night, I initially thought it *was* Alex. Granted, later we were told that the masked figure couldn't have been her, but I wondered, what if it actually *was* Alex? Well, for one thing, it meant that Byron had to be in on it, as he'd vouched for her being in the bathroom."

"None of this makes sense to me," Peter groused.

"Of course it doesn't," I said, patting his leg. "You haven't been here. But trust me, it makes sense to us. Once I realized that Alex had been in the costume, I wondered where Byron had been. It struck me that we were assuming who people were based on their costumes, and that who we thought was Richard might not have been Richard."

"No, seriously. I'm getting a headache," said Peter.

"I'm almost done," I said. "I looked at the pictures I took that night, and sure enough, the Richard at the ball wasn't wearing his pinkie ring. But when we found Richard's body, the ring was there. So . . ."

"So Richard had been killed in the hallway earlier, and Byron had taken his place," finished Aunt Winnie. "And then Byron and Alex kept talking about Richard's paper as if that was the reason behind his murder."

"Exactly," I said.

"Well, thank God it's over," said Aunt Winnie. "I called Cora and told her the good news. She wanted to take us all out for dinner, but I told her that you two were busy. I'll give you some time alone."

I smiled at her. "Thanks, Aunt Winnie. I don't think I could take her or Izzy right now."

"That's what I thought." Aunt Winnie stood and checked her reflection in the mirror. After fluffing up her red curls, and adding an ample amount of red lipstick to her already stained lips, she turned to us. "You two go have some fun. See the sights of Bath. Or stay in," she said with a wink. "I'll be back later." Giving us each a light kiss, she headed out the door.

Once the door had closed, I turned to Peter to wipe the smear of red lipstick off his cheek. He did the same for me. As I looked at his face, and stared into his amber-colored eyes, I realized that this life that I was trying to figure out and perfect was sitting right here in front of me. My life was with Peter. It didn't matter to me anymore that I was between jobs and forced to live with my sister because my apartment had a mold problem. What mattered was being with Peter. "I love you, Peter," I said as I snuggled in close to him.

"I love you too, Elizabeth," he said, wrapping his arms tightly around me. I closed my eyes and breathed in his familiar scent—Tide and a hint of Burberry cologne. We lay curled together in comfortable silence, lulled by the faint hum of the air vent and the muffled voices of people talking out in the hall. I don't know when I'd felt happier or more at home.

"Do you remember that question you asked me before I left on this trip?" I asked.

"Do you mean when I asked you to move in with me?" he said.

"That's the one. I was wondering, do you still want a roommate? Because I'd like to change my previous answer, if I may. I've discovered that my feelings on the matter are quite the opposite."

Peter didn't respond. Surprised, I looked up at him. His face was very serious as he stared down at me. "Well, funny you should mention that, because I was thinking about that, too, and I want to change the question."

My heart began to pound. "You do?"

Peter nodded and slid off the bed. Getting down onto one knee, he pulled a small velvet box out of his pocket. "I've been carrying this around for weeks," he said. Flipping open the box to reveal a sparkling diamond ring, he looked up at me and said, "Elizabeth, will you marry me?"

I started crying, of course. "Oh, my God, yes!" I said as I leaned over to kiss him.

Peter took the ring out of the box and slid it onto my finger. Then he pulled me close and said, "Dearest, loveliest Elizabeth."

I laughed. "Did you really just quote *Pride and Prejudice* to me?"

"I did."

"That's kind of awesome, you know."

He grinned. "I like to think so."

I kissed him again. In the past week, I had discovered two bodies and engaged in a sword fight with a killer. I didn't have a job, and I didn't have a place to call my own, but I had Peter.

Life was good.